Dalí Tamareia has everything—a young family and a promising career as an Ambassador in the Sol Fed Diplomatic Corps. Dalí's path as a peacemaker seems clear, but when their loved ones are killed in a terrorist attack, grief sends the genderfluid changeling into a spiral of self-destruction.

Fragile Sol Fed balances on the brink of war with a plundering alien race. Their skills with galactic relations are desperately needed to broker a protective alliance, but in mourning, Dalí no longer cares, seeking oblivion at the bottom of a bottle, in the arms of a faceless lover, or at the end of a knife.

The New Puritan Movement is rising to power within the government, preaching strict genetic counseling and galactic isolation to ensure survival of the endangered human race. Third gender citizens like Dalí don't fit the mold of this perfect plan, and the NPM will stop at nothing to make their vision become reality. When Dalí stumbles into a plot threatening changelings like them, a shadow organization called the Penumbra recruits them for a rescue mission full of danger, sex, and intrigue, giving Dalí purpose again.

Risky liaisons with a sexy, charismatic pirate lord could be Dalí's undoing—and the only way to prevent another deadly act of domestic terrorism.

Dalí

E.M. Hamill

This is a work of fiction. All characters, places and events are from the author's imagination and should not be confused with fact. Any resemblance to persons, living or dead, events or places is purely coincidental.

Published by
NineStar Press
PO Box 91792
Albuquerque, New Mexico, 87199
www.ninestarpress.com

Warning: This book contains sexually explicit content, which is only suitable for mature readers, and scenes of violent death.

Print ISBN #978-1-947139-58-9
Cover by Natasha Snow
Edited by BJ Toth

For Michaela, Tyler, and Arin: different shades of the same spectrum—all amazing young people who give me hope for the future of the human race.

Acknowledgements

This book is the product of generosity on many levels.

I would like to thank the Tumblr genderfluid community, specifically Andropologist, for boosting my signal when I asked for help developing my book's characters. Several people answered my questionnaire and helped me make the fictional souls in this story more believable, honest, and I hope presented in a respectful light. I am grateful for their willingness to help.

My critique partners once more went above and beyond. I would like to thank Michael Mammay for giving my first draft the tough love it needed and some excellent advice on action scenes, Colleen Halverson for pointing out some serious late-draft issues I hadn't considered, and James Stryker for letting me know I was on the right track with this book. My alpha and beta readers braved many levels of mediocrity and still encouraged me to finish: thank you to Janean Dobos, Ashley Miller, and Katharine Henry Alexander.

Grandmaster Wannabe Ninja Katharine and her husband, Kudo Sensei JD Alexander of Iron Forged Martial Arts, also gave me some excellent advice on structuring my *zezjna* sequences. Any inconsistencies in martial arts philosophy or execution are completely my own.

Developmental editor Jami Nord was hugely inspirational, encouraging, and full of writing wisdom. *bows down* Thank you so very, very much for your help in sensitivity reading, my endless questions, and for encouraging me to take it "from jalapeño to habañero!"

One

HUMAN BEINGS ARE assholes. I should know. I'd become one in the last few months.

You'd think the near extinction of our entire species after the pandemics and global poisoning our last world war inflicted might let us all pull together. Even with galactic war breathing down our necks, when almost everyone realized the human race constituted less of a threat to each other than some of the other things out there, we continued to be dicks.

Those attitudes started problems—in particular, Europan attitudes, of the New Puritan variety. I no longer possessed the self-control or sufficient fucks to avoid adding fuel to their fire.

His voice floated over the excited din of the crowd and the pregame show on the holographic screens above the bar.

"Abomination."

I sighed and turned my head. The Team Europa-jacketed hulk next to me exuded a cloud of loathing against my empathic nets. I raised one eyebrow at him.

"Really? You can't come up with anything more original after fifteen minutes of shit-talking?" The conversation behind me started as a diatribe against the rally for third-gender rights, held outside the arena and glimpsed on the main holo screen. I didn't pay attention to either until the comments got louder and were meant for my ears.

"Faggot."

"How very twentieth century of you." I downed another of the six shots the robotic bartender dispensed in front of me. I wasn't looking for trouble, only anesthetic. Outside, a cluster of media bots interviewing star athletes had driven me into the bar to hide. The presence of mechanized paparazzi still unsettled me. I didn't want them in my face.

The annual Sol Series tournament games between Mars and Europa bordered on legendary for their savagery. No one took rugby as seriously as a gritty Martian colonist or a repressed New Puritan, and the bar overflowed with both, waiting for the station's arena to open. Spectators gathered around us in the bar, drawn by the promise of a fight, glittering eyes fixed on us. My empathic senses drowned in their excitement and fear, even with the numbing effects of synthetic alcohol.

He invaded my personal space and leaned closer, face centimeters from mine. His breath carried a trace of mint and steroid vapors. Great. A huffer, his molecules all hyped-up on testosterone. He stood over a head taller than me, about twenty-five kilos heavier. His fists would do damage. His minions stood at either side, more meat than smarts. Neither spoke. Their mouths hung open while he harassed me, and I expected shuttle flies to crawl out at any time.

"You're nothing but an A-sex freak."

"Better. Still lacks originality." I threw back the last shot. "How about androgynous freak? Hermaphrodite? No, those words are probably too big for you."

The titter of laughter from the crowd only pissed him off. "Go fuck yourself."

"Technically, I can't. But I can fuck anybody else in this room. Can you?"

Shocked laughter rose from the circle of spectators. The guy clenched his fists and flexed his muscles. I continued, "Do I scare you?" I swiveled on the stool to face him and changed posture, crossing my legs in demure modesty. My voice rose into a husky, suggestive alto as I leaned one elbow on the bar. "Or do you want to find out what's under my kilt?"

I hit a nerve. His eyes went blank, black, and his rage flooded over my senses. The crowd gasped and took a step back. Minion One caught his rising fist and spoke. "Jon, don't you know who..."

Jon's lip curled. "It's an atrocity. It should have been killed at birth."

"I prefer the term changeling." I stood, and the circle around us got wider. The potent mix of hormones surged through my bloodstream as they altered my chemical makeup and bulked strategic upper body muscles. I let a cold smile form on my lips and dropped into a Zereid martial arts stance. Jon took half a step back as I became more definitively male in ways he recognized. "Oh, go ahead and hit me, by all means. A good fight is almost as good as sex."

"Break it up."

The crowd parted into nervous brackets with security's arrival. Caniberi lumbered into the midst of the circle with the boneless roll space-born started to get after generations in orbit. He cast a sour eye in my direction.

"Dalí, why is it always you?"

"Just lucky, I guess."

The constable growled at me. He turned to Jon. "You can't play in the tournament if I throw you in the brig for violence. Move out."

Jon stared at me a minute longer. The threat of not getting to beat the hell out of some hedonistic Martians made him reconsider. He and the minions moved away, but he threw one more sentence in my face like a javelin.

"You'll be alone, changeling."

The truth in his words knifed through me all the way to my gut and cut me deeper than any microsteel blade. "I'll be waiting."

Caniberi squinted at me as the crowd began to disperse. "Dalí, do I need to talk with the Captain?"

"No, sir. Leave my father out of this." He'd dealt with enough from me already. My mother was now away on the diplomatic mission I'd been suspiciously—but rightly—deemed unfit to assume. Without Mom there to buffer the uncomfortable presence of my grief between us, Dad was lost.

"One of these days you're going to push the wrong buttons and end up hurt, or worse. Some things the medical officer can't fix." His gaze softened. "Drinking and getting the shit beaten out of you won't bring them back."

"I'm well aware of that, sir." My voice came out sharper than I intended. One of the best officers on the station, Caniberi had known me a little over a decade, and he never hesitated to kick my ass if I deserved it, no matter what gender I chose at the moment. This time, he just stared at me with an odd expression. His pity broke in tepid surges against my senses.

"Get out of here. I don't want to arrest you again."

I turned and left the bar. With the bots still hovering outside, I ducked my head to foil their facial recognition apps and fought my way upstream from the arena.

The shakes hit me in the aftermath of the hormone flood. The synthetic alcohol in my system warred with my normalizing chem levels and sour nausea threatened. I grabbed one of the rails lining the corridor and took several shuddering breaths as my muscles cramped, rearranged, and settled back into the lean, sexless frame where I am most at home.

The crowd jostled around me and headed toward the game. My empathic nets buzzed dully with their anticipation and excitement, but the sense of being watched pushed at the back of my mind. A familiar presence tripped a memory and an emotion.

The watcher knew me.

I turned my head. The Zereid made his way toward me, head and shoulders above everyone else, long, muscular limbs wading with passive grace through a river of human bodies as the crowd shifted for him. An eddy of cautious glances swirled and vanished downstream.

Oily quicksilver eyes without lids narrowed, their shape signifying the equivalent of a smile. His resonant voice buzzed in my ears. "He is the size of a cargo bot, you know. Even the arts we learned can't change gravity. He might kill you."

"I won't let it go that far." I shrugged. I actually hoped I'd bitten off more than I could swallow this time.

But the presence of my childhood friend undid me. A lump rose in my throat, pressure in my head, and I closed the distance between us. He gathered me in against cool flesh. I was locked in arms capable of crushing a human like a piece of foil but which held me with careful tenderness. Against his enormous chest, I felt like a small child, even though in developmental terms, Gor and I are the same age. His concern brushed my mind with affectionate familiarity.

"I see you, Dalí," he murmured. "I mourn with you."

I breathed in the scent of Zereid. Gor smelled of his homeworld—rain and earth and copper clung to his leathery turquoise skin and short, downy fur even in absentia. Homesickness washed over me.

I'd lived on Zereid most of my life. My mother, Marina Urquhart, served as ambassador for fifteen years. Dad's career required he return to Sol Fed, and rather than separate our family, Mom resigned her appointment. My differences were clear, even to my third-gender mother, but there, we were aliens. I wondered what it would be like to have more friends who blinked.

When we got back to our own kind, I found out I was still an alien.

Gor pulled away. In the tarnished silver of his eyes, like antique mirrors, my unkempt reflection stared back at me. His dismay at my mental and physical state, impossible to miss, sighed against my mind.

"How did you hear?" I said.

"Your mother. "

"Of course."

His head cocked. "I tried to come sooner, but the travel permissions into the colonies are daunting."

"No, I understand." I wanted to sit and talk with Gor. I eyed the bar, but couldn't go back in there yet. "Come on. We can go to Dad's quarters. He'll be on the bridge." My own cramped space wouldn't accommodate Gor's height or his bulk.

We squeezed into the private lift and rode up to the command deck. My thumbprint opened the door to the Captain's suite, and Gor made a sound of wonder as he ducked through the port.

Three levels of transparent alloy shielding overlooked the U-curve of Rosetta Station. Shuttles buzzed in and out of bays like honeybees in the hydroponics domes, ferrying passengers to huge starliners docked on the outer limbs.

"An inspiring view." Gor gazed out the window.

Ochre planet-shine from Jupiter's face illuminated the room, the swirling storms in the gas giant's atmosphere familiar to me now. I never found them beautiful, only an echo of the chaos in my head. I dropped into one of the chairs facing the viewport.

Gor eased himself into the seat opposite me. "You're in crisis, Dalí."

I couldn't hide anything from him. Even if I wanted to, he was a telepath; his empathic senses much more attuned than my own modest abilities. Our friendship spanned far too many years, our trust well established. Lying to him would betray our oath of crechemates, a Zereid custom similar to old Earth tradition of blood brothers.

"Today would be the second anniversary of our wedding." I stared at my hands. I still wore a ring on each of them, the ones Gresh and Rasida gave me.

"I remember. The love between you and your mates deserves celebration."

Triad marriages with two members of the same sex and one of the opposite were common. The female population had not rebounded as fast as the male. But mine was the first triad marriage to include a changeling spouse under the new laws we helped to bring about. The legislation was both praised and vilified by hundreds of other citizens while we exchanged vows beneath the domes of the lunar capitol. My parents, Gresh's mother, and Gor celebrated with us. Rasida's mother refused to attend the wedding of her only daughter.

The three of us had been inseparable, invincible. Without them, I staggered, incomplete.

Our child would have been three months old now.

"Don't say it."

Gor's eyes elongated in confusion. "What?"

"That they wouldn't want me to be like this."

"I did not come here to admonish you for grieving."

I gave a short laugh. "What did you come here to scold me for?"

"For ceasing to live. Abandoning the larger destiny for which you trained."

"Ambassador?" I dug a vape out of the pocket of my coat and thumbed the switch, inhaling illegal chemicals deep into my lungs. His gentle reproach against my empathic nets rebuked me without a word.

"You were sure of your calling as a peacemaker six months ago." Zereid reverence toward conciliation is, ironically, unforgiving and unbending.

"I was certain of a lot of things then." I exhaled a cloud of spicy mist. If any of the scent remained, I'd catch hell later for vaping in Dad's quarters.

"There are always those who work against peace, even in their own hearts. As you are doing now."

"I don't know if I believe in peace anymore."

"Because you do not possess it."

"Stop feeding me platitudes, brother."

He spread six-fingered hands wide. "What would you have me do? Tell me. Your pain is mine to share, beloved friend. Allow me to help you. Your rage is fearsome but undirected. You point it at yourself."

"I was supposed to die, not them." I cursed the terrorists who missed their target by eight minutes. When I decided not to address the media bots and chose instead to hold a private farewell with my family, I put myself ahead of schedule. I should have died with them. Even though the bastards failed to kill me, they destroyed me.

"Come home." Gor waited for me to answer. I didn't. He continued. "Madam Ambassador thinks Zereid would be a place of healing for you.

You can study at the temple with me again, be teacher and student. This year's crop of younglings is a challenge." His vocal pipes fluted in laughter. "As we were."

"That isn't much of an incentive." A grin tried to tug at the corners of my mouth, stiff and out of practice with the expression. "I'll think about it."

"Will you?" His doubt hovered between us.

The port slid open again and my father thundered in—Captain Paul Tamareia—"The Captain" to everyone on the station, even me at times. I stood at automatic attention, swaying a little. Gor rose too.

"What the hell were you thinking?" he demanded. "And turn that goddamned vape off."

I complied. "A misunderstanding, sir."

"Misunderstanding, my ass. Six shots of the synthetic piss that passes for whiskey says it wasn't." He turned to Gor and bowed. "Welcome aboard Rosetta Station, honored friend. Forgive me for not greeting you first."

"Captain Tamareia." Gor bowed back.

"How long will you be staying? I insist you use my quarters as your own. Stop by the constable's office and he will register you for my door. I'm afraid most of the cabins are small, and we're overcrowded with the tournament."

"My thanks, sir. My travel clearance is good for the next two weeks, and then I must return." Gor nodded at us. "I should collect my belongings now. I will go to your constable on the way back."

"It's good to see you, Gor."

"You as well, Captain." He put one enormous hand on my shoulder. "Dalí, please think about what I said."

Gor let himself out. Dad and I both understood he made a graceful exit so we could shout at each other in peace. Zereids don't carry a whole lot of baggage. They don't wear clothes.

"Did you need to pick a fight with the number eight of the bloody Europan rugby team?" He tossed his personal data device on the table. "Do you even know who he is?"

"Other than a prick, no."

"Jon Batterson. Does the name ring a bell at all?"

"Batterson." I blinked through mental processes made sluggish by the vape. "As in President Batterson?"

"Light dawns. The heir apparent to his self-righteous little robotics empire." He ran both hands through his hair. I inherited my dark-brown waves from him, but Dad's customary high-and-tight showed little hint of curl. Mine now fell to my shoulders in a shaggy, tangled mane. "Do you realize the mess I would have had to clean up if you really let loose on him? Even if he is built like the ass end of a freighter, you could put him on the injured list."

"It wasn't my intent."

"From what Caniberi told me, you were about to unleash hell on him. You sure stirred up some crap. The president is coming to the game tonight. The constable didn't know who he was either, or he might have thrown you in the brig to prove a point." He sat down with a thud on the steel bench and sighed. "Dalí. Come here."

I sat next to him and braced myself.

"It's been six months. Your leave from the diplomatic corps is finished, and if you don't return, you'll be dismissed. This has to stop. When you go back to your life, you're going to encounter people like Batterson on a daily basis. Your reputation and your career are at stake. You can't do this anymore."

"That life's over."

"Don't throw it away. You did so much in so short a time. You have a gift for understanding, and you will be a formidable ambassador. Sol Fed needs you in the negotiation chamber at the Remoliad. Luna is a better place because of your work."

"Because of Gresh's work. Because of Sida and our child. They were my reasons for everything. I'm not sure I feel as strongly for the rest of the human race."

"Then you need to find another way to deal with their deaths. I won't watch you destroy your future. You worked too hard for it."

"Tell me how, sir." My fury rose. "Tell me how I can deal with it because I'm looking for an exit."

He stiffened. "What do you mean?"

"Nothing." I rose and stalked away. He started to call after me, but the communication tones went off.

"Captain Tamareia, report to the bridge. The president's shuttle is incoming."

"On my way. Dalí!"

I ignored him and ducked through the port.

Two

I HAD TO pass the terminal's arrival gate to reach my assigned quarters in the lodgings district—nothing but a tiny room with a bunk and a desk. More than I needed. I hunched my shoulders and pulled the collar of my coat up. It wasn't enough to evade electronic eyes.

Goddamned media bots. The week after the bombing, they descended upon me every time I stepped outside my door, wanting tears, statements, something juicy to regale the holo viewers at home. Charges of destruction of the networks' property got dropped after I was diagnosed with PTSD. But no one else could verify what I'd seen the media bot do in Luna Terminal. They were all dead.

Six months later, the things still recognized me whether I leaned toward male or female, but followed me at a safer distance. This one hovered outside the gate to spy for any late celebrities who might sneak in after the championship game began. It buzzed and floated in my wake.

"Ambassador Tamareia? Would you care to make a statement on the latest developments in the Senate regarding the Remoliad negotiations?"

"No. I'm on bereavement leave." I didn't turn around.

"How about a statement regarding Sol Fed's stance on third-gender reproductive rights?"

This was a human voice and made me pause. I turned slowly. "Kiran Singh. Waiting for the next big human tragedy?"

His answering smile was brilliant and manufactured for holo audiences, white teeth blinding against dark-brown skin. Tall and slender, Singh's features shared the same androgyny as mine, the kind of facial structure that earned a double take. His plum-colored kurta glittered with embroidery, the tips of shiny black boots visible beneath its folds. I hadn't seen Singh since the memorial service on Luna, but I'd been barely cognizant of anything in those first days of mourning. Except when I punched Singh in the face. I remember that.

"Yours?" I jabbed a thumb at the patient, hovering bot.

"It's my network's."

"Make it go away or it's scrap."

"Stand down, Geraldo." The globular bot obeyed and floated back to the gate.

Singh stood in front of me. The smile faded. "You look like shit."

"Thanks. Good to see you too." I wanted nothing more but to go back to my room and surround myself with a cloud of illegal vaping chems. I turned away.

"Seriously, Dalí. What the hell?"

"What do you want, Kiran?" I kept walking.

"Stop and talk to me. We used to be friends at university."

"We were never friends. Is this off the record?"

"Give me a statement against the New Puritan Movement. The NPM's stance on our reproductive rights is nothing less than selective genocide under the guise of recovering our species. Your opinion still matters to Luna. You can help us make a difference."

"I don't agree with your form of journalism or your tactics. Gresh's opinions were the ones that mattered."

"Gresh was the judicial heart of the equal rights movement, but he wasn't a third. You were the voice. You still could be."

"Not for you and the Third Front." Kiran and his activist friends played along the borders of extremism, where Gresh and I had preferred reason and legislation.

"Dalí. Listen to me." Singh grabbed my arm. I wrenched it away but stopped walking. He moved closer. "I know the bastards got you ousted from your appointment to the Remoliad. The NPM is poison, and it's gaining momentum in the Senate. Do you even watch the news?"

"Not if I can help it."

"So you've given up."

"What do you want from me?"

"You do know that isolationist prick Hyatt won the nomination, don't you?"

"What nomination?"

"To be Head of the Senate, Dalí! Where have you been?"

"In hell."

"Okay." Singh's voice quieted. "I understand. But you need to wake up. Our rights to be treated as the equal of every other Sol Fed citizen are being threatened. Europa introduced new bills into Senate deliberation. With Hyatt's election, they're going to pass and make parthenogenesis mandatory for our reproduction. Guess whose research they're using to fuel the hysteria?"

"Dr. Atassi's, I presume."

"The witch has been busy. They're going to use the law to eliminate the entire third gender."

I blinked at Singh with disbelief, even in my still-numbed state. "That isn't legal under galactic statutes. It'll never pass."

"Wake up! Sol Fed isn't Remoliad yet, and if the NPM gets its way, we never will be." Kiran stepped closer to me. "Changelings are disappearing from the Colonies, and nobody is investigating. They're ignoring hate crimes. In our government's eyes, we don't serve any greater good to further the human race if we can't reproduce."

"Maybe they just wanted to disappear."

Singh's expression grew ugly, and his disgust pricked my empathic senses with needle-sharp derision. "You never did get it. You think more like a galactic than a human being. You were never one of us."

"We've had this argument before."

"The more things change, the more they stay the same. It still doesn't touch you. You're a cold bastard, Tamareia."

I turned my back, but Singh called out, "What if I told you I could connect the NPM to the terminal bombing?"

I stopped and wheeled on him. Two steps brought me within arm's length. I grabbed the front of his jacket and pulled him in, snarling, "If that's true, why didn't you tell the authorities?"

"Take it easy!" He slapped my hands away and licked his lips, his eyes darting away from mine as he straightened his kurta. "Word has it that Batterson Robotics is expanding into illegal weapons technology. I heard rumors the NPM formed its own little militia, funded by Batterson himself."

"Rumors." I gave a bleak laugh. "Prove who killed my family, and I'll show you what a cold bastard I can be. Until then, stay the fuck away from me, Kiran."

EVERY NIGHT, I stood over the graves of my husband and wife. I screamed until my throat bled and scarlet fell like rubies into the mounded silt of lunar soil. I recognized it as a dream only because they didn't have graves. None of the victims did.

I didn't sleep much anymore. Instead, I prowled the underbelly of Rosetta.

Every space station has a place no one admits to knowing about, ignored by the crew because it keeps the ugliness from spilling over into public areas. Spacers who haven't seen planetside for a long time get...hungry. On Rosetta Station, the place they go to satisfy their hunger is the Labyrinth. It's a maze of ducts, plumbing, supply lines and tanks running under the metal skin of the bottom level, which constitute the veins and arteries of the station. Beneath my feet, less than an arm's width away, lay the vacuum of space, frigid and infinite.

In the shadows, makeshift stalls got set up in a hurry after the maintenance droids went into hibernation. Illegal vaping chems filled racks beside other contraband items promising a minute or two of oblivion. Real alcohol distilled in the cargo holds of somebody's ship—not the synthehol they serve in the bars upside—sold by the dram and quickly disappeared. Pornographic holos from off world flickered in tantalizing glimpses, only a second or two to stir the juices and tempt a buyer. Fights were common, weapons forbidden, but blades from all over the galaxy found their way to hand for the right price.

The night's game over, the Labyrinth teemed with strangers. Visitors with more money than sense to avoid this hellhole sought a risky outlet for excess energy before they shuttled home.

Men and women who wanted more intimate trade lingered among the tanks and narrow pipe-lined alcoves. It could be dangerous. Perverse appetites grow in the silence and solitude of space, especially on the slow ships taking a year or longer to transport their cargo from off world. More than once, a chilling corpse blocked the maintenance droids' track when they came back online.

The delicate balance between violence and release lets me forget.

I wore a veil of sorts when I went to the Labyrinth. A hood hid most of my face and left only my eyes exposed. The temperature stayed cold enough against the outer hull of the station that it didn't appear out of place. Once my empathic senses or physical cues told me what they wanted me to be, my body settled into the gender with rising anticipation of a few minutes of unbridled, old-fashioned, down and dirty sex. No lovemaking happened down there in the dark. Few words were exchanged, no money given. For false love, the paid companions had an office upstairs. This was catharsis, need born of loneliness. Sometimes, they groaned someone's name aloud. I kept my names inside, like a silent prayer.

In the faint light, he hesitated, a tall, athletic man with shoulders almost too wide for the narrow space between the tanks. His eyes scanned around him in quick movements. When he saw me, his steps faltered. He wasn't feral enough to be a spacer newly returned from a jaunt. I tilted my head in invitation, leaned back against the pipes leading into the alcove, and waited until he approached me. I turned and led him into the jungle of conduits and hoses behind the tanks until we reached the darkness at the end, away from the crowds on the other side.

I pulled him against me by his belt, my fingers working the clasp. His hands went to my waist, pushed at the edge of my shirt until they found skin, and moved upward. Seeking a woman. By the time his hesitant hands reached my ribcage, my small breasts awaited. Hormone surges drove the change, fueled by my own building excitement and my body's instinctive reaction to his pheromones. His palms brushed over my sensitive nipples, and I shivered as his mingled relief and lust spilled against my mind. I'd guessed correctly.

The kilt was gender neutral and long enough to delay access while the blood-filled tissues beneath my mons prepared to assume a female role. In my neutral state, my genitalia passes as female to an exploratory grope against the front. For a short period, early in my arousal, I'm caught between genders. He was more interested in my breasts. Both hands went up beneath my shirt and kneaded the soft flesh. The tricky clasp of his belt parted at last, and I slipped my hand inside to cup the hardening length of him. He gasped.

Commando. Even better. I shoved his trousers down around his thighs.

The hood fell away against my throat as I knelt. He rocked against my mouth with a muttered oath, steadying himself on the pipes overhead with one hand and the other fisted in my hair. I kept up the rhythm until his breath shuddered. He pulled away and yanked me to my feet. His mouth collided with mine in bruising urgency, the slow heat of volatile liquor on his tongue.

One hand raked up my thigh and found me bare beneath the kilt. A guttural sound escaped him as he lifted me off my feet and shoved my back against the wall of conduits. A grunt of pain emerged from my lips, but I wrapped my legs around him and locked my boots together as he fumbled with the material between us. I was ready. My fingers guided him to the place he sought, my own breathing quick and ragged now. As he buried himself inside me, I grabbed the pipes above my head for purchase, straining against him and meeting each thrust violently as I sought oblivion.

My pleasure came from both physical sensations and the empathic shock of orgasm; my body clenched, nerve endings exploded. The biting cold of the Labyrinth slid away, and the shredding grief for my lost loves evaporated as I experienced the moment of climax in my own body and the body invading mine. My mind burned, consumed and blinded to all outside sensations and emotions. For a moment, nothing else existed.

But it only lasted seconds. The tsunami crashed back to shore, wearing me away with its relentless motion.

The rules of the Labyrinth were clearly not familiar to him. Trapped between the wall and his body for too long, I was forced to speak.

"Put me down."

Dazed, he lifted his head from the curve of my neck and shoulder. "Oh. I'm sorry."

I used the pipes above to maneuver myself away and settled my feet on the floor. Only a few seconds were required to straighten the kilt and pull the hood back up over my head, but I didn't refasten it yet. He seemed to fumble with his belt forever, and my patience wore thin. He was too big to go around, and I needed to be someplace warmer.

"Excuse me."

"No, wait, please. Let me buy you a drink."

I laughed. Couldn't help it. "You're new here, aren't you?"

He missed my sarcasm. "I'm here for the tournament. I play for Europa."

Oh, shit. A New Puritan trolling the Labyrinth. What in the seven hells was he doing down here? I asked him as much. "You'd be safer upstairs. How did you even find out about this place?"

"I came down with my brother and some teammates. They came after the tournament last year. We won tonight, so we'll be here another twenty-four hours before we leave for the finals. Maybe...I could meet you again?"

"I don't think so." Young and naïve; great friends he had, to leave him down here alone. I squeezed past him, and the idiot caught my hand.

"At least tell me your name."

I actually hesitated a moment. I'm not certain why. Long enough for my escape route to be cut off by his friends, drunk on cargo bay hooch.

"I saw him go this way," one slurred, his voice familiar. The hackles rose on the back of my neck as light flashed into the alcove. I turned away and hurriedly fastened the hood over my face again. Shit.

Jon Batterson and the minions stood in the narrow passage. "Hey, the boy's finished popping his cherry. Well done, little brother."

This couldn't possibly get better.

I ducked my head and tried moving through them, but one grabbed me. "Hey, where you going? You got time for another?"

"Wait a minute." Batterson spun me around and ripped the hood off my head. His eyes bulged. I stared back at him and gave the same cold smile I had in the bar.

My would-be gallant stepped between us—well-intentioned, but once again trapping me down the goddamned alcove. "Jon, what are you doing? Let her go."

"Congratulations, Brian." Jon glared at me past his brother's shoulder. "You just lost your virginity to a changeling."

"I...what? No, she's..." Brian turned around and searched my face in the harsh glare of the flashlight. I could see him now, as young and naïve as I'd thought. Confounded, but not angry. Not yet.

"Get out of here, Brian." Jon's voice drawled in monotone, his face blank.

"I'm not going to—"

"No, you really should." My voice deepened with each word as I allowed the softness of femininity to slide away and be replaced with my neutral side. There was going to be blood. Mostly, mine. I ignored the pain of change and let the expectation of a fight begin to carry me over into masculinity. Brian gaped at me in disbelief until Jon pulled him out of the alcove.

I leaped to grab the pipes above and drove a double-footed kick to Jon's chest as he reached for me. Propelled into his buddies, they staggered back, but I only managed to create a roadblock for myself. I scanned desperately for some means of escape between the tanks and spiderweb of conduit and found none.

Zezjna, the Zereid martial art, requires space. I tried to adapt. Someone's nose crunched under the heel of my boot, and I delivered a solid blow to Batterson's solar plexus before the three of them pounded me into the ice-cold floor. My jaw cracked beneath Jon's fist. His massive hand dwarfed the knife he pulled from his boot, glinting in the faraway light. He slammed the blade through my ribcage.

What an anniversary. Gresh, Rasida, and I might spend it together after all. Relieved, I welcomed the black hole that swallowed me.

Three

MAINTENANCE DROIDS FOUND me and sent out an emergency call before I bled to death. The cold of the Labyrinth probably saved my life.

I woke up in increments in a medical pod, the first fragments of awareness indistinguishable between nightmare and reality. Phantoms darted out of the dark to stab me again, and Jon Batterson's voice growled in my ear, *Make sure it doesn't wake up.*

I remembered Gor: an impression of turquoise skin filled my blurred vision as his mind touched mine in reassurance. Dad sat beside me, sorrow etching his face with more lines than he'd earned in the last six horrendous months.

In my delirium, Rasida and Gresh visited me too. Sida took my hand, her dark eyes filled with tears. I tried to speak around the tubes in my throat, but she shook her head, blue-black hair glinting in the harsh white light of the pod.

Not yet, Dalí.

Gresh's eyes held love, but his expression was set and without compromise. I knew the look. He wore the same one when I almost turned down the appointment to the Remoliad because of Rasida's pregnancy.

You have a responsibility. He'd said it then, too. I struggled for reference. Real, or drug-induced fantasy, I didn't care. I wanted this contact. *I know it hurts. Use the pain. I promise it will get better, Dalí. I promise, love.*

Now, wake up. Wake up.

"Dalí? Wake up."

The female voice demanded my cooperation. I opened my eyes and swallowed a painful gulp of air. Tubes no longer choked me. A face swam into view, and the woman smiled.

"You're awake and breathing on your own. Do you hurt anywhere?"

I began to shake my head. Movement sent a sharp, nauseating ache through my skull and made me groan and heave. Agony streaked through my chest. She checked the display of firing pain receptors on the overhead screen and tapped with rapid, precise fingers on her PDD. Medication flowed through the alarming number of subdermal nanopatches that covered me. Relief came almost at once.

"Thank you," I managed. "I'm not dead."

"You were close. You had a fractured jaw, a hemothorax, broken ribs, and a concussion. The knife wound almost earned you an artificial heart. We transfused you twice with synth-blood replacements. I think that covers everything. The chest tube came out this morning. The bones are set and should be healed by the end of the week, but it's best to let the brain heal on its own. I'm afraid you'll experience some pain, headaches, and dizziness for a few days more."

I didn't recognize her. Pale blonde tendrils escaped the tidy knot at the back of her neck, blue eyes mild and curious. "Who are you?"

"Doctor Tella Sharp. Call me Tella." Her voice softened. "You've been unconscious for four days. I had to keep you in a medical coma for a while. Do you remember what happened?"

I squinted. "Yes." Mostly.

"I need to ask you a couple of questions. Constable Caniberi will want some information as well." She hesitated. "Were you raped? I found the DNA of four different men on your body, but only one semen type."

"No. No, the sex was consensual. The fight, too, I guess."

"I'm sorry?"

"I didn't go down to the Labyrinth without knowing what could happen, Dr. Sharp."

Her brow creased. "I just want to make sure I'm not missing anything. I studied third-gender anatomy, of course, but each person's genitalia varies according to their dominant sex." Her fair complexion bloomed with rosy color as she discussed my genitals. "You don't have one."

"No. I'm changeling. I'm neutral until I assume male or female."

"And you can control this at will?"

"Yes."

"That's fascinating."

"One way of putting it." The meds kicked in with speed. My speech slurred. "I'd be happy to give you a demonstration when I'm all healed up. For science."

Dr. Sharp tapped a few more times on the display, grinning. "Go back to sleep. The pain should be better the next time you wake up. I'll spare you the constable until then. I may not be able to hold your father off, though."

I let the drugs pull me back under.

DAD DOZED AT my bedside in the medical pod when I opened my eyes again, a PDD clutched against his chest. I studied him for a minute. His dark hair was streaked with iron, more gray than I remembered. My throat knotted in gratitude. Dr. Sharp said he'd been there, and I knew he'd been on duty every day. He seldom took personal time off except when Mom was in residence.

"Dad," I croaked.

He sat up with a start, and his relief sang in my senses even through the haze of medication. "Hey. Do you need a drink of water?"

"Please."

Dad held the tube for me as I sipped. Coolness spread over my cotton-dry mouth, down my parched throat. I couldn't get enough, but he drew the liquid away.

"Dr. Sharp says not too much at first. How are you feeling?"

"Better." I paused. "I'm sorry. I was stupid. I know I've been difficult to deal with."

"Don't, Dalí." He cleared his throat. "If you wanted an exit, I would have found you a nice airlock instead."

His eyes gleamed at me. Shock, then a chuckle bubbled up in me. He smiled back. Knives sliced my lungs as I laughed, but I couldn't stop. I'm not sure when laughter turned into tears, deep, racking sobs that burned in my chest. My father moved and placed his forehead against mine, stroking my hair until they passed. It was a long time.

When he sat back, Dad's eyes were red. He grasped my hand between his, pressing it. "You can't stay here. It's not helping you."

"I know. But I can't go back to Luna. Not yet." *If ever.* I swallowed. "Gor asked me to come back to Zereid for a while."

"I want you to go with him. Dr. Sharp says you need more time, so I pulled some strings. Your leave is extended another six months, but you should go as soon as you're released from medical." He hesitated.

"Yesterday, Sol Fed fired on a Nos Conglomerate ship between Saturn and Neptune Station. The Nos are threatening a blockade of the Colonies."

I sucked in a breath and held it. The pain in my ribs sharpened my fuzzy thought processes. The Nos Conglomerate constituted little more than a loosely unified band of humanoid traders and merchants—read "pirates," according to the Remoliad. Early encounters with them pushed shockwaves through the fabric of Sol Fed's long-held beliefs of creationist privilege. Few visible differences between our species existed. Subsequent, unfortunate conflicts with our scout ships proved they not only resembled us, they could reproduce with humans. The idea of alien-human hybrids sent a faction of people already unnerved by increasing numbers of third-gender humans into outright paranoia. The NPM and isolationist movements emerged, fed by dire predictions against the survival of the human race.

Sol Fed's recent decision to demand previous authorization for any ship just passing through our outer system was a point of contention in the membership negotiations. It was our right, but pompous, hardly being good galactic neighbors. Nos ships were well armed and outnumbered our fleet. We weren't strong enough to defend ourselves, not without the Remoliad's help. We couldn't afford to pick fights, but we did anyway.

Now they were within striking range of the inner Colonies.

Strange to think of things outside the scope of my own pain again. It would take some time. My eyes kept fluttering closed. Dad kissed my forehead, something he hadn't done since I was a child.

"Get some sleep. I'll see you tomorrow."

THE CONSTABLE BLUSTERED in as my first visitor of the morning, DNA identifications in tow. Caniberi was relieved when I told him I would not press charges, but at the same time pissed as hell he couldn't do anything about it. Taking on the most powerful family in the New Puritan colony of Europa did not top my list of priorities at the moment.

My priority consisted of getting out of the pod and the white, flappy smock that left my ass out in the ventilation. I stayed surrounded by goddamned artificial medical assistants with the Batterson Robotics logo displayed on their chassis. Anxiety did not relinquish its hold on me even when Gor came to visit. He spoke with the doctor, who reprogrammed the bots to stay out of my personal space. It was better afterward.

The pain lingered, but became more tolerable. When Dr. Sharp believed my claims of improvement, she let me leave the bed. She allowed me a set of scrubs but confined me to the medical bay.

Even walking around the pod proved more difficult than I imagined. The good doctor remained quite opinionated about my recovery, and I chafed under the restrictions, although, I grudgingly admitted she knew what she was doing.

She was also more than a little curious about my uniqueness among the third gender.

"May I ask you some personal questions?" became a mantra the week I convalesced under her care. I didn't mind answering, if only to make Tella Sharp turn shades of pink. I suspected she'd led a sheltered life. She was young, quite lovely, and if I had to guess, in her first practice after residency somewhere civilized. I picked up little from her in my empathic nets. Her focus and control usually kept her emotions buried beneath routine. Rasida was the same way when she worked, the elements of her private life compartmentalized in the deepest parts of her mind. I'd found the fiery, passionate personality beneath Sida's scientist alter ego. I wondered about Tella's.

"So, do you view me as an interesting genetic mutation, or the knell of doom for the human race?" I asked questions of my own, sometimes rather tartly.

"I find you interesting as a person who just happens to have a fascinating genetic trait." She let my sarcasm roll off. We were becoming comfortable enough with each other not to take offense when either of us got salty. "I read a summary of a paper last year that suggested it's a corrective mutation rather than a malignant one. I found it easier to agree with than the doom and gloom predictions."

I grew still. "A natural progression allowing transgenderism to correct itself."

"That's the one. Their arguments were rather passionate but logical. People whose gender identities didn't match their birth sex appear in some of Earth's earliest recorded history. The concentration of intersex and transgender individuals in the Hijra colony on Luna, where the first refugees from Earth were evacuated, was the clear beginning of a bottleneck." Her brow creased. "What is the scientist's name? I feel like I should know it."

"Rasida Gresham-Tamareia." The name fell from my lips like an invocation.

Her hands ceased their busy flow over the touch screen. "Your wife," she said.

"They called her the most brilliant geneticist they'd seen in years. The government tried to recruit her, but she chose to work for the university, instead, and continue the study. It's how we met."

Rasida published the paper after six years of research and painstaking analysis of her data. I'd volunteered as a test subject during my junior year and fell in love with the dark-eyed grad student whose work subverted the claims of NPM-sponsored scientists.

"Her final hypothesis about changeling traits?" Tella inquired.

"A self-terminating mutation in this corrective flux." I smiled without mirth. "It isn't likely to proliferate, since we can't contribute to the reproductive process without genetic assistance. Changelings will be a brief note in the history of our species, rather than the permanent addition the NPM's doomsayers predict. But her new work...now, that's something that would have shaken some of these isolationist assholes to the core."

"What was she working on?"

"She proved we have a common ancestor with the Nos."

"What?" Tella's shock was clear. "Why haven't I heard about this before? That's important research."

"She'd won a grant to further the study before I was appointed to the Remoliad. It was one of the reasons she and Gresh decided to stay on Luna during my mission." I swallowed, hard. My emotions were in turmoil, memories coming in a rush I couldn't stem.

"Your husband practiced as a human rights solicitor, didn't he? Was he third gender?"

"No. Gresh—Andrew—was very much male."

"You were his wife?"

"No. Gresh liked men. I was husband to both of them."

"Oh." Her complexion flushed crimson as she worked things out.

Small minds leap to pornographic images—yes, mine too—but it wasn't like that between the three of us. Gresh and I were already committed by the time I fell in love with Rasida. They were close friends. Since I am incapable of reproduction, Gresh and genetic manipulation allowed a way for me to contribute to the laboratory-assisted conception of our child. While all three of us were biological parents, only I shared Rasida's bed. We were a boring, normal, married threesome who loved each other fiercely.

I expect never to find such a level of communion again.

"Tell me more about Gresh and Rasida." Tella watched me, aware I was struggling against a loss of composure. I took a breath.

"They—I—" Tears threatened and burned my eyes. I still couldn't talk about them with clinical detachment. I turned my back on Tella, embarrassed. Her hand lay softly on my shoulder for a moment, and her sympathy flowed over me. She left soon after.

The physical symptoms of withdrawal from the illegal vapes played themselves out while I was still unconscious, but I struggled with the psychological sequelae now. I had no access to chemical crutches that dulled the pain. I shut out Tella's attempts to engage me in conversations about the loss of my loves. The subject remained off-limits until I surfaced from nightmares in a cold sweat, my own scream echoing back from the walls of the pod.

The robotic assistants that monitored my vital signs were set into alarm by my racing heart and buzzed around me. Their presence increased my panic. I shoved one away, and it collided with the other. They both made annoyed electronic chittering sounds. I sat in bed, panting. Tella padded in from her quarters adjoining the medical pods, sleepy and concerned.

"Dalí, what's happening?"

"I'm sorry I woke you, Dr. Sharp. I'm all right." My voice sounded hollow in my own ears.

She studied the readouts on the screens for a second before she waved the complaining bots away with a flap of her hand. They withdrew in sullen, artificial silence. She drew the chair up beside the bed.

"You have nightmares every night. What are they about?"

"The explosion at Luna Terminal." I ran a shaking hand over my face, damp with tears I hadn't known I shed.

In my nightmares, I see Rasida's blue gown and Gresh's red hair as they float side-by-side, motionless in space.

In reality, I saw nothing but the first explosion. Spots filled my vision with blank, white blobs. My shuttle rolled over, pounded by the force of the blast. By the time the pilot regained control of the craft, nothing remained but a cloud of debris. The amputated limb of the space terminal hung by twisted girders. Everyone inside the arm of the terminal who wasn't incinerated by the blasts suffocated, exhaled into the void above the argent sphere of Luna by a rush of evacuating air.

Tella leaned forward. "I'm so sorry. I read about it in your file, and I can't imagine your pain. I'm willing to listen if it helps. Tell me what you loved most about Gresh and Rasida."

"I can't yet." Hot tracks followed the course of the first.

"All right. Then tell me what drove you insane. What made you argue with them?"

Surprised, I stared at her. She waited. I stammered, thinking.

"Ah...Gresh made this terrible dish he loved, some kind of tank-grown seaweed thing, but Sida and I couldn't eat it without gagging. He'd take offense when we went out to a restaurant instead. He sulked."

"What about Rasida?"

A smile crept at the corner of my lips. The pain stayed level and didn't rip me to shreds. "She hated my kilts. She preferred me to dress in a sherwani, when I wasn't in uniform, but she'd buy wild prints that made people stare at me more than usual. I complained and told her I wouldn't wear anything with print or embroidery except at our wedding."

"What did you wear for your wedding?"

"A scarlet sherwani with gold embroidery. Her choice. Gresh insisted his be more muted, though. Dark gold, like honey." I closed my eyes. "Rasida's gown was like a flame, crimson and orange and yellow. I married fire and honey. It was fitting."

It was the first memory of a joyful time, since their deaths, that didn't send me into a spiral of despair. I opened my eyes and looked sidelong at Tella.

"You tricked me. And I thank you."

"I have my moments." She rose, yawning. "Do you want something to help you go back to sleep?"

"No. I think I'm all right." Strangely, I was.

"Call if you change your mind. Good night." She left the room, and I lay back, holding the fragile memory of our wedding day close in my thoughts. I only dozed, but the dreams were muted, the rounded edges of sea-worn stones instead of jagged shards of glass.

Four

"HOW DO YOU see yourself?" Tella asked me on the morning she removed the last of the nanopatches from my skin.

"What do you mean?"

"Male? Female? Both?"

"No one ever asked me that question." I thought for a moment. "I see myself as 'neither.' I'm something different altogether." I winced as one of the patches threatened to take skin with it. "Ouch."

"Just hold still. You're lucky you don't have much in the way of body hair. So, your determination of gender when you interact nonsexually is based on what people want from you? Nurturing female, warrior male; that sort of thing?"

"It's a little more than that. I have a high degree of empathy. Not enough for psi-ops, but enough to give me advantage. I learned to rely on it in the way the Zereid do. Gor's people depend upon empathic sense to relate to each other. My friend can't show a lot of facial expression." I wiggled my eyebrows in demonstration.

"It caught my attention."

"It helps to get hints of what people feel, and what they want, especially in sexual situations. Another advantage to growing up on Zereid was their culture lacks societal gender expectations. Pair bonds are fluid and not exclusively heterosexual except for purposes of reproduction. Everyone is expected to do what needs to be done, from military service to caring for younglings. Living there meant freedom to be myself. I wasn't pushed in any direction in regard to sexuality. I don't think third-gender individuals who grow up in the colonies possess that sense of self beyond the two usual genders. They view their neutrality as a burden rather than a comfortable alternative and struggle to fill one of those roles."

"You don't?" She glanced at me sidelong. "You just said you look for hints to tell you what your lovers want. You wait to figure out where you fit into other people's needs. Where do your own come in?"

I opened my mouth to answer and didn't find one. Not one I wanted to share at the moment, anyway. "Did anyone ever tell you you're irritatingly perceptive?"

"Once or twice." She wiggled the next nanopatch out of my skin and examined the pelt of hair-thin needles to be certain no strays got left behind. I thought about her observation for a moment.

"I didn't struggle with it until we came back to Sol Fed and started to date my peers. I think I was the frequent subject of sexual experimentation."

"That must have been terrible for you."

"Sarcasm, Dr. Sharp? No, I never complained, and I'll be the first to admit I rarely hesitated. I still don't. I like sex." I enjoyed the view of her fair skin warming with tones of pink as she concentrated on lifting the edges of the last two patches. "But I never had to be cautious about who I am outside the bedroom until now. The NPM and their views on species preservation... I got quite a shock when I discovered I'm a genetic abomination."

"We're not all like that, Dalí." Her voice chided softly. "The Europan sect is pretty scary, even for me."

"Aha. I knew you were a virgin." The final patch nested low in my groin, the only area I do have body hair. She wasn't gentle this time. I whistled a Zereid profanity through gritted teeth, my eyes watering.

"You deserved it," she said primly. "I was married. For a while."

"What happened?" I stood up and put on my own clothes while she tapped more information into her PDD.

"Those gender roles you talked about? I couldn't conform to the 'go forth and multiply' part of New Puritanism, and it isn't negotiable with my husband. The survival of the human race is apparently dependent upon his progeny. I'm not ready for children. He put me aside—the guiltless word for divorce."

For the first time, I caught something of her emotions in my empathic senses. Sadness. Anger. Even fear. "I'm sorry."

"I'm not." She slid the screen away. "So, that's it, then. You're free. I want to see you in a week to make certain your heart's fully healed before you start any kind of training programs."

"I'm leaving for Zereid tomorrow with Gor."

"Oh." She hid her disappointment well, but the flare of it spun poignantly in my senses and touched me in an unexpected way. We'd become friends, separated by a doctor-patient formality, but somewhere, it tangled with a mutual spark of attraction.

"Follow-up with the ship's doctor, then. Your inoculations are all up-to-date. I'll transmit an encrypted copy of the records to your station file."

"Thank you, Tella. For everything." I paused. "I don't know when I'll come back, but I'll be in touch."

"I'm afraid I won't be here long. This is only a temporary assignment until the new station medic arrives. I'm picking up a surgery appointment on Mars. One of their militia reserve medical officers is shipping out to the base on Enceladus in a few weeks. It's a fresh start in a new place."

It was my turn to be disappointed. "This is goodbye, then."

She smiled at me. "I'll attach my new contact information to the records."

MY NARROW, CRAMPED quarters never bothered me while numbed by the intensity of my grief and chemical crutches. Tonight, it seemed to be closing in. I found myself eager to leave Rosetta Station behind.

Restlessness kept me tossing for an hour or two before I surrendered and sat on the side of the bed. I'd given my vapes to Gor for disposal. I didn't trust myself not to pick them back up. I considered going for a walk but feared the demons I'd exorcised for now still haunted the corridors and underbelly of the Labyrinth.

A chime sounded on the port, signalling someone requested access. The glowing clock read after 0100 hours. Enough wariness remained in the wake of my brush with eternal sleep to check the view screen for a hint of who waited outside. I'd burned a few bridges with some of the crew as well.

It was Tella. My pulse sped up.

A touch on the plate, and she stepped in, her cheeks pink. She apologized. "I'm sorry it's so late. I thought you might want a holo copy of your medical records, instead..."

I thumbed the door closed. I didn't need to read her emotions to know it wasn't the reason she'd come. The holo card she held out fell to the floor as her arms went around me, her mouth covering mine. I devoured her lips; my hands tangled in her hair. Our clothing made a pile in front of the door when we took the two steps to bed.

She pushed me down on the mattress. Blood surged and filled the sensitive tissues between my legs, and when her hand stroked me there, I shuddered in sensory overload. Every nerve ending that normally rearranged itself was still concentrated in a deliciously inflamed area with nowhere to go but detonation.

Tella began to trail kisses down the side of my neck and jawline, my chest. She bit gently at my nipples, and my breath caught in a groan.

"Tella..." She covered my mouth with hers and kissed me again, bringing the pace down even further from its frantic beginning. Making love to me. Change hormones sent rampant little chemical bombs through my bloodstream, but as yet I had no clue toward Tella's sexual inclinations. I pulled away and begged, "Tell me what you want."

"Isn't it obvious? I want you, Dalí. Just you."

Her eyes smoldered as fingers swirled around the swollen flesh between my thighs and eased beneath the fold of skin over my mons, where tissue awaited the chemical signals for external or internal arousal. Her touch elicited a spasm that rocked my head back into the mattress, and my external erection leaped into full engorgement. "Oh, god! Where did you learn that? I don't think my heart is ready for this."

"Trust me. I'm a doctor."

The pressure of her hand teased and stroked me to rigid, a purr of approval in her throat. "Different than I thought it would be. Thicker, and so smooth."

The path of her tongue down my stomach gave me little warning before her mouth enveloped me. Blind with sensation, heat and softness an excruciating pleasure, I couldn't form words or thought. It didn't take long for her to bring me to the edge and push me over. My body shook in violent tremors, a groan torn from deep in my chest. When I could see again, her lips curved in a complacent smile, pale hair tousled around her face in a golden halo. Playful and self-satisfied, she slid her body over mine and back up for a soul-grazing kiss. Time to teach her an advantage to changeling anatomy: no refractory period.

I rolled Tella under me, my arms beneath her hips, her surprised laughter transported into a gasp as I eased into her, still rock-hard and ready. My head bent to her breast, circling the swollen bud of a nipple. I sucked it into my mouth in gentle counterpoint of my movement inside her.

"Oh!" Tella's fingers tightened in my hair. "How long does it last?"

"As long as I want it to—with the right stimulation."

"Conserve your strength." Long legs wrapped around my waist. "You promised me a demonstration of both genders."

Her enthusiasm inspired me. We proved my repaired heart capable of withstanding orgasm not once, but three times. Tella's final tally was four.

"I swear I don't make a habit of seducing my patients," she murmured afterward.

"I'd hope not. I don't think many would survive it."

She chuckled low in her throat, and her hand traced the scar near my sternum.

"Why did you decide to visit me, then?" A tinge of guilt in her aura made me wonder. The question hung between us for a long moment before she answered.

"I like you a great deal. You fascinate me, and you break my heart, all at once. I think we're in the same place. I can't pretend I understand what it's like for you, but I see the same expression on your face I see in the mirror. We're both adrift and more than a little lost."

"I don't know who I am anymore. It's one of the reasons I'm going back to Zereid for a while, where I can just...be. But it's easier now, knowing I have a friend. I don't have many."

"What about Gor?"

"Gor doesn't find me attractive in any gender."

"His loss. You're beautiful."

"So are you." I stroked pale hair away from her eyes. "Thank you, Tella. You gave me another gift tonight I didn't expect." I kissed her again. She returned it with warmth. Things began to get interesting once more, but before we reached the point of no return, the mechanical voice of her com badge interrupted officiously from the pile of clothes in front of the door:

"Dr. Sharp, report to medical pod six. Maternity."

"Baby on the way. I need to go." She rose from bed, my hand trailing her arm until our fingertips parted reluctantly. Tella skimmed into her clothing and pulled her hair back into a knot. She picked up the holo card from where it had fallen.

"My contact frequencies are in the records. Let me know when you've reached Zereid safely." She placed it in my hand and bent for another kiss. "I wish you peace," Tella whispered. She was gone as the port hissed closed behind her.

In the remaining few hours of early morning, I slept dreamlessly for the first time in six months.

GOR DIDN'T EXAGGERATE about the permissions required to travel in or out of Sol Fed since the Nos fired on our patrol ships. My diplomatic credentials earned me relatively easy clearance, but it still required separate permissions from my home colony of Luna, Rosetta Station, and the Zereid Embassy.

The Andari-registered *Bedia*, a bulbous, two-hundred-passenger vessel, hosted several oxygen-breathing species on board besides the humans embarking at Rosetta. The diminutive, fish-like Andari flickered about in schools of three or four. Family groups of Zereid moved in a serene pavane through the tubular atrium, and at least one tawny-pelted Ferian slunk in feline grace through the corridors of the passenger quarters.

Holo screens mimicked windows, showing recorded views of the vast starfields through which we traveled. Before the advent of exotic matter drives, a gift of technology from our Zereid allies, travel from Luna to the last outpost of human civilization on Neptune Station could take months. Now it takes only days. But Zereid lies six weeks away, a series of four Einstein-Rosen bridge jaunts—what the galactics call 'dark space' travel. At top speed between wormholes, time still crawls to the countdown of the voyage clock. Carefully programmed climate adaptors prepare the passengers for the gaseous mix of Zereid's atmosphere little by little during the trip, and if you're desperate, you can watch the numbers creep up and down. Even on the starliners, in relative luxury, there is only so much you can do to stay busy.

Once the ship's doctor cleared me, I began to refresh my *zezjna* skills in the gymnasium with Gor. If he expected me to earn my keep and teach younglings in the temple their basic forms, I had to be in better shape. A seven-year-old Zereid is nearly my equal in height and weight and just as strong.

Zezjna is based on empathic instinct and visceral sensation, eschewing deadly force to neutralize your opponent's threat. Yes, ass-kicking on occasion. Strength helps when an opponent is just over a foot taller, but I don't boast the muscular power of a Zereid. I do claim an advantage. I can bend, roll, and tuck myself out of many of the attacks with sheer agility. On a good day, anyway.

These were not good days.

I hit the floor for the eighth time in our session and groaned. My ribs creaked under the strain.

"Put on the body armor."

"I don't want it." I knew Gor currently treated me with the same care he did his youngling charges, and it rankled my pride.

"It is either that, or re-break your ribs. Put it on."

I belted it on with sullen compliance. I wasn't behaving any better than his students, to be sure. I faced Gor across the mat. Training ended quickly, with my face plastered on the pads, after the next pass. Fire enveloped a dislocated shoulder.

"We will stop. I am sorry. You are not listening inside, my friend." He helped me to my feet. "Tomorrow, you meditate instead. Body and mind must work together, not in opposition."

The degree of beating I took only proved my concentration still suffered. He dropped my physical training back to every other day for the first week as I reacquainted myself with the mental disciplines of *zezjna*. Afterward, I started to hold my own again.

On the days I nursed bruises and the raw aftermath of dislocations, I reoriented myself to what had happened since the bombing. As much as I hated to admit it, Kiran Singh held the moral high ground when he called me out. I was appalled at how out of touch I'd been. I kept up my nocturnal schedule and visited the library, when the rest of the ship slept, to read or scan archived news holos from the Fed.

It was the missing-persons reports I found most disturbing.

It's impossible to wander out of climate domes without someone aware you're leaving. Especially with heightened security due to the conflict with the Nos, DNA identification is scanned at every terminal and doorway. The vanished individuals didn't report back to work, to university, to militia training, or return to their partners even though their ID never showed a departure. No bodies were ever found.

Sensational journalists like Singh weren't the only ones who speculated hate crimes. I knew one of the missing by name—Akia Parker, a human rights solicitor like Gresh. His case was classified as a possible homicide, based on threats he received during an investigation into the Dickensian conditions of some of the protein processing plants on Mars. Other disappearances got chalked up to "high-risk lifestyles"— the insinuation clear it was their own fault.

Intrusive media bots buzzed and harangued their loved ones with metallic-voiced requests for statements. The anguished eyes of these people haunted me. The sight of the globular bots hovering around them brought an unbidden vision.

In the terminal window overlooking my waiting starliner, I spotted them: Rasida's blue dress a jewel set in gray steel and glass, Gresh's red hair a beacon. One hand on her rounded belly, Sida placed her other hand on the pane. I pressed my palm against the window of the shuttle. Gresh put his arms around her as she dashed away tears. The insistent media bot maneuvered into the window beside them. And it erupted into a white-hot nova of flame and shattered glass...

I swept the holo off the screen with a convulsive movement. I'd made headway, but unexpected things still triggered a miasma of bewildered pain and rage. Anxiety ebbed, but the troubling facts of these reports still bothered me.

Without fail, all eleven of the missing were changelings. After a decade of living among my own species, particularly on Luna, a bastion of liberal arts and sciences, I'd met only a handful of other changelings in the third-gender community. Few acknowledged their difference in high profile like Kiran Singh and me, even in the Hijra quarter, that most bohemian enclave of the Colonies. The suggestion these people would openly flaunt their changeling qualities seemed doubtful. There were perhaps only six hundred third-gender individuals with this mutation scattered throughout Sol Fed.

Statistically, these disappearances could not be coincidental.

Five

I TOOK MEALS alone or in our cabin with Gor and avoided public areas during the rest of the passengers' waking hours. But the captain of the liner invited 'Ambassador Tamareia and guest' to dine privately with her one night. I hesitated before accepting.

Technically, I remained on leave from the Diplomatic Corps even though I traveled under my credentials. I'd packed and unpacked my dress uniform six times before shoving it back into my bag, irritated with my indecision. I neither wanted nor required any formal receptions, but Captain An'ksh could help bring me up to speed on the situation with the Nos, free from our media's filtered view. I keyed in accommodation instructions and informed Gor he would be my date.

I drew my hair back into a low queue and dressed in the dark-blue tunic. The silver crescent of the Lunar Militia gleamed on my left shoulder. The golden sunburst of Sol Fed blazed on my right, and green laurels of diplomacy encircled both cuffs. I hadn't worn the uniform since the memorial service. It didn't feel right anymore.

Gor didn't dress up, of course. He made a concession to formality and deference to the tender sensibilities of other species with a priestly sash, draped around his neck and crossed in front to hide his marsupial pouch. His blue nether regions were still exposed fore and aft.

We were shown into the Captain's dining room and issued personal translators. I rested the microphone patch in the hollow of my throat beneath the banded collar of my tunic. Gor's enormous hands dwarfed the delicate tech. I assisted him in placing his mic between the twin nasal cavities on his forehead and set the tiny, nearly invisible earpiece against the aural opening near his jaw.

As we approached, Captain An'ksh bowed her smooth-skinned head to us in greeting. "Ambassador Tamareia. Welcome." The translation from her patch, a beat behind her sibilant native language, sounded in my ear. "Honored Gor, I see you. Please join me for drinks. We are waiting for one more guest."

An Andari pair, their throat-gills fluttering rapidly, stayed close to Captain An'ksh and moved gently in her wake as she spoke to us. The captain, by necessity, embodied an alpha status among her people. They followed her at a distance. Their graceful movements twinned with hers even when they weren't watching her directly, a dance to silent music. I found interaction with schools of Andari hypnotic and oddly calming.

"I am glad Sol Fed petitioned to formally join the Alliance, but I do not understand why it is taking so long." The Captain handed us slim beakers of an emerald liqueur. The fluid held a fragrant bouquet of chlorophyll and flowers, pungent and sweet on my tongue. "With Nos pirates attacking your ships, I fear there is little time to lose."

"Each of our colonies has its own government in addition to the elected leaders of Sol Fed. They all must agree to abide by the treaty. There are some reluctant parties who believe an independent future is more desirable for the human race." I left out my strong opinion these holdouts were motivated by xenophobia and the threat of profit loss. Refugee status in the Remoliad Alliance would allow any of our new allies to provide us with things we were unable to get on our own: building materials; food; advanced technology. President Batterson and his robotics empire didn't want free tech streaming into the Colonies—profits would plummet. Greed will undoubtedly be the downfall of humanity.

"Your species needs the protection and support of the Allied forces, but until you request assistance, we cannot interfere. That, too, is part of the treaty."

"What is your view of the conflict with the Nos, Captain An'ksh?" I asked.

"The situation escalated without any warning. Most strange. Your government's new requirements to pass even through the edges of the system seemed to provoke them. I understand why permission is necessary to enter the inner Colonies, but to simply claim the entire sector as sovereign space without colonization seems..."

"Rude?" Gor suggested.

"Unconventional, to say the least. The Nos themselves are so divided, there has been no formal statement regarding war from the Conglomerate's governing body, if one could even call it such. The clans cannot agree on anything."

A message arrived as we talked, and the Captain nodded briskly when one of the attendants murmured in her ear. She turned to us. "Our other guest is unavoidably delayed and will join us for dessert. Shall we dine?"

The round table represented a work of art. A flexible surface area adjusted before each being to accommodate tall Zereid knees and diminutive Andari physiques. Her attendants delivered the first course, a platter of greens and the heavy, red, bean-like staples of the Zereid diet, portioned into disks the circumference of my head. Gor tucked in immediately and picked up a slice with delicacy despite the enormous size of his hands.

"The custom of dining with the Captain is not an Andari tradition," Captain An'ksh confessed. "I learned of it from my human first officer, and I thought it charming. As I am something of an amateur anthropologist, the event gives me an opportunity to get to know other species as we do what we all must do regardless of our origins: consume nutrients. This at least, is something all life forms share."

"I count myself fortunate I grew up in the Sol Fed Embassy on Zereid. I met many species. My mother taught me the first step to alliance is finding common ground."

"Forgive me if I do not understand, Ambassador, but I can see few physical differences between humanity and the Nos. Would it not be a good beginning to peace?"

"One would think so, but instead, we hated each other on sight."

"Miscreants, the lot of them." Gor made a sound of disgust. "They boarded a Zereid relief ship not long ago and stole supplies meant for the Colonies."

"Your people could receive so much more with the refugee status Remoliad membership would bring." The Captain's gills fluttered in bemusement.

"I cannot disagree, Captain." We remained our own worst enemies. Like President Batterson, Edward Hyatt, the new Head of the Sol Fed Senate, had a personal business potentially affected by Remoliad aid. He owned much of the hydroponics industry on Mars. Of all the colonies, Mars most needed the building materials the Alliance could provide to abate the crowded tenements. But with relief supplies of food easing demand on his processing plants, Hyatt's stakes would also be diminished. His vehement isolationist stance was not as steeped in dogma as the NPM's, but was no less baffling.

The salad course was removed and replaced with the main dish, an Andari delicacy. "I wished to represent all our cultures at this dinner," the Captain told us. "This is a meal we serve to welcome friends, as it is difficult to make and conveys the regard of the host. I did not prepare it myself—I beg your forgiveness. My chefs are experts and can manage preparation with twenty-four hours' notice." She glanced at Gor. "The dish is completely vegetarian, honored guest."

She poured green-gold oil from a beaker over the deep pan. The contents erupted into movement; long, cylindrical tendrils splashed sauce on the table. Captain An'ksh showed us how to use calipers to capture the wriggling stuff in the dish. She speared one writhing creeper with the pointed arm of the utensil and bit the ruffled end of the vegetable with her smooth dental plates. The vine went limp. The dish reminded me of giant asparagus—if beefy asparagus went rogue and tried to escape the dinner table.

Once our meal was subdued, Captain An'ksh admitted, "I have an ulterior motive for inviting you to dine, Ambassador. I received a report this morning after we emerged from dark space: the Nos detained and searched another passenger liner originating from Rosetta Station. They were waiting on the opposite side of a wormhole when the ship came out."

Gor and I exchanged troubled glances. "Do you have any idea why they would detain a passenger ship?" I asked.

The Captain's throat gills opened and closed in a staccato pattern, the equivalent of a negative headshake. "The reports are sketchy. The crew and passengers were held in the main dining area under armed guard while a squad of Nos searched through the cargo bay. They were looking for something but did not find it. They did not hesitate to stun anyone who resisted. None were killed. I am concerned for two reasons: first, the other ship is also Andari registered. Second, they departed at almost the same time as the *Bedia*, but in another direction. I cannot help but wonder if they detained the wrong vessel, and if there is something on mine they seek."

I pondered this as she continued, "I am worried. Our next dark space jaunt terminates inside a Nos trade corridor. Should anything occur, may I call upon you for assistance as a military advisor and negotiator?"

I suppressed a sigh. "Captain, you should know I am currently on leave from the Diplomatic Corps. I was recently widowed and not certain I'm fit for duty."

Dismay fanned her gills and brushed my mind softly. "I had no idea. My sincerest condolences, Ambassador."

"Thank you." I considered a moment. "Should we be detained, I will assist as best I can."

"I can ask no more. We shall continue to hope your assistance will not be required."

"Are we armed, Captain?" Gor asked.

"No. We are not."

The captain's attendants returned with the delayed sixth guest in tow. My breath stopped. With them was a ghost.

The woman who stood in the doorway resembled Rasida so much I almost stumbled to my feet in shock. Gor's head swiveled to me in alarm at the surge of emotion against his empathic nets. The Captain rose to greet the new arrival.

"My friend?" Gor questioned with concern. I managed to nod my head and confirm I was all right.

As my sense returned to me, it became obvious she was not Sida. Unfortunately, I did know her.

Captain An'ksh motioned to the table at large. "Welcome. We are about to begin dessert. Will you join us? This is Dr. Yesenia Atassi."

Dr. Atassi took the chair opposite. Her eyes swept Gor with a thin smile, and when she reached me, the expression faltered.

"Dalí." Her discomfiture rivaled mine. I bowed my head in cool greeting.

"Dr. Atassi."

The Captain looked between us. "You are acquainted with each other already? How splendid."

"Yes." Dr. Atassi recovered quickly and sat down. It was anything but splendid, but if she behaved herself, so would I. The steward took our plates away and replaced them with a bowl of fresh fruit grown in Sol Fed hydroponics.

"Dr. Atassi, what is your field of study?" Gor inquired as we started dessert.

"I am a geneticist."

"I believe you told me you are to speak at the Remoliad?" The Captain prompted.

"I have been asked to present my work in support of treaty exemptions allowing genetic manipulation of our species. There is a threat constituted by genetic drift in the human race as it recovers."

"It sounds fascinating. Will you tell us about it?"

The left side of my mouth twitched and threatened a sardonic smile as I waited for Dr. Atassi's reply. She didn't look at me, but at the Captain instead.

"The recent bottleneck of our species allowed a genetic mutation to proliferate, one which affects the reproductive system. An increasing number of humans are now born with both male and female sexual characteristics. Some are calling it the rise of a third gender, instead of the threat it truly is."

"Why is it a threat? The Cthash have three genders."

Gor bit into an unpeeled banana. Relieved to have something to distract me from the litany of bigotry disguised as science, I showed him how to release the fruit from its skin.

"Yes, but their third gender provides an enzyme critical to fertilization. When these individuals reproduce with a normal human"—here, I almost choked on the liqueur—"the genes in the mutation often result in what are called changeling traits. It can imitate both genders for sexual purposes but serves no role in reproduction. These mutations are sterile, without any true reproductive organs at all. If allowed to go unmanipulated, the ability of humanity to sexually reproduce itself could be severely reduced within a few dozen generations."

"Really? Why, it sounds disastrous," Captain An'ksh said. I could not stay silent now.

"Dr. Atassi's theory"—I made certain to stress the word—"has been challenged by a number of scientists. It's based on her projections alone with no real hard data to support it. One scientist disproved it with her own calculations."

"As you are aware, I stand by my research." Her animosity against my empathic senses showered over Gor as well. He was mystified, silver eyes growing round with curiosity.

"Oh, I remember." We glared at each other.

The captain broke the uncomfortable silence at last. "I understand it is customary to conclude this event with a pledge. In the spirit of peace, may we agree we will endeavor to learn more about the similarities between us instead of the differences."

"Hear, hear," I muttered, and raised my glass as well.

"To understanding." Gor agreed. Dr. Atassi lifted her glass but said nothing.

I excused myself not long afterward. I thanked the Captain for her hospitality, and urged Gor to stay as long as he wished. I left the translator patch with the attendants.

My long, irritated strides didn't carry me back to the solitude of our cabin, but to the gymnasium, where I stripped off my dress tunic and boots. I vented my frustration in violent, controlled bursts of *zezjna* against the immovable punching bag until my breath caught painfully and my knuckles were bruised. Exhausted, I crumpled to the mat and lay there until sob-like gasps subsided into something like normal breathing.

I looked up at Gor, who'd eventually found me. "I thought I was doing better. I'd rather go back to being numb."

"The scabs get scraped off and bleed again. It will happen." He paused. "Who is the female, Dalí?"

I closed my eyes. "Dr. Atassi is Rasida's mother."

"Ah." The flute-like quality of his voice sighed with a note of comprehension. "She despises you."

"The feeling is mutual."

Six

THE INEVITABILITY OF another encounter with Dr. Atassi was only a matter of logistics. Three weeks remained in the voyage; too long to hide, and nowhere to run.

In the middle of the ship's "night," when the other passengers slept, the deserted library hummed to the drone of the ship's engines. The viewscreen in front of me scrolled with the latest reports of skirmishes between the Nos and Sol Fed. I let the information flow past me, my thoughts scattered elsewhere. I didn't expect to hear her voice at this hour.

"I've never forgiven you and Andrew Gresham for turning my daughter against me."

Yesenia Atassi moved to sit in the carrel adjoining mine and faced me over the screen. Her appearance posed less of a shock this time, the differences clear to me now. Hard lines pulled her mouth downward, where Rasida's had always tugged upward with hidden joy even in her most serious moments. The daughter's dark eyes had sparkled, and the mother's were flint-hard as they regarded me.

"Good to see you, too," I said dryly.

"You used her to further your cause."

"I loved her, and we did nothing of the kind. Rasida made her own decisions based on her research. She chose to work with us because she didn't believe in discriminatory laws against third-gender citizens."

"Because she was infatuated with you." Her lips pressed together in a thin line. "From the time she met you, it was always Dalí this, and Dalí that. Rasida wanted your approval. She would say anything."

"You hold so little regard for her skills as a scientist? Odd, when I think you taught her everything she knew before she even came to university. Sida refuted the data because hers disproved it. You can't even consider you might be wrong?"

"Because I'm not."

"Because the NPM would cease to support your research facility if you did."

"You think I'm some sort of mercenary scientist?"

"No. I think you're a dogmatist."

"I'm no Europan."

"Perhaps not, but they certainly love your work. I've had it hurled at me more than once."

Dr. Atassi's lips thinned. Her eyes sketched a round of the library, and back to me again. "She was pregnant."

"Yes."

"Gresham's?"

"And mine." I set my jaw. "The child was related to all three of us."

"You edited out the third-gender mutation?"

"No. We didn't."

Her predictable disgust fumed against my empathic nets. "You inserted changeling genetics into an otherwise normal genome? What would it have been?"

I clenched my fist under the carrel and took a deep breath to tamp down my rising anger. "Human—and loved more than anything in the universe."

"There is a reason changelings are sterile, Dalí. The mutation isn't meant to reproduce itself."

"Apparently not, Doctor. That verdict was delivered with a bomb in the Luna Terminal."

I swept the holo crawl off the screen and stalked out.

Embers of grief and rage, never extinguished, but only banked beneath a wall of ashes, threatened to reignite in an inferno. I had no way to numb myself against it this time. I'd left the chems behind on the station. I wanted to vape so badly I shook. My heart raced. Cold sweat broke out on my forehead.

I lurched into the deserted atrium. The moment I turned into the silent promenade, I staggered to avoid a collision with a tiny obstacle, my headlong flight interrupted.

A Zereid youngling crawled through the padded benches, all sparkling silver eyes and blue fuzz. Her mother sat nearby, and I mumbled an apology in their language. The adult's eyes separated in surprised delight.

"I am sorry. I did not expect anyone to be about at this hour. I cannot keep her still at night since she became mobile," she explained. "She wants to explore and keep the rest of our group awake."

The youngling gazed up at me, her size comparable to a one-year-old human child. Her mind, guileless and open, brushed against mine. A strange tightness built in my chest. I returned the acknowledgement and knelt beside the infant in helpless fascination. She reached out for me, laughing. I took her into my arms because she wanted me to.

She snuggled her head beneath my chin and yawned. Her warmth and the sweet, milky scent of her fuzzy head filled me with an unanticipated longing.

"She likes you." The Zereid mother smiled and cocked her head in recognition. "You are an empath?"

"Yes." My throat constricted, my voice hollow. "How old is she?"

"She was born at the end of winter. It will be mid-summer when we return."

Only a little older than ours would have been. I cradled her sleepy head. This precious little being shattered me. Her mother rose quickly and laid a cerulean hand on my shoulder in acknowledgement of my distress, her empathic broadcast warm and concerned.

"You lost a child," she said. Her quicksilver eyes clouded with shared sorrow. "I mourn with you."

I was undone by this stranger's sympathy, her compassion. The youngling lifted her head and gazed at me. She sensed my grief, unable to comprehend it, but raised a tiny hand to touch my wet cheek in wonder. It left my remaining composure in shredded, bleeding ribbons. Blinded with tears, I gave her back to her mother and stumbled down the first corridor I came to. Every step I took seemed to drag. The weight of mountains crushed me.

Somehow, I found my way back to the cabin I shared with Gor. As I staggered over the threshold, he caught me, sat on the floor, and held me. All the demons came howling out of my head: the loss, the fucking unfairness of it all, the sudden realization of my own near-death experience on Rosetta. The Zereid can't cry, but they mourn, sharing the burden of grief between them. He bore mine and didn't flinch. Affection surrounded me, his sorrow a balm against my raw heart, turquoise skin damp with the salt of tears and all the other slimy things accompanying an emotional meltdown. It takes a true friend to deal with those kinds of bodily secretions. He never complained.

The storm ebbed, leaving me weak, lightheaded, and hollow, scoured of the months-long darkness held inside. Gor picked me up, as if I were an infant myself, and tucked me into the berth. I slept for two of the ship's days. Each time I woke, Gor's reflective eyes gleamed in the dim light, watchful and steadfast. On the third day, I dragged myself out of bed.

"Where do I go from here?" I asked him.

"First, eat. Then we train. One step follows another. One day follows another." He touched my head, and his reassurance flowed into my mind. "It is a beginning."

A WEEK OUTSIDE Zereid space, our ship entered the narrow corridor claimed by the Nos Conglomerate.

Most passengers slept through the uncomfortable parts of dark space travel, but with my ridiculously off sleep cycle, I became familiar with them. Dropping the EM bubble around the vessel resulted in quick acceleration. I ignored the stomach-flipping sensations as the *Bedia*'s engines wound up for superluminal speeds. We were free of the wormhole. Travel to the next point near Kadrel, the home of Remoliad Alliance headquarters, and our final dark space jaunt lay ahead.

Before the engines reached full power, an explosion rocked the ship.

Lights flickered. Klaxons wailed as I steadied myself, legs braced wide. Across the cabin, Gor sat up quickly in his berth when the vibration of rapid deceleration set in.

Attention, passengers. Remain in your cabins. To avoid injury, lower the restraints on your sleeping platform and await further instructions. The automated voice from the com beside my berth repeated the message in Sol Standard, echoed in Zereid's musical language by Gor's screen. A white light began to glow on mine, and I pressed my hand against the plate. "Yes?"

A human voice spoke Sol Standard. "Ambassador Tamareia? Captain An'ksh regrets your assistance will be needed after all. Can you join her on the bridge?"

Minutes later, my footsteps echoed in the corridor leading to the command deck. The door was sealed. A simple port without any reinforcement, it only reminded me this vessel was not built to withstand an attack. I pressed my palm to the scanner. One of the crew blurted a stream of burbling syllables I suspected meant "Identify yourself."

"It's Ambassador Tamareia."

The door slid open. An Andari crewman pointed a sidearm at my abdomen until Captain An'ksh motioned me inside. The human officer met me and nodded crisply as the door resealed.

"Ambassador." He handed me a translator patch, and I donned the earpiece hurriedly.

"What's happened, Captain An'ksh?"

"They were waiting for us when we came out of dark space and fired over our bow before we could go to FTL." The Captain's webbed fingers, sheathed in sensors, spread in the air in front of her. A heads-up display of space around the starliner appeared between us. She circled an area behind the ship. "There."

The radiation levels depicted outside the hull stayed evenly yellow and green, until a blink-and-you've-missed-it flurry of orange blurred and faded.

"Drive emissions," the human officer said. "They roughly match those of a Nos Conglomerate frigate. Usually a crew of fifty or so. Moderately armed, not enough to destroy our ship, but cripple it if they want to."

Captain An'ksh motioned to him. "My first officer, Commander Rion Sumner." We exchanged nods. In his midthirties, his powerful build and the way he held himself made me think career military, but he wore a generic Andari starliner uniform.

"Were you a militia pilot, Commander? I'm impressed you know their specs."

"No, sir...or...ma'am?" His brow creased in uncertainty. I'd chosen a calf-length, blue kurta and trousers instead of my Corps tunic. If we were about to be boarded by the Nos, a Sol Fed uniform would be a likely target.

"Ambassador is fine." He understood, and I noted a shift. It wasn't disrespect, simply a lessening of formality. My empathic nets read nothing negative from him; in fact, I sensed nothing at all. Odd.

"I used to pilot a freighter until I got tired of losing cargo to these bastards. It's how I got to know them. I thought passenger liners would be secure. More fool, I."

"Did you receive any demands?"

"We've been ordered to come to full stop so they can land a shuttle." Captain An'ksh sighed. "I had no other option but to capitulate."

"It's all we can do at the moment. You did say we have no armaments?"

"None, save for the officers' sidearms."

"Standard repulsor fields?"

"Commercial grade, not military. Nothing that will deflect a plasma cannon." Sumner pursed his lips. "But they won't want to risk damaging anything they can sell for a profit at the Market."

"The Shontavian Market?" Like the underbelly of Rosetta, but much more frightening, the Market floated in deep space, its location unknown unless one was issued an invitation to take part. Rumor had it anything was available there—for the right price. "There has to be something on this ship they want. Can you pull up the cargo manifest, please? Are we carrying something they might be particularly interested in?"

The Captain pulled up a list. "Passenger belongings, but nothing declared of great value. Medical devices and some camera equipment. Nothing that appears to be of undue interest."

"What kind of camera equipment?" The hair on the back of my neck prickled.

She consulted the manifest. "Programmable robotic cameras, self-propelled."

Seven hells. Media bots. "What's their final destination?"

"The Remoliad."

My gut twisted. Paranoia refused to leave it alone. "I need to go to the cargo bay."

I hoped I was wrong.

Seven

"EXACTLY WHAT ARE we looking for, Ambassador?" Sumner asked as we descended into the bay. He stopped at a console and removed a sniffer pack from its base. "We check everything for excessive radiation as it comes in."

My instinct told me to trust him, although at this point, I wasn't sure I trusted myself. "At Luna Terminal, before the explosion, I saw media bots behaving strangely. I'm certain at least one of them carried an explosive device. I just...need to know."

He stared at me a moment. I still couldn't feel anything from him— why not? Accustomed to hints caught in my empathic nets, I found Sumner's null frustrating. His expression was strange, though, as if he were resigned to my interference.

He finally swore under his breath and gloved his left hand in one of the sensor sheaths. He flung up a diagram in the air, consulted it. "One of those." He motioned to a group of large shipping containers at the far end. We moved past the supply pallets of food, tanks of water, and personal property belonging to the passengers into the commercial cargo area near the back of the ship.

"This is the one." Sumner held the sniffer out to the container and swept the door. The Batterson Robotics emblem reflected the steady green glow of the probe as he carefully paced the length of the ten-meter rectangular container. "Nothing suspicious here."

"Can we open it?"

Sumner consulted the manifest and keyed a security code into the pad on the outside. It took both of us to move the massive door. Inside, the globular media bots hung dark and motionless in racks, camera eyes blind and shuttered. I counted twenty in all, suspended by twos down the sides of the crate. He waved his sniffer around them and shrugged at me.

"Nothing, Ambassador. They're all clean and accounted for."

I felt a bit foolish. I glanced at another container, which displayed no company emblems, twice the size of the Batterson crate. Electronic readouts gleamed green and red in panels along the side. "What's in this one? This is climate-controlled, but it isn't marked."

He frowned. "The data said medical equipment. Seems awfully large, though, and climate control is excessive."

"Where did it originate?"

"Europa, same as the other. Headed for the trade hub." He raised the sensor, flashing white. "Energy readings say something's active inside." Sumner tapped the same code he used to open the other container. The pad beeped in protest, glowing like a red ember. "Yeah, thought it would be too easy. Hold this." He passed the sniffer to me. "After you've been around these containers a while, you learn their quirks. Always helps to know a backdoor to use in case of emergency."

He pried a side panel off and tapped in a code on the keypad while holding down a thumb switch. The pad beeped and turned green. "Manual combination reset. Works every time."

The doors swung open on hydraulic cylinders, and we both froze at the sight of what lay within.

"What in the..." the Commander swore viciously, his surprise betraying an impressively obscene vocabulary.

Four sarcophagus-like chambers—medical pods. The glow of instrumentation revealed them all to be in use. A robotic assistant buzzed between them. As I stepped into the container, the bot retreated to one side to wait. Beneath the transparent hood of the pod, a genderless, brown-skinned body covered with nanopatches lay motionless against the cushion, their face in repose. The vital signs on the display above read slow and stable.

"They're asleep," I breathed in relief. I checked the next one. "The same. They're suspended."

"Like they used to do on sub-light ships?" Sumner moved between them, his face troubled. "What did we just stumble into?"

"No idea." Each chamber held a third-gender changeling. Most appeared to be in their early twenties; the dark-skinned changeling looked slightly older. I suspected some, if not all, were among those reported missing from the Colonies. The pods only filled half the container. A heavy metal door bisected the crate in the middle.

"Commander." A possibility occurred to me, and the slow burn of rage heated my thoughts. "Does the Nos Conglomerate deal in slave trade?"

He hesitated. "There are rumors the Shontavian Market deals in sex slaves. Nobody outside knows for sure."

Sumner's com chirped, and Captain An'ksh's translation emerged. "We will be at boarding speed in thirty-seven minutes. Is everything all right?"

"May I?"

Still dazed, Sumner handed me the com. "Captain, please send personnel and equipment to transport four medical pods up to the infirmary immediately."

"What did you find?"

"Contraband."

I swept the sniffer over the inside door. The radiation remained within safety levels, and Sumner eased the panel aside.

Eight dark media bots hung in racks. As we walked between them, the sniffer's probe vacillated between red and blue—a pattern designated for the atomic signatures of high explosives.

I raised the com. "Captain, we should use most of those thirty-seven minutes and come up with a plan to neutralize the boarding party."

"How?" The Captain's translation actually squawked. "We're a commercial passenger ship!"

"I don't know yet. Please tell passenger Gor to meet me here." I turned off the com and muttered, "Tell him I'm making this up as I go." I returned the device to Sumner. "Commander, I need a camera. And would you check the passenger manifest? Find out if a representative of Batterson Robotics is on board. Bring them to the cargo bay whether they want to come or not. Don't tell them anything."

APPARENTLY MY DESTINY was to become a thorn in the Batterson empire's side.

Within ten of our allotted thirty-seven minutes, Sumner's crew found the representative and brought him protesting to the bay, flanked by security. His voice carried through the cargo vault even before he came into view. When he caught sight of the open containers, his tone became more strident. I ignored his presence until my video records downloaded into the ship's memory for safekeeping. I reactivated the camera and set the device on top of the pod closest to the door, where it would pick up the tirade.

"I will be lodging a complaint with the Andari Trade Commission for opening goods en route to our customers. Batterson Robotics will not be responsible for any damage to these media bots, and you and your captain will be footing the bill for repairs, Commander Sumner."

"Ambassador, this is William Farmer." Sumner appeared ready to deck him as I stepped out of the container.

Surprise, surprise. I recognized him as Minion Two, Batterson's silent buddy in the Labyrinth. He could talk, after all.

He continued to bluster about damages and violations until he looked directly at me. The words died, his mouth once again hanging open. His shock at seeing me alive washed across my empathic nets.

"Son of a bitch. You," he managed.

"You are about to be charged with arms smuggling and human trafficking, Mr. Farmer. I suggest you shut the fuck up."

Sumner's eyebrows shot up, and he appraised me with new respect as Farmer babbled, "I don't know what you're talking about."

I propelled him by the front of his jacket and forced him into the open container. The medical pods still waited for transport; the mechanical assistant hovered between them as the ship's doctor checked readouts and vital signs. The panel behind remained ajar, the deactivated media bots clearly visible.

He gaped at me, stricken. "What is this?" Genuine discomfort, there; he didn't expect to see this cargo, but he recognized it. Sweating now, Farmer swallowed and motioned to the marked Batterson crate. "That's my cargo over there. I'm only a glorified delivery boy. Europa One Network is covering the treaty negotiations next month at the Remoliad. I'm supposed to show them how to program our media bots."

"Really? You can show me how to program them, instead." I smiled, a conscious echo of the last time he'd seen me. "Let's start with these." I pushed him past the medical pods and he resisted.

"I want a solicitor."

"You don't have time for a solicitor. We are less than thirty minutes away from being boarded by a Nos Conglomerate frigate."

"I don't—I didn't—I'm only an employee. They told me to get these containers on board. I had no idea what was inside this one. Do you think I'm stupid enough to bring bombs into a starliner I'm a passenger on?"

He had a point. But I did think so.

"Tell me how to activate the bots."

"Easy. Our new system is the most user-friendly yet. One push of a button and go..."

"Cut the sales pitch and show me."

Reluctantly, Farmer walked into the racks of bots and pointed. "This button. Power up and the system comes online immediately. They're fully voice programmable and they broadcast on standard frequency."

My brain fired on a level it hadn't in months as the outline of a plan took shape. "They use recognition software. Facial, team logo, helmets."

"Of course. Upload an image, or point it at a holo or a real person and activate the scanner, here. The image will be registered, and the bot will stay with the target."

"Target?" I questioned softly.

"S-subject."

I hated him even more. "I assume they work in all environments, including space." He confirmed this with a shrug of one shoulder. "Will they communicate the scanned subjects to each other?"

"They're networked to share information. If you leave them on standard frequency, you can give them remote verbal instructions."

"Unless they're armed, they won't explode; correct?"

"Yes. At least, I think so. I don't deal with that part of the product."

"Who does?"

Farmer clamped his lips shut.

"Tell me how to arm them."

"Are you insane?" His panic crested against my mind.

"These are the only weapons we have against a Nos frigate, Mr. Farmer. I suggest you tell me how to arm them."

Farmer sighed and closed his eyes. "Scan in your target. Transmit a single digit "8" to the bots. They'll arm. To detonate, transmit the word "boom." To disarm, single digit "0." He cursed bitterly. "Goddamn Batterson. He set me up to take the fall on this."

I bit back what I really wanted to say. "Commander, lock up Mr. Farmer until the threat is neutralized. If the Nos want to know who's responsible for this cargo, direct them to the brig."

"You can't do this!" Farmer wrenched his arms away from the diminutive Andari security officers and turned directly into Gor's solid blue chest. He stared up in surprised terror. My friend glanced down at him mildly.

"Do you need assistance, Dalí?"

"No. Mr. Farmer is leaving now." A crowd of medical and crew came to evacuate the pods as security escorted him away, still complaining about his rights. "How much time before we're at full stop, Commander?"

"Twenty minutes. What are you thinking?" Sumner narrowed his eyes.

"What will the Nos be armed with when they board?"

"Usually low-powered sidearms and stunner prods. Less risk of damaging goods."

"I think it's safe to assume this is what they want. Will they inspect the cargo here or on board their ship?"

"They'll want to confirm if it's here before they move it. Sickbay may not be the safest place for them," Sumner hazarded as the first of the changelings was rolled out. "Where would you look for someone in a medical pod?"

"Can they be hidden somewhere else? These people are defenseless in their condition. They'll need someone to guard them."

"I can't imagine them going into the library...no." He snapped his fingers. "The Captain's dining room. Both doors can be secured. We can post guards inside where they won't be seen."

Captain An'ksh's voice broke in from the com. "We've been ordered to move all passengers and crew not in essential functions to assemble in the atrium."

"Did they ask you for a passenger manifest?" With An'ksh's negation, I continued, "Then it's unlikely they'll miss me. I'm going to stay behind in the bay and use one of the unarmed media bots to record what's happening."

"You can't stay down here alone." Sumner grumbled. "Captain, permission to remain with the Ambassador?"

"I'm afraid I need you up here, Commander." Her uneven voice carried anxiety in its syllables before translation.

"I will stay," Gor offered, and I flashed him a grateful smile.

"I hoped you would. Captain, there will be a broadcast coming over the standard Sol Fed frequency. Record and secure the data, please."

"Understood, Ambassador."

Turning to the crew, I directed, "Make this crate appear as if the pods were never inside. The medical assistant goes with them. We have less than twenty minutes before everyone needs to be in place. Let's make it quick. Commander, may I borrow your com and your sensor glove, please? Your priority on getting back to the bridge will be to get me an image of the Nos frigate to scan into these bots."

"What are we doing, Dalí?" Gor questioned.

"Help me get eight bots out of the other container and switch them out. Then, we find an airlock."

Eight

CAPTAIN AN'KSH'S CREW did their job thoroughly, and the container lay bare of extra tech by the time Gor and I shut the sliding panel on the newly racked media bots.

I jabbed the power switch on another one of the unadulterated robots. A little tune played, sapphire light swelling in the lens eye.

"Thank you for choosing Batterson Robotics, excellence in media, medical, and personal robotics technology."

"Shut up." I scanned the container with the media bot and instructed it to broadcast an uninterrupted image of the crate and its surroundings. Gor took the bot to high ground in the bay's catwalk and left it concealed in an area thick with cables and hardware.

Carefully, I switched on the bots hiding explosives in their globular mech compartments. The Batterson Robotics logo gleamed on the instrument panel, but these bots omitted the inane little greeting. They hovered in place, lens eyes unshuttered, waiting for instructions. Even immobile, they made my chest tight with loathing. Seven fucking hells, but I hated these things. The idea some piece of shit had blithely typed in the word "boom" to kill my family and more than one hundred others in the terminal filled me with cold fury. We herded the obedient bots into the portside refuse airlock and ordered them to stay.

Sumner's voice came over the com. "Ambassador, their shuttle is prepared to dock in our bay. Once aboard, they will most likely enter through the atrium. I estimate your position will be swarming with Nos in less than ten minutes."

He certainly sounded like military. "Understood, Commander. Do you have an image of the frigate yet?"

"I'm sending a holo now. It's on our port side."

I spread my palm and activated the heads-up. A rotating, three-dimensional graphic of the blocky frigate appeared in the space above the sensor sheath.

"Perfect. You'll register the port side airlock opening in a few minutes. Can you silence any alarms or announcements in the cargo bay for the duration of their boarding?"

"Done."

I pressed the scan button on the bot. A red grid enveloped the holo image as it swept and registered the target. A blinking white light appeared on its spherical face, and one by one, the others lit up too, blinking in unison. I lifted the com and adjusted the band to standard frequency instead of the ship's.

"Extreme close-up of subject. All angles. Hold position and wait for further direction."

"Acknowledged." Robotic voices chimed back in chorus. I punched the airlock door control and the inner port hissed closed, sealing itself.

"Ambassador, the Nos are on board. This will likely be our last transmission before they take the bridge." The Captain's voice was tight.

"How many?"

"I counted fourteen, armed with small weapons as Commander Sumner predicted."

"Stay safe, Captain. Comply with their demands and tell the crew and passengers not to resist. Airlock opening in thirty seconds."

The button counted down in small red blips without the normal sensory display of flashing lights and klaxons. Bless Commander Sumner. Through the window slit on the inner door I watched eight media bots float out into space as the door opened. Their little propulsors would do the rest. They weren't coming back on board. I closed the airlock and returned to the container. Gor shut both doors without reengaging the security pad.

"I hear them." Gor lifted his head, his aural openings more sensitive than my own ears. "I think it's time to hide."

"Who said anything about hiding? *Zezjna* rules of war."

In the faint light, Gor's reflective eyes glittered as he regarded me. They elongated and the distance between them increased in a Zereid expression of anticipation. I grinned back.

WITH WEAPONS BRANDISHED in tense, jerky movements, eight humanoids entered the bay. Black armor contrasted harshly against skin tones ranging from fair to pallid, but even so, they would be difficult to identify in a crowded Sol Fed station based on appearance alone. Up close, eyes the color of ice gave away their species.

But something else bothered me. This was a boarding party. I expected to pick up excitement or even hostility from the pirates. Nothing tugged at my senses except for Gor's calm presence beside me.

"Dalí..." His empathic nets spread wide, sending ripples through my own. "There is something I should tell you about the Nos."

"What?"

"They are nulls. They have no empathic or telepathic broadcast."

I stared at him in accusation. "That might have been something to mention before you agreed to my plan." If I couldn't sense my opponent's intent, the important advantages *zezjna* held for me evaporated.

"It will be a good exercise for us both."

As I suspected, the group went directly to the container we'd left unlocked. Shouts erupted when they found it empty. The leader of the party fumbled out his com.

"Eminence Yarol." Translation came through the patch I still wore. "They're not here, either."

"What?" His communicator blatted. "This is the right ship!"

"The transport vessel is here, but nothing is inside. Correction." He paused as a subordinate came out of the container, gesticulating. "The hardware is here. The other assets are not."

"Oathbreakers!" the voice hissed. "Prepare it for transfer. Search the other containers."

The band fractured. Two made for a floater platform on the opposite end of the bay. Four began to force their way into different cargo containers. The last two split up, one to poke among the food pallets, and the one who appeared to be in charge headed for the control room where we were concealed.

"Now what?" Gor breathed in a near-silent whisper.

"We lock the doors." I pressed a combination into the panel.

"Those were not the control room doors."

"I know."

Zezjna rules of war: incapacitate the enemy without killing him. Gor took out the leader as he entered the room. His enormous hands clapped both sides of the Nos's head with a resounding smack. He eased the unconscious body to the floor, and I concealed his sidearm in a drawer.

We exited the room silently in opposite directions. Gor kept to the shadows of the huge containers, his bulk difficult to conceal anywhere else, while I slipped into a low crouch and ghosted the edge of the pallets. Adrenaline triggered my change hormones; my upper body and legs ached in the anticipation of battle.

Until I turned the corner, I didn't realize a Nos stood there. We both stared in surprise, but I recovered first. I delivered a blow to the throat to paralyze his vocal cords. A second strike to the temple rendered him unconscious, sprawled across the pallet. I pulled him off and left him behind the mound of foodstuffs, stowing his weapon out of reach between the stacked pallets. I didn't want him to wake up and shoot me.

The next raider carried a stunner prod in his hand. He shouted and swung at me, the crackle of energy passing within millimeters of my body. My kick slammed into his knee with a sickening crunch as the armor and joint bent in the wrong direction. He had time to scream before I slammed him headfirst into the side of a container. The impact echoed through the bay with a loud *bong*, and he crumpled. I heard other voices shouting in Nos. A beam from an energy weapon sent sparks and red-hot chips of metal flying over my head. I scooped up the stunner and ducked behind another pile of pallets.

I caught sight of Gor lurking behind a nearby freight container and held up two fingers. He raised three. Showoff.

Three remained. One turned left instead of right as he emerged from the narrow space between containers and missed a clear shot at me. He got the stunner prod shoved between the waist and thigh plates of his armor. The charge sent him convulsing to the floor. The one hiding behind the container's open door burned a shot close enough to char my sleeve. I knocked her weapon away with a sweeping blow from the stunner as her arm came around the side. The gun dropped from her paralyzed hand, but she got in close and grabbed the shaft of the weapon with the other. I trapped her hand and dropped, pulling her off balance and down to the metal floor where we grappled for possession.

A startled shout went without translation as the last raider crashed into the container next to us. I struggled to keep my prisoner on the floor. She was as strong as me and determined to have the stunner.

"A little help here?" I managed as Gor reappeared. He picked her up and tossed her into the open container. The breath left her lungs in a *whoof*. I recovered her fallen sidearm and pointed it at her. Alabaster eyes glinted, narrowed, but the Nos trooper stayed down.

"Well, that was fun," I panted. My ribs drummed a dull complaint in time with my pulse.

"What do you want to do with the rest of them?" Gor asked. He wasn't even winded.

"We'll lock them all in the container for now."

He carried our prisoners into the container by twos, tucked under his arms. I stripped the leader of his communicator and put the device in my pocket. Some of the Nos began to stir as we closed the door and locked it. I lifted the com Sumner had given me and transmitted the digit "8" to the bots I hoped now surrounded the pirates' frigate outside to port.

Received. Armed.

"My friend, do you know what you're doing?" Gor inquired.

"Nope."

The com speakers in the cargo bay blared in unexpected volume with Captain An'ksh's sibilant voice. Both of us scrambled for cover, startled. The translation sounded in my ear.

"Ambassador Tamareia, turn your com back to ship's frequency."

I cursed and did so. "Yes, Captain?"

If it were possible for an Andari to sound breathless, she did. "Ambassador, please return to the bridge. We have secured the ship, but the Nos are threatening to fire. I'm not sure what to do next."

Nine

IN THE ATRIUM, four bloodied Nos pirates lay on their stomachs at gunpoint. Medics tended to wounded passengers and crew. Some of the lingering crowd glimpsed Gor and me, and a strange current of excitement followed us down the corridor as we hurried to the bridge.

When they let us in, Sumner grinned at us with arms crossed over his chest. A Nos with hands cuffed behind his back sat scowling at his feet. The Andari security officer covered another prisoner with his sidearm; the Nos's weapon hung comically large at his side. Confused, I turned to Captain An'ksh.

"What happened, Captain?"

"We inadvertently began to broadcast the media bot's live footage to every screen in the ship, including the main holo where the passengers and crew were held. It had a most unusual effect on them. They watched you two neutralize the threat in the cargo bay, and seemed to realize they outnumbered the Nos. The struggle was over in minutes, but not before shots were fired. One of our prisoners managed to alert their ship before Commander Sumner subdued them. The frigate threatened to fire."

"Is their ship doing anything?"

"No. They appear to be oblivious that they're surrounded by camera bombs." Sumner tapped a screen. The main viewer showed the Nos frigate to port. "We can't even pick them up on our scanners because they're so small, but they're broadcasting on Sol Fed frequencies." He toggled between screens. Eight views of the frigate's hull, close enough to show scratches in the ship's outer skin, proved the bots accepted my instructions.

I brought the com I'd liberated from the Nos out of my pocket. "It appears negotiation is in order." I moved closer to her and whispered out of earshot of the prisoner, "Captain, you should do this. I don't want to imply Sol Fed played any part. We'd better portray this as a passenger action until we reach Zereid."

The com in my hand began to bark. "Report. Is the ship and cargo secured? We are picking up Allied military vessels in this sector."

Captain An'ksh brightened at the news. "Commander Sumner, would you verify this?" She turned to me. "If you will tell me what to say, I will do my best."

After a moment's coaching, she threw down the gauntlet, her gills fluttering. "Attention, Nos Conglomerate frigate. This is Captain An'ksh of the Andari vessel *Bedia*. Your boarding party is in custody. You violated Andari trade codes and Remoliad Alliance statutes with your illegal detention of my ship."

Silence filled the moments after her bold announcement. I imagined chaos on the bridge of the Nos frigate.

"Confirming two Alliance vessels are in the vicinity, Captain. Should I hail them?" Sumner asked. The Captain indicated her assent. She spoke again, her voice stronger.

"Alliance ships are en route to our location, Nos frigate. I suggest you disengage before they arrive, and we can settle this without military action."

"We can still disable your ship and your life support systems, Captain." The voice on the com snarled at her. "By the time the Remoliad's ships reach you there would be no one to rescue. You are an unarmed vessel."

"At this moment, eight explosive devices are within millimeters of your hull," Captain An'ksh said with brilliant nonchalance, belying the constant motion of her feathery gills. "I would consider us armed, Nos vessel. I demand to speak to your captain."

Another moment of silence ensued. "Eminence Yarol. I command this ship." The untranslated stream of speech, clipped and furious, lost something of its annoyance in transit. "You will release my crew."

"You are in no position to make demands of me, Eminence." Captain An'ksh exuded more confidence by the second. "How shall we settle this? I am willing to return your crew with assurances you will leave us to continue our voyage to Zereid without molestation."

"We do not believe your claims regarding the explosives, Captain." His aggressive tone suggested he couldn't be certain.

"Tell them to take a look at the broadcast. Maybe a close-up of their hull on camera will give them reason to believe," I said. The Captain did so.

More silence.

"Captain, Alliance vessel *Nova One* states they will reach our position in fifteen minutes," Sumner informed her.

"Do the Nos know?"

"I'm certain they do."

Minutes ticked by, and Captain An'ksh became more nervous. "Why haven't they responded? Commander, are their weapons at full power?"

"Powered, but no targeting of their main cannons, and their position remains unchanged."

"They're probably weighing their options. They don't have many. If they want to avoid a confrontation with Remoliad forces, they'll respond soon enough," I reassured her.

"With cannons or with capitulation? Should we power up our lifeboats?"

Eminence Yarol's sullen reply came over the com before I answered. "We accept your terms. Return my crew to their shuttle. We will depart as soon as they are aboard. Disarm your explosives."

"Can we trust their word?" An'ksh looked to me and Sumner.

"We can time this to the last minute, and there won't be opportunity for them to do anything but leave before the Allied ships get here. I think they'd rather avoid the military." I still wondered why Remoliad ships conveniently happened to be in the area, and why Sumner remained so composed in the face of all this for a freighter pilot. "Notify them we will disarm our explosives once the Nos are en route to their ship."

"Will he accept this?"

"Captain, we have his balls over a fire right now. He'll accept anything," Sumner told her.

His statement, the captain's confusion, and apparent unfamiliarity with humanoid male anatomy drew a snort of rather undiplomatic laughter from me. "As you said before, Captain An'ksh, Eminence Yarol has no room to protest. He'll do as we say."

She repeated our caveat to the Nos captain. He accepted with an obscenity-laden slur against the Andari species, but the confrontation was over. Captain An'ksh gave orders for the prisoners to be returned to their shuttle under armed guard and sank down into one of the instrumentation naves, the movement of her throat gills so rapid in her relief they blurred.

"You, Captain, are a force to be reckoned with." I bowed to her with deference. "Your performance was flawless."

"I never expected to be raided when I became a starliner captain," she said faintly. "And you and passenger Gor are the heroes of the hour, Ambassador Tamareia."

I'd forgotten in the heat of the negotiations and groaned inwardly. "And how, exactly, did it get broadcast to the entire ship?"

"I hit the wrong button," Commander Sumner confessed. I raised an eyebrow, and he dared me to contradict him with the hint of a smirk. This man was never just a simple freighter pilot. Something of my suspicion must have shown on my face, because he flushed, straightened, and said, "Captain, I will oversee the transfer of the prisoners to their ship."

"Yes, thank you, Commander."

He turned to Gor and me. "Do any of the Nos locked in the container need medical attention?"

"Their injuries are minor," Gor assured him. "We were careful not to damage them permanently."

I AVOIDED THE atrium and let Gor make an appearance. The ovation down the main hallway echoed in raucous glee. Even I felt the heady joy of the passengers from a distance and knew my friend must be basking in it.

Instead, I went to the Captain's dining room where the four changelings lay in stasis. The guards let me in without question and regarded me with something like awe. Whatever Sumner's motives in broadcasting the footage throughout the ship, he'd cursed me with notoriety. I wasn't ready for it.

The ship's doctor nodded in greeting. In the course of my clearance examination and subsequent training injuries, he'd become familiar with me. "Ambassador."

"How are they?"

"Stable." The Andari studied me. "They are all neuter, like you. Is this significant?"

"I'm afraid it might be." In the nearest medical pod, the changeling's hair lay against their shoulder in a long braid, heavy and black as starless space. The one beside them held someone fair-skinned, blond hair buzzed close to their head. I remembered this person from the holo vids. They hadn't returned to their post after leave two months ago.

Condensation on the transparent windows gave evidence of the chilled temperatures inside the chamber. "Can you tell how long they've been suspended, Doctor?"

"The drug reservoirs are almost full. I would estimate four to six weeks. Not long before we departed, perhaps."

"How much time will it take to bring them out of suspension?"

"Forty-eight hours to do it under protocol. Any less and we risk shock and death. Shall I begin the procedure once we move them into the infirmary?"

"I think we should. As soon as they start to wake, contact me, please. They may be frightened to find themselves on board a starliner, so far from home."

My com burped static. "Ambassador Tamareia, the prisoners are back on the shuttle and prepared to leave. Alliance ships are less than three minutes from us. You may want to disarm those bombs."

"I'm transmitting now, Commander." I tuned the frequency to standard broadcast and transmitted "0" to the media bots.

Disarmed.

"Group together and maintain a position two kilometers from any vessel in the area. Do not follow subject as it leaves. Await further instructions."

Acknowledged.

I turned the com back to ship's frequency. "They're disarmed and moving out of the way. I didn't want to bring them back on board, but we'll need them for evidence."

"We'll let the Remoliad handle them." A pause. "Very well done, Ambassador."

I moved away from the doctor, removed my translator patch, and closed it in my hand. "Ears only, Commander?"

Another pause. "Go ahead."

I guessed him as Sol Fed intelligence, or even psi-ops, given how easily he blocked my empathic senses. "Who are you?"

"No one of consequence."

My brow creased. "I've seen that old holo vid, too. Unless you're the Dread Pirate Roberts, I think you're lying."

"Then you'll know the next line is, 'Get used to disappointment.'" Real amusement gilded Sumner's voice.

Fair enough. He had a sense of humor and great taste in ancient movies. I wouldn't jeopardize his cover. "Understood."

"Will you be interviewing William Farmer yourself? He seemed surprised to see you."

"Mr. Farmer and I have a virulent history, Commander. It wouldn't be appropriate. I might need assistance with the investigation." I didn't trust myself enough to guarantee Farmer's well-being. I wanted to use him as a punching bag.

"I'll be happy to help. Sumner out."

The Nos frigate left in a hurry before our rescuers arrived. Their own shuttle squeaked aboard seconds ahead of firing engines, running away from the *Bedia* and its approaching rescuers.

Remoliad officers from *Nova One* thoroughly scanned the bomb-enhanced tech and made records of them for my evidence collection. At the last, the media bots were neutralized into a cloud of tiny particles by a four-letter word transmitted over a hand-held com.

I forced myself to witness the explosion with a clinical eye, without reliving the moment at Luna Terminal. It took every scrap of self-possession I had. I turned away to find Sumner studying me, his eyes the dark blue-green color of Zereid's ocean moon. His expression appeared to take measure of my reaction. I looked away first, frustrated, incapable of relying on my empathic sense to gather clues about him. He stayed a flat null most of the time, barely even there. If he did wear a psy-shield, it wasn't evident.

Captain An'ksh and I gave copies of the data filmed in the cargo bay to the captain of the *Nova One*, but I kept my own records and holo vids of the unmarked crate, medical pods, and manifest I'd collected. It was Sol Fed business, and for the sake of formality, I'd file my report in the Embassy as well. But something told me it could disappear from government files. An encrypted holo card lay secreted in my private belongings.

I had no illusions it would be easy to take down the Goliath that was Batterson Robotics. It would require one hell of a slingshot—and some pretty big fucking stones.

Double entendre intended.

Ten

THE SLEEPERS BEGAN to rouse from chemical hibernation under the cautious regimen of the ship's doctor. First to wake, the soldier blinked at me with groggy incomprehension.

"You're safe," I assured them. "You're in the infirmary on an Andari starliner."

Blue eyes searched my face a moment, taking measure of my androgyny. "You're a third?"

"Changeling, like you." I paused. "I'm Dalí. Who are you? What colony are you from?"

"Alix Nilsson. Luna."

"Alix, do you remember what happened before you were placed in suspension?"

Furrows appeared between their eyes and across the brow. "I'm not sure. I was at one of the tournament games with my buddies at Olympus. We just finished war games at Valles Marineris with their Militia and we got leave for a couple of days before we ship back. Jeeze, I must've been on a bender. I remember getting in a fight, and I think I got laid out. Am I still in medical?" Alix struggled to sit up. "Why am I on a starliner? I'm supposed to be back to camp at Tranquility. Did war finally break out or what?"

"Not yet, but it's close. You were suspended over a month. We're about two weeks away from Zereid."

"Zereid?" The voice from the pod beside Alix's surprised both of us. "That's light years from home! What am I doing here?" The black-haired changeling blushed, their hands crossed over their chest. Panic crested against my empathic senses. "What is this?"

I motioned to the Andari medical staff. They brought linens to the bedside. The changeling, rapidly becoming a she, wrapped herself in a sheet as Alix, still neutral and nonplussed at their nudity, sat up on the side of the pod, groaned, and held their head.

"We're still trying to determine what's going on. We discovered the four of you in a shipping container just prior to being boarded by a Nos frigate."

"The bastards are boarding Allied ships now? What the hell?" Alix's head came up.

"What's your name?" I asked the other changeling.

"Emme Yang. I'm from Mars."

"Do you remember anything?"

"I think... I don't know. The last thing I remember was being in a hospital, maybe?"

"So you were all in a medical facility?" I struggled to put a pattern to this.

"I wasn't. I remember what happened to us." Anger tinged the voice across the infirmary. The older changeling was awake and motioned to the now-stirring figure in the other pod as they sat upright. "It was a flat-out abduction. Shay and I were held in the lab for a month with four others before these two came along. I'm not sure what colony we were in, but I'm pretty sure the guys were Europan. Be glad they didn't have time to experiment."

"What happened?" I crossed to talk to them as the Andari medical officers offered water and checked their patients' vital signs. This changeling had already assumed male anatomy, shoulders taut and tense as the muscles rearranged and bulked under dark skin into a more powerful upper-body mass.

"Testing out the merchandise. They kept us pretty drugged up." He motioned at the pod beside him. "Those animals were particularly rough on Shay."

"You're both from Luna?"

He grunted in affirmation. "I know who you are. Dalí Tamareia, right?"

"Yes."

"I admired your work for third-gender rights before you became an ambassador. I worked with Andrew Gresham a time or two. Akia Parker. I'm a human rights solicitor for Sol Fed."

"I remember your name. Gresh thought highly of you." I shook the hand he offered.

"I'm sorry for your loss. He was one of the good guys."

"He was. Thank you." I turned back to the subject at hand. "Do you have any idea why they took you?"

Dark eyes stared into mine, red fury in their depths, and Akia nodded curtly. "I overheard them talking about some kind of market."

"Why would they want to tangle with a solicitor? They had to realize people would notice you disappeared."

"I made some powerful people angry. With my profession I led, as they say, a high-risk lifestyle." Akia shrugged in Emme's direction. "I suspect we all made poor choices, or we wouldn't have been taken so easily."

Emme blushed miserably and pushed a stray lock of black hair behind her ear as Akia continued, "But where are the rest?"

Others? My heart sank. "Only four of you were in the container with some other contraband."

"Then four more are out there, somewhere." Akia's face sharpened with anger. "I think interest in changeling sex slaves exists among the galactics, and we're being sold by our own species. You and I need to talk, Ambassador."

IN ZEREID'S ORBIT, it became possible to transmit messages back and forth to the Embassy. I begged a favor from Captain An'ksh and used her ready room to conduct a private communication before we docked with the terminal. I contacted Michael Martinez, who had taken over my mother's post ten years ago as Ambassador. I alerted him four Sol Fed citizens sought asylum in the Embassy until they could return safely home. I also gave him a rundown of the prisoner detained aboard the *Bedia*, and the severity of his crimes.

"I've already been contacted by legal counsel on behalf of Mr. Farmer," Martinez informed me, his mouth turned downward in a sneer. "He is to be released on his own recognizance upon arrival."

"How did they find out?" I demanded. "He was only allowed to transmit a message this morning under the supervision of the first officer."

"Footage of passengers liberating the vessel from Nos pirates already made the rounds of most Alliance media a week ago. You and Gor are viral heroes, I'm afraid. The passengers aren't staying quiet about it in personal communications."

I drummed my fingers on the instrument panel in irritation. "Convenient they suspected Mr. Farmer might need a solicitor upon his arrival to Zereid. I trust nothing of the human or arms trafficking suspicions got mentioned in the media?" I almost hoped Kiran Singh would get wind of this.

"No. Nothing." Martinez fell silent a moment. "Dalí, there's something else you need to know. I was contacted a few days ago by the Diplomatic Corps. I am required to inform you your leave of absence does not allow service in any official capacity during your stay here on Zereid, nor does it allow you to investigate crimes against or committed by Sol Fed citizens."

"Really." I allowed frost to edge my voice. It gave Martinez pause. If I hadn't previously realized how deeply President Batterson's empire and the NPM were burrowed into the government, I did now. "That didn't take any time at all."

"You are to turn all official copies of evidence records you made over to me when you arrive." His eyes narrowed at me. "Do you understand these instructions, Ambassador Tamareia?"

In my rising anger, I almost missed the odd stress on the syllables of *official*. "I understand, Ambassador Martinez. I hope you will assist with the investigation on my behalf."

"As much as I am allowed. Those four citizens will be safe here. I give you my word." Martinez ended the call.

In the cramped quiet of Captain An'ksh's ready room, I contemplated transmitting the resignation I had already composed to the Diplomatic Corps. In the end, I didn't transmit. Not yet. My commission could still be useful, and I'd be an idiot not to keep as many weapons in my arsenal as I could.

SUMMER HAD REACHED its zenith in the hemisphere where Gor and I grew up together. The craggy mountains loomed, backlit against Zereid's warm oceanic moon. Sharp scents of open air, not the recycled, conditioned air of starships and climate domes, burned the tissues in my nose and lungs. The dizziness of acclimation, and in some measure, the emotions evoked by this homecoming, made me sway on my feet. I closed my eyes, my heart too full for words.

"Welcome back, beloved friend." Gor touched my head.

Here no associations of loss or conflict existed, only memories of childhood and adolescence. I spent the first night in the unsheltered balcony of the outer temple, open to the wind and elements, looking up into cloud-swaddled stars.

The next day I hiked through deep, wooded lavender valleys behind the temple and reveled in the weightless embrace of a frigid lake. I swam until I was exhausted and hauled myself out, dripping, to shiver on the rocky edge and listen to the cry and moan of flightless birds scudding over the surface of the water.

The chief priestess called me to her a few days after my arrival. She sat behind me and her soft hands encompassed either side of my head as she assessed my mental state. I could not resist her if I'd wanted to, her empathic and telepathic skills far beyond anything I could ever hope to master. But I desperately needed her assessment and guidance. I let her examine the raw, bleeding places I still refused to probe. She wandered the barren areas scrubbed away by floods of grief and self-destruction, tested what was built shakily upon the old foundations, and sifted through the broken piles awaiting some kind of restoration.

"Gor told me he was frightened for you when he first arrived on the space station," she said. "Your will to live appeared fragile, and you sought an end to pain with reckless behavior. But something changed your path. Tell me."

"I almost got what I wanted. I nearly died. In the place between living and dying, I saw them. My family." I closed my eyes briefly. "They seemed to tell me I had work to do. And I discovered others who need my help. But, priestess, I don't know if the path of *zezjna* is what I seek. I'm restless. Peacemakers should have a sense of what it is to be at peace. To negotiate in the Remoliad, I need a reason to believe in the future of the human race. I no longer have the optimism or faith my species will do what is right. Gor is correct to be concerned. I'm lost."

"You must find what still anchors you to life. Your crechemate always followed the path of priesthood, but that is only one road. *Zezjna* also allows for the protection of peace by whatever skills you are given. This is a parallel journey. Think on this as you stay with us. Teach the younglings, find your balance, and begin anew. Allow yourself to be what you are now without shame. Accept the anger and doubt and sadness for what it is. You may find yourself back where you started, but if not, you will find a new starting point. What is meant to happen will happen. Peacemaker—or peacekeeper."

Eleven

TO MY STUDENTS, I was a curiosity only because I wore clothes and blinked. Two months into my routine of meditation, study, and morning *zezjna* drills with the younglings, I almost recognized myself again and lived without unconscious adaptation of my body for others' benefit. But cynicism now gave an edge to my personality, too many rough edges to smooth out.

Time passed, and late autumn arrived in shades of plum and fire below the temple. My leave of absence would run out if I didn't go back soon, but I couldn't bring myself to give a fuck. The resignation still waited on my PDD, a tap away from an uncharted life.

"Dalí?" One of my young charges came to me, eyes turned away in shy respect.

"Yes, Kla? What is it?" Two eight-year-old males sparred in front of me and tested the boundaries of "not killing your opponent." I wondered if I should separate them.

"Another hoo-man is here."

I looked up, startled. I hadn't sensed anyone else. In a sea of Zereid thoughts and emotions, a human presence should have been a siren. Inside the shadow of the inner temple, Rion Sumner leaned in casual repose against one of the massive stone pillars. He regarded me with those odd, sea-colored eyes. Damned null. He didn't wear Andari insignia this time. His gray uniform proclaimed Remoliad Alliance. The plot thickens.

"Thank you, Kla." I motioned to the two students who grappled on the mat in front of me. "Will you come find me if they start to bleed anywhere?"

"Yes, Dalí." She giggled, a pure trill of delight.

I crossed the courtyard, a wary smile on my lips. Sumner pulled himself out of the lazy slouch and met me halfway.

"Is this the part where you challenge me to a battle of wits to the death?" I asked.

"No, this is where I come to tell you I'm looking for the six-fingered man, and I recruit you for the Brute Squad."

"Tell me." My body tensed, and he straightened, surprised.

"Did anyone ever tell you you're terrifying at times?"

"Me?" I laughed, taken aback. "When?"

"Just now. I barely mention our proverbial nemesis, and you morph into some kind of avenging angel. Impressive, but scary as hell. You did it with Farmer, too. He nearly pissed his pants when you told him to shut up back in the cargo bay. Can we talk in private?"

I motioned him to the end of the balcony, away from the students. The mountain peaks rose behind us, laced with early snow. The bite of wind was stronger here, but we sat on the wall above the valley, the trees below aflame in the morning light. "You probably suspected my assignment to the *Bedia* was temporary. Before that, I really did pilot a subspeed freighter through Nos trade routes for a year. I almost died of boredom and won't be volunteering again. I've been a mercenary, a drug runner, and a dozen other professions. Deep cover is my specialty."

"You aren't Sol Fed intelligence or psi-ops like I thought. What are you? Remoliad intel?"

"Yes and no. If you ask the Remoliad, we don't exist, although we hold commissions when it's convenient. We're a multi-species cooperative. No independent alliances with any race, but we've made more than a few enemies. Individual citizenship is forsworn to become citizens of the galaxy, so to speak."

Pieces fell into place with abrupt realization. "You aren't entirely human, are you, Commander?"

Defensive posture started to turn his body to steel and flesh but relaxed before he became immoveable. "No. I'm a hybrid."

"Nos and human?" My empathic senses flattened against a null in his presence every time, the same as I'd experienced with the Nos raiders on board the starliner.

"My mother was one of the Europan Militia officers captured in the first military skirmish with the Nos on a Sol System trade route about thirty-four years ago. She wasn't exactly welcomed back to Europa with a half-breed child in utero. She volunteered for an out-system posting as soon as possible after I was born. Until Sol Fed petitioned for Remoliad membership, I'd never been back. My mother considered herself an exile until the day she died."

"I'm sorry."

"So am I, for your loss. I never had the opportunity to express my condolences once I realized who you were. In the holo vids, I'd assumed you were male." He grimaced. "I hope I'm not being insulting. I hadn't met a changeling before."

"No, I used to present more as masculine, especially when dealing with Colonial governments." I shrugged. "This is who I am."

"The others on the ship seemed to pick male or female. You don't?"

"When it suits the moment. For changelings in the Colonies, it's a survival measure. Excuse me a minute." From the other side of the courtyard, Kla motioned to me urgently as she hopped up and down. I went to separate my overly enthusiastic students. There was only a little bleeding involved. I sat them both down on the balcony to meditate awhile. The time approached for the class to end, so I gave instructions to the rest to stack away the mats and padding and told the younglings they were dismissed as soon as they finished.

"You knew who I was. Why?" I returned to the conversation without preamble. "Does this have something to do with Luna Terminal?"

"In part. We keep a close eye on the Shontavian Market. Anything shady in the galaxy usually shows up there first. We've been watching strange cargo activity originating from Rosetta Station. During my stint as a freighter pilot, I hacked into one of the crates and found miniaturized explosive devices tucked into media bots, like the ones you discovered on board the *Bedia*. I tagged the shipment. Operatives tracked them to the Market. They were sold and shipped back to the Colonies on a passenger starliner. The ship docked at Luna Terminal a week before the explosion."

"Who bought them?" My nails cut half-moons into my palms and reminded me to breathe. I relaxed my fists.

"We're working on that." Sumner's mouth formed a grim line. "I was already undercover on the *Bedia* for...different reasons. We had no idea about this shipment of explosives or the human cargo, but we've since verified they were headed for the Market. I asked to head this investigation instead. Which brings me to the reason I'm here."

"I'm listening."

"Thanks to Akia Parker, we know another shipment is out there. We found them. My insider confirmed four medical pods aboard a slow freighter. The Nos are fighting among themselves, waiting for their chance to board as soon as they enter the trade route. The payout must be astronomical if they intercept the cargo."

"Did you confirm if Batterson Robotics is involved in this human trafficking operation?"

"New information makes it a certainty. We'll let them stew about how much we know for now. We're concerned about who's on the receiving end of the deal. We want to find out where the other changelings are going, if it's slavery, or something worse. We need someone who can infiltrate this very specific situation."

"I'm still listening."

"My contact on board the freighter agreed to engineer a mechanical emergency requiring assistance and repair. We rescue one of the kidnapped Sol Fed citizens and insert you into a medical pod with an implanted personal tracker. You ride to the end and assume an undercover position." He grew sober. "It could be brutal. I can't guarantee your safety. We don't know who or what's waiting on the other side. We set a prearranged time for extraction. Then we come bust up the operation, rescue the others, and we all go home. Less negotiation. Maybe more ass-kicking." He gave me a knowing half smirk. "You appear to enjoy that part."

"How long before you need an answer?"

"We leave in two days. It's important to catch up with the ship before they cross into Nos trade routes."

"I'm due back at the Diplomatic Corps in four weeks."

"I'd say you were procrastinating. You won't make it." Sumner paused. "I'm asking you to join my team, Dalí. I'm impressed with what I saw. Your deductive reasoning, your skill at physical combat, diplomacy...even your changeling traits could be an invaluable asset to us. Your concern would be the protection of the galaxy and its citizens as a whole. Are you interested?"

The path of the peacekeeper stared me down.

For the first time in almost a year, a sense of excitement flared in a burst of electricity behind my sternum.

"One condition."

"Name it."

"I'll accept this mission. But when they find out who planted those explosives in Luna Terminal, I want to be there when they're taken down. It's personal."

"Here you go again. Scary as hell." Sumner appeared to consider a moment and nodded. "It isn't my decision alone. But I will give you my word—when we move on the party behind the bombing, you will be involved."

"What assurances do you need, Commander—if that's still your appropriate designation?"

"It is. You should transmit the resignation you've been hoarding. You'll find the wording changed to transfer your credentials to the Remoliad and an unnamed independent party."

"How—?" I narrowed my eyes at him.

"You were thoroughly vetted. That's all I'll say for now. From this moment on, you leave your loyalty to Sol Fed behind. What we do may not always be in the best interests of your home system."

"My home system doesn't appear to be concerned about its own best interests."

Sumner extended his hand, and I gripped it firmly. "Then welcome to the Penumbra, Dalí Tamareia."

Twelve

GOR UNDERSTOOD WHY I would take the risks, but he still worried about me. I confided the details of my new assignment to him alone. My secrets—all of them—are safe with my crechemate. Even the ones I don't want him to know.

"You do plan to come back from this mission?" Liquid-silver eyes turned a dark mirror against me, the question a gentle rebuke.

"I don't have any illusions about how dangerous this is."

"That is not what I asked."

His gaze pierced me. A wry smile pulled the corners of my mouth into a twist. "Damn you, brother."

"You still have nothing that anchors you to living. I fear it is too soon to take on such responsibility."

"Those people in stasis can't wait for me to get my shit together."

"Agreed. But I cannot help but weigh the implications of your choice. Is it merely another way to seek an end to pain?"

A growl escaped me. "You will never let me forget, will you?"

"Can you blame me for worrying? Your light was nearly gone. It is a small flame yet, though it grows brighter."

Pale illumination from the ocean moon cast cyan shadows on the temple balcony and reminded me I only held the darkness inside at bay. It still whispered through my head at night, in dreams of shattered glass and vaporous exhalations of bodies into the vacuum of space.

"Will you keep these safe for me, brother?" I tugged off my wedding bands. The indentations in my skin remained, grooves worn into my flesh to match the memories of Gresh and Rasida, seared into my neurons. Their cool weight slid from my palm into his leathery hand, and he enfolded my wrist with six inescapable fingers, the rings held between us. I tightened my grip on his hand.

"Promise to return for them, beloved friend."

"I will."

The next morning, I said goodbye to the younglings, repacked my bag, and left my Diplomatic Corps uniform behind.

With my resignation transmitted and irretrievable, I contacted my mother from the Embassy on a secure channel. No words described my admiration for Marina Urquhart. Every step she took in her career was for the love of her home system or her family.

And here I was, privately renouncing one and taking leave of the other.

"Dalí!" This wasn't the formidable Ambassador on my holo screen; this was definitely Mom, a line of worry between her eyes. "I'm glad you contacted me. Paul said you were better, but your dad just tells me what I want to hear." Her auburn head cocked, studying my projection on her side of the communication. I'd inherited those fine, high cheekbones from her, but not the pale complexion. "I haven't seen you wear your hair so long before. It suits you. So, tell me."

"What do you want to know?"

"If you're really better."

"I'm working on it." I paused. "My behavior was nothing short of erratic for a while, and I'm sorry. That's the reason I contacted you. I'm about to do something stupid, and I don't want you to think the worst."

"More stupid than fighting Nos pirates with Gor? I did catch the news holos."

"You might say so. I just resigned from the Corps and transferred my credentials to the Remoliad."

The statement would be enough to provoke a strong outburst from my father, but my practical mother hardly blinked. "You're staying on Zereid."

"No. I'm taking on a new mission for an independent party."

This did merit a reaction. "Oh, Dalí. That's code for mercenary."

"Could be." I still wasn't sure what the Penumbra was, exactly, but it sounded right. "This is something I don't feel I can turn down."

"Does this have anything to do with the citizens Mike Martinez is sheltering in the Embassy?"

"I was informed my help is not needed." Even on a secure channel, I remained cautious. "You heard about the new law the Senate passed?"

"I did." She grew solemn. "It's a point of contention in the negotiations."

"Kiran Singh called the legislation selective genocide."

"I never thought I'd say this, but I agree with him. Making laws against reproductive rights for any minority population sets a dangerous precedent. Fortunately, the Remoliad recognizes their argument is flawed."

"They have a few more millennia of genetic science under their belts than Dr. Atassi does."

Mom smiled in hesitant caution. "You won't believe this. I introduced Rasida's paper as a counterargument against her work. She is actually collaborating with Remoliad scientists to confirm the data and move for new genetic research studies to be done."

"Is hell freezing over?" I guess our little chat on board the *Bedia* made her think. "Good for Yesenia. If their pet geneticist withdraws her support, those bastards might lose traction in the Colonies."

"It's wonderful to see you smile, even vindictively."

I laughed outright. "My manners are still off-line. It's probably better I find a new career."

"Be careful. Will you contact us soon?"

"When I can. It might be a while."

"I was hoping you'd relieve your old mother here when you said you'd transferred your credentials. I suppose I'll stick around."

"Don't let them put one of Batterson's cronies in the negotiation chamber."

"Not a chance."

"Will you tell Dad? I'm burning too much of Mike Martinez's subspace budget as it is."

"I will. I love you, Dalí. There's light in your eyes again, and it makes my soul glad."

"I love you, too."

I TURNED IN my government credentials to Martinez, who received them with a somber nod of understanding. He jerked his head toward the terrace behind his office. A strong sense of déjà vu overwhelmed me as I passed through those doors—I'd spent so much time on this veranda as a child I recognized every stone, every mortar line. I could almost touch the ghost of gangly, adolescent me, leaning against the wall overlooking the mountains. The night before we departed, I stayed outside for hours, excited to return to Luna, but weeping for the only home I'd ever known. An echo of the hollowness of heart struck me now. I would come back to Zereid whenever possible. But Sol Fed would never be home to me again.

Martinez faced me. "Dalí, I don't know what you uncovered, exactly. I'm not allowed to examine the evidence you collected, but I've learned enough from Akia Parker to realize something dark is happening. I've been instructed to send them home, but none of them want to go. They're afraid."

"With good reason, Mike."

"Enough for you to resign." Martinez regarded me solemnly. "Are the actions of one family, even the President's, so dangerous?"

"For most people, it probably isn't; at least not yet. But if you're third gender like my mother or a changeling like me, Akia and the others...yes, it is. Our rights to procreate are being taken away. The leader of Sol Fed regards changelings as less than human. Somebody with ties to his company tried to sell those people to the Shontavian Market. It should bother anyone with an elementary education of Earth's history. If we can't control our own reproduction, what rights can they take from any citizen?"

"You always fought for third-gender rights in the Colonies. Why are you running now?"

That stung a little. "I'm not. I'm following the trail."

"If it leads to the Market, you might not come back."

"I'm aware of that." I took in the city, the faraway, erubescent mountains, and a deep breath. "Mike, will you promise me you'll protect them, no matter what happens?"

Martinez's eyes softened a bit. "You have my word."

"Even if it means defying an order? They might say anything to get them back to Sol Fed."

"I won't allow it. Akia Parker already developed a contingency plan if they try to force them out."

"Is Akia here?"

"I can't blast him out of the library. He's here."

"I want to talk to him before I leave."

"You remember where it is." Martinez extended a hand, and I shook it firmly. "Be careful, Dalí. There are places in the galaxy that don't follow any laws but their own. You're used to civilized behavior and reason. Outside the Remoliad, you won't find much."

"I think I need to be less civilized for a while."

I found Akia burrowed into a holo viewer carrel, so deep in a data flow he didn't notice my approach. I stopped a few meters away and said his name softly. He startled, his dark face rigid in surprised fear before he realized who I was.

"Tamareia!" He got up and gave me a hard embrace. "How are you?"

"Good, thanks. Can I talk to you? We should go for a walk."

"Yeah, sure." He understood. The watchful cameras and attendants of the Embassy would make it difficult to say anything we didn't want overheard. We passed through the gate and down the street. The tower of a *zezjna* shrine rose above the busy path, the stairs almost uncomfortably tall for human beings. My thighs burned with the fire of lactic acid by the time we reached the first level, and Akia panted beside me. I took pity on him and he laughed softly as we sat on the edge of the steps.

"Damn, I need to go out more. Full gravity still kicks my ass."

"You'll get used to it." I hesitated. I'd thought a long time about what I prepared to do now. I would disobey a direct order from the diplomatic corps, but I was no longer their Ambassador. I dug into the pocket of my jacket and pulled out a holo card. "I want to give you something."

"What is it?" He stilled.

"On the surface, a copy of Shakespeare's *The Tempest*. Embedded in the text are the videos I collected on the *Bedia*, including my conversation with William Farmer. Find Caliban's lines."

"I thought this was suppressed." He turned the card over in his hands.

"They told me to turn in the official copies of my inquiry. This isn't official. This is raw data."

He gave a low, evil chuckle. "Thank you. Thank you. You could get fired for this."

"Too late. I already quit. I start a new job tomorrow."

"You going back to Sol Fed?" Akia frowned.

"No. I don't think I will."

"I understand. Knowing what we know, it doesn't seem like home anymore."

"There's a favor I need to ask. I want you to make a copy and get it to Kiran Singh as soon as possible."

"I hate that little asshole. You sure you even want the Third Front in on this?"

"Somebody declared war on the third gender. We didn't start this, but I hope you and Kiran can finish it."

THE SHIP WAITING on the outskirts of Zereid's busy spaceport was small and predatory. This one had a lethal, dagger-like design I'd never seen in person.

"Is this a Kadrelian blockade runner?" I stopped and gazed in admiration at the sleek ship. Sumner gave me an affirmative raise of eyebrows. I'd gained some points.

"Meet *Thunder Child*. She's our best friend, transport, and home between worlds. She can house a crew of thirty, but there's only twelve on board for this mission. Atmospheric and EM travel capability. Wicked fast." His voice held the pride of ownership, more than a little enamored with the vessel. Sumner gazed at it with a lover's eyes.

"Is she armed?" No guns were in evidence, but the ship's pedigree made me suspect otherwise.

"We keep a few surprises under wraps. She's heavily modified. Our weaponry is hidden when we're planetside." He stroked the side of the craft lovingly, long, sensitive fingers spread wide. "I missed her. Piloting the *Bedia* was like maneuvering an asteroid."

"If you're done making out with the ship, Sumner, we need to take off," an oddly accented voice from the gangplank interrupted. A pale, reptilian-scaled face peered out at us; bright-green eyes gazed disconcertingly in opposite directions—one at me, and one at Sumner.

"You're just jealous," the latter shot back. "The rude one is my second in command and my copilot. Ozzie, meet Dalí Tamareia, our new team member."

"One of the civvies who took down the Nos boarding party?" He spoke Sol Standard without a translator, no small feat for a lipless Cthash. Ozzie extended a three-fingered hand. I met each taloned digit with two fingers and a thumb. "Good to finally meet you. You impressed the boss, for sure. I'm Ossixiani clan Sustrix. Ozzie for short."

"Hello, Ozzie. Your diction is excellent, by the way."

"Thanks." Only a slight hiss trailed at the end. The reptilian grin disconcerted me, and revealed sharp little teeth in two rows. His pleasure at the compliment brushed my mind with warmth. If it hadn't, I would have been concerned he'd take a bite out of me.

"Ozzie speaks almost a hundred different galactic languages, so if you need a tutor, he's the one to go to." Sumner waved me up the gangplank. I shifted my bag and took a last breath of the petrichor and copper-tinged atmosphere into my lungs, one final glimpse of crimson autumn mountains so I could remember Zereid when I needed peace.

Sumner keyed the ramp closed behind us as Ozzie hurried forward to the cockpit.

"Take your pick of empty cabins and strap in." Sumner pointed down a narrow, almost vertical stairwell in the center of the ship. "Plenty to choose from. Even at full crew compliment, nobody has to double up unless they want to. Environmental suits are underneath the bunk in case of emergency. Stow your bag there until after takeoff. The screens will go live when we engage EM drive and artificial gravity. Afterward, you're free to move around. I'll find you."

He turned to follow Ozzie. I made my way down the stairs and caught glimpses of other oxygen-breathing occupants strapped into cushioned jump seats as the engines began to whine. I picked the first cabin devoid of any sign of claim, stowed the bag and dropped into the seat to fasten the five-point harness across my chest.

The thrust of launch pushed me back into the pads. Outside the tiny slit of the starboard window, ombre sky and mountains wheeled in a dizzy, slanted blur. Once more, I left Zereid and its serenity. I hoped some of it would stay with me. This planet was my home in a way the Sol Fed Colonies had never been—never would be again, without Gresh and Sida.

But I felt myself coming back to life. I had a purpose again, at least for the duration of the mission. I closed my eyes, and the thrum of the starship's engines vibrated through muscle, bone, and sinew—the pulse of my new home between worlds, leaving the atmosphere of Zereid behind.

Thirteen

THE SMALL SCREEN with the voyage clock illuminated about twenty minutes into our flight. Twenty-six hours until intercept of the freighter—Sumner hadn't bragged about the ship's speed. *Thunder Child* made the transition to superluminal velocity so smoothly I almost missed the telltale vibration as the exotic matter drive kicked in. My body settled back into the seat and no longer strained against the harnesses. Queasiness brought on by the initial zero gravity lessened. I unstrapped and tested my footing. Not full grav, but enough to keep my boots on the floor.

Sumner appeared in the doorway. "You good? No problems with half grav?"

"None. I did a rotation in the militia at zero grav. I can find my space legs again." More air than usual brushed the back of my thighs, the black kilt's pleats suspended a bit further from my skin. I'd already added a set of formfitting shorts underneath in deference to the gravity change. I should be polite at first and avoid giving any of my new crewmates an unexpected third-gender anatomy lesson.

"We need to get a couple things out of the way. Ozzie might speak dozens of languages, but the rest of us are less capable. The best way to solve the issue of communication is a neuro-translator implant combined with a micro-com. All of my crew has them. Quick surgery, local anesthetic."

"That's fine." I'd considered having it done when I reached the Remoliad, once upon a time.

"We'll insert your personal tracker, too. Come on; I'll show you to medical. Some of your briefing will happen there by necessity."

"When will I go under?"

"Doc says about eight hours prior to intercept. It has to be as quick an exchange as possible in case the Conglomerate isn't in a waiting mood. We obtained one of the pods from the *Bedia* for you to take your nap in."

We went back up to the top deck. Crew were active at their stations now, performing routine tasks. I noted a pair of Andari, a Cthash with darker scales than Ozzie, and to my surprise, a yellow-haired Nos, his tall frame hunched over a holographic navigational display. They all glanced up at me with varying levels of curiosity, but Sumner led me aft to the wide door of the medical bay. He stopped, but didn't key the port.

"Before we go in, I need you to understand something. I hand pick my crew based on their expertise and their knowledge. We were lucky enough to come in contact with someone who's been on the inside. What they did in the past is no longer relevant. They work for me now. I didn't know a connection existed between you until yesterday, but I expect everyone to function as a team for the duration of the mission."

Mystified, I followed him through the opening door.

Inside the steel-and-white medical bay, in blushing, pale-tressed glory, stood Tella Sharp.

"I don't believe you two need an introduction." Sumner leaned against the doorway. "I'll give you fifteen minutes to sort it out as best you can. After that, you receive your implants whether you worked it out or not, and we all go for briefing back on the command deck in one hour. I'll be back."

The port closed behind him. Tella's discomfort and embarrassment slid against my mind, tinged with shame.

I took a step forward. "What is this about?"

"You probably thought you'd never see me again. Neither did I." Her arms clasped herself tightly across the chest.

"It's good to see you. I'm not sorry about what we shared, Tella, and I don't expect anything from you. I don't understand."

"There are things I need to tell you, and we don't have much time." She motioned to her narrow workspace. We faced each other over the desk.

"My temporary assignment to Rosetta Station was not an accident. It put me in a position to monitor the people in the cargo containers. I'm the one who placed them in suspension."

Cold flooded me. "You?"

She nodded jerkily. "The patients came to me under sedation. The hibernation process is complicated, and he'd tried to initiate it with only robotic medical supervision. He didn't want them to die...like the first three did."

Oh. *Oh.*

"That's why you were asking me so many questions. You were...collecting data." I ran a hand over my tightening jaw as heat built in my face and chest. "You hid it well. I never sensed you lied, or I didn't want to know. You have the blushing virgin role down to a science."

"It began that way. But it changed. I do care about you. I understand we might never be friends again, and you may hate me when you learn the rest. He wanted me to make it appear you didn't survive your injuries. You were meant to join the people in the container we're intercepting."

"Batterson. Jon Batterson is your husband." *Make sure it doesn't wake up.* The voice hadn't been a drug-induced hallucination. He'd been there. One more reason to maim the bastard if I ever crossed paths with him again.

"I couldn't do what Jon wanted, not once I read your file and saw what you'd lost. I'm so sorry, Dalí." Her eyes filled with tears. "The Batterson family is terrifying. You don't even know what they're capable of. They wouldn't let me go to Mars to start a new life if I refused. They could end my career with one communication to the medical corps. I wanted out of my marriage and off Europa."

"You helped them destroy people's lives to gain your freedom."

"You don't ask questions. You do what they tell you and pray you don't make them angry. Bill Farmer is probably running scared right now. I don't think he'll be going back to Sol Fed. Neither will I." She raised her head. "I saw the holos of you and Gor on the ship. I knew what you were fighting for, and at least four of those people would be safe. But I didn't put you in the container. Jon won't let that go."

"How did you contact Sumner?"

"I didn't. He contacted me. I programmed the med assistants and the pods. My MD identification numbers are in there—there's no way around entering them. Commander Sumner found me on Mars and offered amnesty and transport out of the system if I'd help with the investigation. I was just waiting for the Battersons to come silence me. I didn't see any other options. I know I did something unforgivable. I want to try to make this right."

She'd hidden her lies so well before. "Can anyone else program the medical pod?"

"Are you insinuating I'll kill you in your sleep?" Her indignation railed against my empathic nets. "If I wanted to leave you in a medical coma, I would have back on Rosetta like Jon told me. I could have let you die and avoided the entire issue. I am a doctor. My career and what's left of my integrity are all I own, Dalí. Unless they get another doctor on board, you can't finish this mission without me."

I had my answer. The outburst of passion was as real as it got, and I found half a smile tugging at my mouth. She wouldn't kill me.

"I'll work with you, Tella."

The door slid open. "Everything okay now?" Sumner shifted between my smirk and Tella's angry, defensive posture, her face red rather than pink.

"It's fine, Commander. I'm ready for those implants."

"Up on the table. Take off your shirt and jacket." Her words ended in sharp consonants as she stabbed an index finger at the examination platform, avoiding Sumner's questioning gaze. I complied with her instructions and lay back on the cushion. Tella shoved my head to the side.

"Whoa." Sumner crossed his arms. "How do I stay on your good side, Dr. Sharp?"

"Obviously not by sleeping with her," I muttered.

"Shut up and hold still." A hypospray left the area behind my right ear sterile, cold, and numb. She took more care with the insertion of the tiny, delicate, obscenely expensive tech she drilled into the mastoid bone. The whole process took less than ten minutes. By the end of the procedure, she wasn't quite as pissed off, but held up another hypospray in my line of vision and informed me with exaggerated sweetness, "Antibiotic to prevent infection, not poison."

"Yes, thank you."

The personal tracker proved less traumatic. Under the skin of my left axilla, the micro tech presented a small lump beneath my fingertip. Upon cursory inspection, it wouldn't arouse suspicion.

"The anesthetic will wear off in a few hours. If you need something for pain, tell me." Surgical implements hit the metal tray with a clash as Tella swept clear her operating field and carried them away.

Sumner, who stayed for the procedures without further comment, finally spoke as I dressed. "There's a little time before the briefing. I'll give you a quick tour. Doc, you remember where the command deck is, right?"

"Yes. Give me some time to sterilize these instruments, and I'll be there." She ignored us as we walked out. Our steps rang against the corridor in silence until the commander said quietly,

"I'll assign my interspecies medic to the bay when Dr. Sharp puts you under."

It hadn't escaped me how he'd remained in the room, nor how the good doctor had a translator earpiece instead of an implant. "You don't trust her either."

"No. I don't."

BRIEFING TOOK PLACE around the holographic map I'd glimpsed earlier. Minus Ozzie, who was busy piloting the ship, we gathered in the octagonal command center. Tella sat apart from the rest of the crew. Three different languages bounced back and forth until we arrived and added another. One of the Cthash came to me and hissed politely. Sumner translated.

"This is Tommi, my medic and communications officer. She wants you to test your translator com. It'll activate and deactivate with a direct tap, if you'll try now."

I thumped the tiny bulge behind my ear and murmured conversation took on a second level. Humming frequencies of translation were carried through bone to my cochlea. "Hello, Tommi. Is it operating correctly?"

"Seems to be. The com will cover a couple of kilometers in open areas, a bit less depending on terrain or how deep in a ship you are. Turn it off when you want privacy or the entire crew will know what you're up to." Tommi gave an openmouthed grin like Ozzie's, toothy and disconcerting. "We won't let you forget it. Believe me. You'll pick up the habit soon enough. Welcome aboard."

"This is my core team," Sumner said. "They're with us on every mission." He waved at the Nos. "Melos keeps more engineering and navigational information stored in his head than I'll ever hope to remember. He is also our ticket into the Shontavian Market."

The black-clad Nos gave me a curt nod. His pale eyes glinted in the blue light of the holo display. I returned the greeting. Sumner went on, motioning to the Andari. "Ka'pth and Ra'sho are my intelligence team. They know what color underwear the head of the Remoliad is wearing on any given day. Don't try to hide anything from them, or they'll take it as a personal challenge.

"You already met Tommi. Ozzie is her brother. Their other sibling, Ziggy, is my weapons officer and head of security."

"Welcome, Dalí. You will fit in nicely—did you notice the Commander has trouble with names over two syllables?" Ziggy's eyes swiveled and fixed on me as Sumner grinned and shook his head in a beleaguered fashion. "I hear you fight *zezjna*. What weapons are you checked out on?"

"Standard Sol Fed militia pulse rifles and sidearms. Zereid archery."

Ziggy made a huffing sound, unimpressed. "Any blade skills?"

"Militia hand-to-hand training, but it's been a while."

"It might help you through, where you're going. I'll give you a refresher after the briefing."

"Sounds like Dalí's got a busy day. Let's start. This is the first sortie of what promises to be a complicated and protracted mission. Dalí is our primary undercover operative. We will intercept the Sol Fed cargo freighter *Gojira* in..." Sumner peered at the voyage clock. "Twenty-four hours and seven minutes at our current speed. Our contact on board engineered an emergency for which they requested assistance before they reach the Nos trade corridor. We will pull alongside the freighter and duplicate their trajectory. This will be a time-sensitive mission. Everything needs to be in place and ready to go as soon as we match speed.

"Dalí will go into suspension about eight hours before intercept. We've constructed a cover for the pod to disguise it as one the instrument coffins a repair crew uses. Ziggy, Dr. Sharp, and I will wear repair team coveralls. The starboard airlock closest to the container we're looking for will be opened by our contact on the *Gojira*. We'll connect and complete the transfer. One of the pods will be extracted and Dalí's will remain on board. We hacked ours so its activity matches the duration of the others. Dr. Sharp and Ziggy will reprogram the medical assistant so no gaps in data are evident. Once the hibernation pods are activated, Dr. Sharp says they can't be opened until it's time for the occupants to wake up. It would be better if we could give them their own tracking implants, but we'll settle for tagging their pods."

"What if the Nos attack while the ship is at boarding speed?" Tommi questioned. Across the holo display, Melos grunted.

"They won't push their luck. After the *Bedia*, they know they're under surveillance in Remoliad space. They'll wait until they're midway or more into the Nos corridor."

"We're sure this cargo is what they're waiting for. Allied freighters passing through weren't molested." Ra'sho's throat gills ruffled as she spoke.

"Ra'sho and Ka'pth managed to glean some intel, and Melos will give us a rundown on everything he's seen in his experiences at the Market. He secured us an invitation at its next rendezvous point. His contact will transmit the coordinates as soon as they're available. He can also answer any questions about the Nos. We have no idea where Dalí will wake up, so it's best to be prepared."

The smaller Andari male began to speak. "The Shontavian Market is an ongoing black-market operation with mention in navigational records and lore for more than a millennia. This self-sustaining economic community is under the control of a ruling caste Ursetu called Lord Rhix. It is an honorary title, passed down to successors—but the frequency of successions suggests that it is not natural death which passes the title."

Ka'pth's sensor-sheathed hand flicked in the holographic map and reference bullets freckled the galaxy. "It's a floating market. These are the dates and locations for which we've been able to verify past rendezvous coordinates. Melos confirms it is not a space station, but a large ship. Old, but obviously not a thousand years old, it possesses military grade weaponry and EM drive. To avoid uninvited guests like Remoliad enforcers and Penumbra agents, the Market is in constant motion. Rendezvous point and time is a closely guarded secret. The location and items of interest are transmitted in a coded message to primary, trusted contacts who in turn impart the information to invited participants. Trade statutes are ignored. Weapons, mercenaries for hire and illegal substances seem to constitute its major business but anything of value can be bartered or sold inside. Concerns over the trafficking of intelligent life forms predate Remoliad slavery interdiction. It got its name from the Ursetu's sale of bioengineered Shontavian mercenaries."

"Did you see anything suggesting slave trade?" I asked Melos.

"Not personally. If it exists, it isn't in the public area of the market. Booths are set up in a three-level bay. The whole area is high security, with mercenary troops primarily from the Ursetu warrior caste, loyal to

Lord Rhix. No sidearms allowed in the Market, but there are plenty of blades and fights. They only break things up when it threatens profit. High-level negotiations take place in another part of the ship behind well-guarded blast doors. I never held sufficient rank to attend these meetings. Talk mentioned certain—entertainments, offered as negotiation points."

"What kind of entertainments?"

"Interspecies relations. Specifically, Lord Rhix keeps a brothel of exotics. To gain his favor or entrance to the Market, he will sometimes accept new concubines as incentive." Melos gauged my reaction. I merely raised an eyebrow.

"There's more. Bioengineered mercenaries remain in his service. Anyone who displeases him or attempts to cheat him is fed outright to the Shontavians or forced to participate in gladiatorial combat as sport. I attended one of these events. Bets are placed on the combatants. Afterward, the victor faces a Shontavian for their freedom. No one ever walks out." Melos's pale eyes met mine gravely. "You're an ambassador, yes?"

"I was."

"Lord Rhix is the ruler of this enterprise, a prince of pirates and smugglers. Whomever may now hold the title, we have no proof they can be reasoned with. Keep your head down and draw no undue attention to yourself. Go in, learn as much possible. We will get you and the others out as quickly as we can. Your fate will not be pleasant if you are discovered."

"How will you contact me when the time comes?"

"We'll communicate with you via the implant when we arrive to set up the extraction," Tommi said.

"It all sounds a bit vague," Tella murmured from her spot outside the circle. Melos glanced at her.

"There are too many variables. We cannot plan until we possess more information."

"We haven't lost anybody yet, Dr. Sharp," Sumner reassured her.

Yet. An empathic echo of the sentiment rose from somebody in the group. Probably me.

Fourteen

I LAY ON my bunk later and browsed the info dump the Andari prepared for me with distracted attention. The voyage clock counted down the hours to intercept and my date with the suspension pod. I tried not to think about it, but my eyes kept straying to the dwindling numbers. My head wouldn't absorb any more information. I sat up and tossed the PDD aside with a harsh breath just as Sumner poked his head around the doorjamb of my berth.

"Dalí, can we talk for a few?"

"Sure." I followed him to his ready room—a spartan cubicle with a workspace and two chairs. Busy holo screens showed the readouts of all ship's systems, patterns of light and data in a dizzying flood. He took the seat behind the desk, and the door slid shut behind us.

"Turn off your com." Sumner tapped his own as we sat down, and I complied. "Are you sorry you accepted my offer yet?"

"No. I'm still committed. Or maybe, I should *be* committed." I rubbed a hand over my eyes. The scope of the mission got blurrier by the minute, stretched further into uncertain territory.

He snorted as he pulled a bottle and a couple of tumblers out of hiding from behind his desk. "We're all a little insane. You fit in perfectly." Sumner poured a generous measure and handed me the amber liquid. He saluted me with his own. "First round is on me. You buy when you get back."

It was real whiskey, smooth and fiery on my tongue, and I let myself groan in appreciation. "Where did you get this?"

"A friend. From another mission." Sumner rolled the whiskey in his glass. "Our network of contacts is widespread. We all have past lives we can tap into. Learn who you can trust on undercover missions and cultivate those relationships. Give them reason to trust you, and they will work with you."

"Like me?"

"Like you. I don't offer them all jobs, though." He set the alcohol down. "There may be unpleasant aspects to this operation. I want to be certain you're fully aware of the risks." Sumner started to color; the deep-red flush crept around his clavicles and worked its way up. "There is a high probability you will be sexually abused by the Nos. It's a method they use to show captives they are powerless."

"The people we're going to rescue already suffered abuse back in Sol Fed. To bring them home, I'm willing to accept the risk."

"What about voluntarily sleeping with the enemy if the opportunity presents?" The flush climbed all the way up to his hairline.

"It depends on the situation." I knocked back a slug of whiskey. "I'll make my own determinations."

"I would never make it an order." He sat back. "And killing?"

"I understood the possibility existed when I was active in the militia." I met his eyes. "If you vetted me as thoroughly as I suspect, you saw my psi-ops eval."

"You're an empath. That's the reason the Zereid don't kill, isn't it?"

"How would you feel about experiencing someone else's death, Commander?"

"If it came down to your life against another's, could you kill?"

It was a cold feeling to search my conscience and realize I could. "Yes."

"I'm going to be blunt. Deep-cover missions can consume you if you go too far, and they can mess with your head. My director almost didn't let me ask you to do this. Your current psych profile, especially the loss of your family, makes you high risk for failure." He met my eyes directly. "They had issues with sending a brand-new agent into a situation as dangerous as this. Unique circumstances being what they are, I don't have a better option. But I think you can do it."

"Make getting the others out your priority. I'm going into this voluntarily. They weren't given any choice."

"You still looking to die?"

His gaze challenged me to answer. "I'd say my ambivalence has tilted to the side of living. I'm not attached to it yet, but I could be."

"We don't do suicide missions."

"It didn't cross my mind. That's the truth."

"Good. If I think you're taking unnecessary risks, I'll terminate your employment and ship your ass back to Zereid. Friend Gor and the kindergartners can sort you out. Survival first. Mission second. You understand me?"

"Loud and clear, sir."

Sumner sat back, satisfied. "When the time comes for extraction, we'll contact you on your implant. Even if it's off, we can activate it remotely and signal you like this." He pulled a PDD from its cradle and swiped across its screen. Three tones sounded in my skull. "If you can't respond without being compromised, we will repeat the signal hourly until you can talk. Initiate contact with the word 'Inconceivable.'"

I laughed outright. "How many *Princess Bride* references do intergalactic spies use, Commander?"

"On my team? Constantly. The Cthash love the movie. Ra'sho came up with the idea to use it as code for this mission. How well do you know it?"

"Five years of university drinking games well. You guys watch a lot of holo vids?"

"Missions are long and tedious sometimes. Most of it is waiting for things to happen. Got to pass the time, somehow." Sumner grinned at me widely. "We decided your designation should be Miracle Max or Buttercup. Your choice."

"Gee, thanks." I thought a second. "It might be useful to keep both an option, if I assume a gender."

"Good idea. Do you appear that much different as a female?"

"Subtle facial differences, and two larger ones." I lowered my chin toward my chest. "If I wear cosmetics, my appearance changes more drastically."

"What about your voice?"

"Do you need a sample for the communicators?"

"Yes." His fingers flew over the PDD. "Whenever you're ready."

"This is how I speak when I'm female." I pitched my voice to ring higher in my head, breathier. I changed my body language subtly and crossed my legs at the knee. "I haven't had trouble with my speech-activated devices recognizing either one."

Sumner's eyes widened. "Wow. Impressive."

"Vocal training and posture, Commander." I took a more delicate sip of the potent alcohol. "No physical changes involved yet."

"Even without it, you're female." His brow furrowed in confusion. He studied my face intently. "That's quite an illusion."

"Human beings look for certain things to determine gender when they can't see what's under the kilt. It took some study. I was seventeen when we went back to Sol Fed. I picked out someone I wanted to be like, someone I found attractive and fascinating as a female. I begged her to be my roommate for a semester so I could imitate her." I smiled, remembering. I uncrossed my legs, sat back and let the space between my knees widen, my forearm resting on one thigh as I confided in the deeper register I used as a male, "Her name was Allison. Intelligent, beautiful, and completely uninhibited. She was my first lover in both genders."

"And now you're a guy." Sumner shook his head. "How do you do that?"

"Perception only. I have no gender; only the mannerisms and voice you expect from a man or a woman."

"On the *Bedia,* and at the temple, I got a strong sense of your personality but neither sex."

"That's who I truly am."

"Fair enough."

I SAT MOSTLY naked on the edge of a medical table and let a still peeved ex-lover perforate my back with hand-sized nanopatches. Not exactly a good time. I was grateful for Tommi's presence. She kept up a steady stream of patter while Tella worked to prepare me for suspension.

"Remember you'll be weak when you come out of it. The parenteral nutrition will keep you alive, but your muscles will waste from inactivity. If they're thinking merchandise, they'll fatten you up a bit before they sell you. Use the time to collect as much information about your surroundings as you can." Tommi's nimble, talon-tipped fingers peeled protective backing off the nanopatches as she handed them to Tella one by one.

"You're right. I hadn't considered that." I winced as Tella pressed what seemed to be a bed of nails into the muscle mass below my left shoulder blade. The needles were only a couple of millimeters long, but there were over a hundred of them in each.

"When is the last time you ate or drank?" Tommi peeled another patch.

"I ate an hour or two after the briefing. Nothing at all in the last six hours."

"We'll be giving you a cathartic in a few minutes to empty your bowels before you get in the pod."

"Sounds fabulous."

"It isn't. Better than waking up with an obstruction, though," Tella said absently as she worked in the cluster of needles directly over my left kidney. I sucked in a breath and thought of Zereid's mauve-frosted valleys.

The third patch over my right flank was just as much of a treat. But it still held second to the joys of the bowel-shaking earthquake I experienced fifteen minutes later. The cathartic efficiently completed the forward and backward evacuation of my entire digestive tract. Sweaty and trembling, I lurched out of the head. Tella handed me a cup of cool, gelatinous liquid.

"Here. Drink this. It will make you feel a little better and help to protect your stomach and esophagus from acid while you're in suspension."

I downed the syrupy stuff. The liquid soothed the nauseated, empty cavern my stomach had become during the great migration.

"Time to lose your shorts," Tommi instructed.

"I thought I already did." I skinned out of the last item of clothing and sat on the side of the pod. Tommi studied me with interest and shrugged, one eye meeting my gaze and the other still on my body.

"I'm sorry to stare. I'm just curious."

"I'm used to it." I couldn't help but shoot a sideways glance at Tella, who turned her usual shade of roses and cream.

"I wondered what function your third gender has in comparison with ours. You know Ziggy is what we Cthash call *ix*." The translator didn't change the word, the sibilant sound unenhanced in my ear.

"The changeling third gender doesn't function in the same way. We don't have any organs for reproduction or fertilization."

"Oh." Her posture changed, coming to respectful attention. "You're more like our wise ones, then."

"Wise ones?" This, I didn't know about.

"Yeah. Our species looks to them as counselors and judges because they can see all sides of things. They..." she appeared to search for an explanation. "They're outside everyone else but considered a special gift from our ancestors. It's a small clan in comparison to the others, but highly honored."

"Interesting." I thought of my past in the diplomatic corps and of Akia Parker's work for civil rights. "Our species doesn't see us quite so positively."

"Time to get in the pod, Dalí." Tella's voice interrupted, soft and regretful.

For the first time, a frisson of anxiety ran through me. Once I went under, I had no defenses, no guarantees, and no real way to be prepared for what came next. It was a terrifying prospect. A shuddery breath betrayed my tension.

"Are you all right?" Tella's concern and her own fear brushed against my mind. She didn't know what lay ahead either, to what she had sentenced the other changelings placed in suspension before me. Her guilt gnawed at the edge of my empathic senses, like grit against skin.

"I'll be fine." My resolve still hung in there, masked by fear of the unknown. I swung my legs up into the pod and lay back against the cushion.

"Turn off your translator com." Tommi placed a gentle, scaled hand on my shoulder. "Keep it a secret, and use the advantage."

I tapped my implant. Tommi and Dr. Sharp continued conversation, the whispery hiss of the Cthash language once more a mystery to me. As Tella began to apply the patches on my chest and abdomen, a strange, floating sensation crept into my head and dulled my senses.

"What else was in the cup, Tella?" My speech stumbled off an already thick tongue.

"A sedative. You probably don't want to be awake for the rest of the catheters. It's all right. Just relax."

Tommi said something, and Tella laughed. "Tommi says sweet dreams."

The drug began to really take hold as Sumner's face appeared above me, ocean-colored eyes swimming against the ceiling panels of the medical bay. "We'll see you on the other side, Dalí. That's a promise."

"What a view to go out on," I slurred. "Did I ever tell you, you have the most beautiful eyes I've ever seen, Rion?"

"Ambassador, are you flirting with me?"

"Dalí has a tendency to proposition people under the influence." Even stoned, I could recognize a proprietary edge to Tella's voice. "Go to sleep, Dalí. We'll take care of you."

"I'm serious," I protested in narcotic honesty.

"Yours aren't too bad either." Laughter tinged Sumner's admission.

"Damned null. I can't tell if you're flirting back." Muzzy thoughts tumbled in attempts to make sense.

"Figure it out later."

My sludgy consciousness dragged me into dreams of floating in a frigid Zereid lake, gazing up at the sky. I dove deep into the dark water, naked and weightless, and drifted until I could no longer hold my breath. I propelled myself upwards toward the light.

I surfaced into disorientation and panic.

Fifteen

STRIDOR DEAFENED ME as I sucked air into my lungs. Bright, white lights. Bitter cold. Voices shouted in a language I didn't understand. Rough hands pulled me out of the medical pod, and I was dragged along.

More shouts. I fought to clear the sticky blur from my vision. Held upright on either side, other hands raked my skin and groped between my legs. I couldn't prevent it, too weak and inhibited while the drugs still coursed in my system. A voice abruptly silenced the others in accusatory tones, and another speaker, high and frantic, seemed to protest.

Iron hands wrenched back my shoulder, and the sting of a hypospray pierced my bicep. Systemic agony—my muscles slid and rearranged, too quickly for comfort. My body flowed between genders in rapid succession, eliciting a dry scream from my throat as tissue burned, swelled and subsided in my breasts and groin. Other sounds around me told me I was not the only one in pain. Someone yanked my hair from behind and forced my head up. Against a swirling vision of ice-colored eyes, someone spoke in puzzled tones before I was dragged again and dropped on a glacial floor with other stirring, groaning bodies.

We were left in silence and darkness.

Four of us huddled together in the cold and clung to each other for warmth. We hadn't been brought out of suspension gently. Violent seizures wracked one of the changelings, and we cradled the jerking body by turns. Even with an unchallenged position in the middle of our human dog pile, their clammy skin did not warm. The pulse I found fluttered an irregular rhythm, thready at best.

Weak and ravenous, anger began to rise as my senses returned, and it became clear our comrade's condition rapidly deteriorated. I groped my way along the wall and located the door. My fist banged on the port, my teeth chattered as I shouted. "Open up!"

I pounded and yelled until I was hoarse. The action warmed my blood and my mental processes. At last, the door hissed aside. I forced myself to stand on rubbery legs and squinted up at the Nos standing outside in the light of the corridor. He leveled his weapon at me.

Naked, I glared from beneath stringy hair and hoped I appeared as scary as Sumner thought I did. I spoke in Remoliad Standard. "Under Allied statutes granting citizens of Sol Fed refugee status, I request you provide us with medical attention, clothing, and food." I pointed to the huddled group behind me. "One of us is critically ill."

The guard gave no sign he understood. He stepped back and jabbed at the controls of the door.

I sighed, felt my way back to the others and wrapped myself around the near-comatose changeling, who moaned something unintelligible. I suspected shock from the abrupt withdrawal of suspension drugs. Some time ago, they had lost control of their bodily functions. We were all covered in their waste, but nothing could be done about it.

"Thanks for trying," one of them said. Their voice held the timbre of practiced masculinity and vibrated as they shivered. The four of us hadn't even introduced ourselves, the terrible intimacy of nudity and captivity more binding than knowing each other's names.

"They aren't Remoliad. I didn't think it would work, but I had to give it a shot." I pressed my forehead against the dying changeling's shoulder and whispered to them, "I'm sorry." I no longer sensed any emotions, only a white noise, unidentifiable pressure against my empathic nets.

The panicked whine of my third cellmate began to fray my nerves. "Why are they doing this to us?"

"I don't know." Confined in a dark metal room, smeared with shit and piss and vomit, I wouldn't learn a great deal.

"I don't remember you from the lab," the deeper voice said.

"I wasn't at a lab. The last thing I remember is trolling the Labyrinth on Rosetta and getting knifed in the chest." My own story constituted my cover. It would have been true if Tella followed through with her instructions.

"You went into the Labyrinth? For fuck's sake. Did you have a death wish?" my companion laughed nervously.

"I guess I did. You know it?"

"Only by reputation. I was a cabin steward on the intersystem shuttles. I heard things."

"What happened to you?"

"I flirted with the wrong passenger. We met for a drink when we got back to Mars, and her boyfriend showed up. He beat the hell out of me. I came to in the lab. God, now I have another reason to hate the Europan rugby team. He was one of the forwards."

I gave a startled laugh. "Seriously? I had a major disagreement with some of the team, too."

"Wait, me too!" the querulous changeling interjected. "I went to a party after a tournament game. One of the guys from Team Europa brought some real alcohol. I didn't realize it was so strong. I woke up strapped to a medical pod."

Well, well. Jon Batterson took his act on the road. Someone on the Europan team took Alex Nilsson in the drunken postgame brawl on Mars, too, undoubtedly. I would never learn the stories of the three dead changelings, whom Tella Sharp verified as among those missing from the Colonies. "Does anybody know about our friend, here?"

The changeling furthest away from me answered. "No. Aja never talked much, but—I got the idea they were a prostitute." They sighed. "The real question is, where are the others? I guess they didn't make it. I don't think we can hope they got away."

"What are your names?" I finally asked.

"I'm Kai. You?"

"Gresh." I'd chosen a name I would remember even under the influence of drugs.

Kai's hand squeezed my arm. "I can't say it's good to meet you here."

"I understand."

"I'm Dru." Our cellmate sniffled and hugged the comatose changeling tightly. "Aja's getting colder. What does that mean?"

I said nothing. We all huddled a little closer until at last Aja hitched a final, rattling breath. I became aware of their empathic absence as the staticky silence dissipated in death. Dru sobbed, but Kai helped me lay the body down gently and arranged Aja's limp hands over their torso in the darkness.

First failure of my mission. What the hell was I thinking when I agreed to this?

I POUNDED ON the door again, but no one came. Each of us took turns banging and shouting until we were exhausted, which didn't take long in our state. We left Aja's body where it lay and moved to a cleaner margin against the opposite wall. The cold floor sucked out our body heat, but we tried to sleep in between bouts of shivers, spooning each other like lovers. There couldn't be anything less sexual than this situation. It was survival.

Maybe hours, maybe a day passed before someone came to remove the corpse. Harsh light blinded us when a scowling Nos medic arrived and gagged in disgust at the condition of the cell. A good deal more shouting and accusatory pointing happened before they moved us into another area that seemed slightly warmer.

We used a lavatory under guard and cleaned the filth from our skin before the Nos grudgingly distributed blankets and placed us back into a different, dimly lit cell. No clothes appeared, but they brought water and ration packets. We fell on the food and water like animals, ignored the unfamiliar flavors of the nutrient cakes and licked the wrappers clean. Someone understood my request, or the Nos acted solely to protect what remained of their profitable goods. The temperature still hovered around freezing in this new cell but at least it was clean, and a toilet of sorts squatted in one corner.

The lurch out of EM drive woke me from restless sleep during my turn sandwiched between Dru and Kai. Dru's head made a painful connection with my nose.

"Are we stopping? Did we stop?"

"Not yet. We're slowing down, though." The vibration of engines still carried through the metal floor into my skull. Rubbing the back of my neck to diminish the buzzy sensation, my fingers came in contact with the bump of my implant.

Idiot.

I tapped it, camouflaging the motion as I sat up.

"Do you have any idea where they're taking us?" Kai asked. He wrapped wiry arms around his tucked-up knees, a shock of black hair falling into almond-shaped brown eyes.

"If I had to guess? The Shontavian Market."

"Are you serious?" Kai gulped. "I thought it was just spacer talk."

"What's that?" Dru asked fearfully, sweeping red-tinged hair back from her face in a practiced gesture. She pulled the blanket around her shoulders to cover her breasts. I wasn't sure it was wise for her to assume a gender—the Nos seemed baffled by our neutrality, and so far none of them had assaulted us beyond a curious grope.

I didn't answer, unwilling to feed her panic. When the cell door slid open, three Nos stood outside. Two guards held weapons leveled at us, and a male who wore the silver torc of Eminence over his black armor stepped in. He spoke Nos and looked straight at me.

"You will offer no resistance upon transfer, or you will be stunned."

The translator kicked in, but I gave no sign I understood. "I'm sorry. I don't speak Nos," I said in Remoliad Standard.

He growled an impatient curse that didn't translate and repeated his order in the language I used.

"Gresh?" Kai's voice rose in a question.

"It's time to go." I tried to sound calm. "Don't resist. They're already nervous."

A second officer appeared in the doorway. "Eminence? We have instructions to land in his personal shuttle bay."

The Eminence paled. "His personal bay? Not the market entrance?"

"Yes, Eminence." The other officer licked his lips nervously. "Shall we comply?"

"You fool. Of course we comply! We can only hope he will not kill us all." Sweat beaded on the Eminence's forehead. He left the cell, and a guard jerked his head at me, indicating we should follow.

That exchange did not sound positive for anyone. Behind me, Dru began to cry in terror as the second guard dragged her out of the cell into the narrow corridor. Her sobs continued to escalate as they escorted us to a shuttle in the Nos frigate's belly, and her captor grew intolerant. She stopped when a gangway in the ship's side extended and began to back away.

"No! No! I want to go home! Please take me home!"

The Nos shoved her forward. Dru went sprawling, and he kicked her in the thigh with vicious force. As she screamed with pain, I reacted instinctively—and foolishly. I grabbed the guard and tried to pull him away. It earned me a stunner prod.

Being stunned is not as comfortable as being unconscious. I wished I were. Muscles contracted beyond the threshold of pain into torture, but I couldn't scream. I could barely breathe. The effects lasted only minutes, but eternity passed in those few hundred seconds as they hauled me aboard and strapped me unceremoniously into a seat, the blanket trailing behind.

"You all right?" Kai pulled the blanket over what was left of my dignity. My nerve endings shrieked as the rough material dragged across skin. I hissed something to the affirmative through gritted teeth.

Dru hunkered down beside us, sniffling, but shocked into silence. The shuttle's engines fired. I tried to shut my mind to the raw anxiety Dru and Kai experienced, only to recognize a good deal of the fear as my own.

Get a grip on it, Dalí. You've already lost one. You're here to help rescue them from this nightmare. I closed my eyes and pictured Zereid's mountains, the bottomless lake, and red-streaked sky. I wondered how long I'd been suspended, what season graced the valley below the temple. The ocean moon might be in full phase now, a disc of sapphire and aquamarine.

My rampant pulse slowed and took my breathing down with it. By the time the shuttle docked in what seemed to be the Nos Eminence's personal hell, I was able to think again and the worst of the pain had passed.

The hollow, black sights of guns—many guns—followed us down the ramp of the shuttle.

Sixteen

THE BAY SPANNED the width of an enormous ship, large enough to hold half a dozen smaller craft. An armored, helmeted host of humanoid mercenaries greeted us. I stared a little at the hulking shape in the back. A Shontavian mercenary. Its faceplate was raised to reveal slick gray skin and a maw full of prongs. Two of its four arms cradled a large caliber pulse rifle. The other pair aimed a standing gun array at our small group. A fighting machine engineered for war by their Ursetu masters, the Shontavians were not bound by Remoliad treaty prohibiting eating their enemies. Or anybody else they wanted.

A visored officer sauntered up to the Nos, his weapon held across the abdomen. "He's waiting for you in the gallery. Bring the merchandise and follow me. The rest of your party stays here."

"You. Come with us." The Eminence barked a dry command at me in our mutual language. His complexion put Luna's ashy landscape to shame. I'd had no idea Nos could get any paler. I gathered Kai and the limping Dru, and we followed, clumped together for reassurance. More of the masked, armored guards took up a position behind us. My bare feet were numb as we crossed the bay; they'd been cold so long I wondered if sensation would ever return. The mercenary officer ushered us into a lift, and after a moment, the doors opened on paradise.

Warmth. Blessed warmth and carpets beneath the soles of my feet, a roaring fire in the center of the room. While only a holographic projection, the heat emanating from the base of the projector was real. Dru gave a cry of longing, and the three of us were pulled toward the vision of flames by pure Neanderthal instinct. The guards let us go without reprimand and prevented our Nos captors from following. I didn't care what was coming anymore. At the moment I would have sold my soul to stay right there.

Beside me, Kai moaned, hands out to the fire. "They can kill me now."

"What is this place? Are we on a ship or a space station?" Dru asked. Almost garish in its luxury, this room appeared to be a lounge or a lobby.

"You are in the private residence of Lord Rhix."

Startled, Dru yelped. Beside us, a trollish vision with an overlarge cranium and clay-skinned, drooping features nodded, his mouth curved in something resembling a smile. My empathic senses read a surge of reassurance as I stared in genuine surprise. I'd never seen this species before. And he spoke Sol Standard.

"Who are you?"

"I am Simish. Follow me, please, and I will see to your comfort."

The Nos shifted, blustering. "This illegal merchandise was seized in a Nos Conglomerate trade route. You aren't taking them from our custody until we negotiate terms." Eminence Odrik's protest dropped in intensity as the mercenaries closed around him.

"He's ready to *negotiate* with you in there." The commander pointed his rifle at a closed door.

The Eminence swallowed, straightened, and began to walk toward the door. His first officer stood frozen to the spot, terrified, and Eminence Odrik took two furious steps back, grabbed him by the arm and dragged him along. If Odrik went down, his subordinate was going with him. It would have been funny had my own circumstances been more promising.

"This way, please. You will be well-treated here as you regain your strength." Simish gestured, and with reluctance, we left the leaping holographic flames to follow him.

The door sealed behind Eminence Odrik and his first officer. It truncated a short, gurgling scream. Dru gaped in horror, wide-eyed, and Simish beckoned us in hasty urgency. "Come."

The mercenary escorts trailed in our wake. "Where are we?" I asked in a low voice.

Simish glanced over his shoulder at me. "Many things are answered by observing and listening. It will undoubtedly be safer for you. I know you must be weak, but we are not going far."

The Nos should have provided us with more formal blankets. We were underdressed for the opulence surrounding us. Artifacts and artwork from all over the galaxy crowded walls and platforms, things strewn about carelessly for which I had no reference. This suggested the abode of a collector. One alcove down an intersecting corridor held dozens of holo displays. I stood too far away to parse what they displayed. Three armored mercenaries surveyed the screens in this security nave with rapt attention.

"This dormitory was prepared for your use while you recover." Simish stopped in front of a reinforced port.

"No, please, not another cell!" Dru whimpered and shrank against Kai and me. Simish paused and regarded us with his sad, droopy eyes.

"They did mistreat you. You're safe here. You can be assured this is not a cell."

"It looks like a lock to me." Kai's jaw tightened.

"Security, not imprisonment. For your protection as much as Lord Rhix's." He placed his palm on the pad.

The door opened with a *whoosh*, a heavy, air locked port leading into a large room. I stared, my steps faltering, and Kai muttered, "Holy shit."

Not as crowded as those outside, this lush room was furnished with couches and chairs one could sink into and be lost. Its crowning feature lay above us. A dome in the ceiling opened to the cosmos, where the galaxy spun out an infinite dance of expansion against the blackness of space. It filled the room with the ebb and flow of starlight, too subtle to tell if it was a projection or a window. The view didn't have the dulling quality of a transparent metal alloy, so crisp I could make out even the dimmest of bodies above me. I caught a glimpse of what lay beyond through this impossible vista. We were on an enormous ship, surrounded by dozens of other spacecraft of varying origin.

Our guards stayed outside. Simish motioned to doors on either side of the common area.

"There are private chambers for each of you. Today will be a time of rest and recuperation. I know you are all malnourished and we will start with simple food. Are any of you in need of immediate medical attention?"

"Gresh has a stunner burn," Kai said. I hadn't even felt it in the cold, but now, a tight, sunburned sting came with the reddened skin.

"And the bastard kicked me," Dru said, exposing her leg from the blanket folds to reveal an ugly, purpling knot above her right knee.

"There are facilities in the chambers with a bath or sonic cleanser available. If you wish to make use of them, I will return with the appropriate treatments for your injuries. There are toiletries, robes, and towels inside."

"A real bath with hot water?" Dru headed for one of the open doors.

Simish bowed to us politely and exited the room. The guards took up position outside as the port sealed itself.

The sound of running water came from the suite Dru chose, her squeal of delight echoing back into the common area. Kai and I glanced at each other in mutual trepidation.

"It may look like a hotel, but we're still prisoners." Kai's brown eyes were wary.

"You're not wrong."

"You remember the fairy tale about the kids who found the candy house in the woods?" He shuddered. "Did you see the Shontavian out there? My god, those teeth. You don't think they're going to feed us to that thing?"

"Why go to all this trouble then?" I frowned, looking around at the overstuffed cushions and furs of unknown animals, the magnificent view above, and the six empty rooms lining the outside walls. "To me, it seems like a room where someone spends a lot of time on their back, if you get my meaning."

"What? No. No, no. You're kidding, right?" Kai's face fell when he realized I wasn't joking.

It wasn't the prospect of being part of someone's harem that troubled me. The vacancies on either side did. If this was the fabled brothel Melos had heard of, what happened to the last set of concubines?

THE WARMTH AND vibration of the cleanser was a religious experience after the cold, unspeakable conditions we'd endured aboard the Nos ship. It left me more clearheaded, but a stranger faced me in the mirror.

My nails and hair were overgrown. I hadn't cut it while on Zereid, and an uncertain number of months in suspension brought the brown waves to the level of my shoulder blades. Coupled with the mass I'd lost in transit, it gave me a more feminine appearance even in my neutral state.

The hooded robe they provided only enhanced the illusion as I pulled it over my head. Soft against the painful burn, it was made of nanosilk material, obscenely expensive and seldom seen in the Colonies. The properties activated with body heat, self-adjusting the length of its hems to cover my wrists and ankles. Two thicker diamond shapes on the cuffs hid additional options. Pinching the left one in my thumb and forefinger changed the robe's color, running through a slow wash of the spectrum. The other divided the bottom portion of the garment. It startled the hell out of me as fabric slid together between my legs and formed loose trousers.

A second press on each button returned the robe to its original white color and design. I left it that way. This unanticipated luxury didn't seem like something a prisoner would wear, at odds with the nightmarish captivity into which we'd awakened. It only made me lean more toward an intended role of concubine versus main course for the Shontavians.

A tap at the outside door alerted me to Simish's return. "I have a topical medication which will relieve the pain and speed the healing process. Do you wish me to apply it?" He showed me a tube attached to a flat applicator.

"No, thank you. I'll do it myself."

"How do you feel?"

I took measure. "Hungry. Weak."

"I am not surprised. You were in suspension for a long time. It must be disconcerting." My trollish attendant set out a cup of water, a bowl of clear broth, and wafer-thin pieces of pastry at a small table in the bedroom. The soup sent up streamers of delicious mist, unfamiliar aromas to me, but at the moment, I found it ambrosia. My stomach howled.

"Eat slowly. You may experience discomfort of your digestive tract if you do not."

I sipped at it, resisting the urge to down the broth in greedy gulps. "Simish, I don't know why I'm here."

"Of course you wouldn't." His sympathy played at the edge of my senses, but I sensed reluctance to share any information. "Rest, and sleep. There are items left in the common area you will find palatable if you wish to eat again. I will return in twelve hours."

"What happens then?"

"You will be presented to Lord Rhix. He may wish to inspect you."

That didn't sound ominous at all.

Simish bowed and left, a being of succinct words. What I did sense from him was benign, but he felt sorry for me. This did not bode well. I trusted Sumner's promise would be kept before we were fattened up for whatever awaited us.

The comforting warmth of the soup and pastry in my formerly empty system provoked an enormous yawn. I stumbled back into the lavatory and applied salve to the burn with unfocused eyes.

The bed was a thing of wonder. I had about ten seconds to appreciate it until sleep flowed over me.

"WE DON'T WANT to keep him waiting. You are expected to behave with courtesy." My little attendant trotted beside me and glanced up anxiously. "Can you do this?"

Be polite to a slave dealer? Sarcasm twitched in the side of my mouth, but I bit it back. "I can govern myself." I'd insisted on going first. I hoped I could give Dru and Kai an idea what to expect and allay some of their fear.

Armed guards arranged themselves in stiff watch before a closed door. "He wants to inspect the new arrivals," Simish informed them. The translator whispered in my head.

"Don't let it get out of hand. We had to clean up after he got done with the Eminence. He's waiting. Go in."

My handler glanced at me several times as he led me through the door into a darker room, as if to assure himself I would keep my promise to behave. On the other side of the chamber, another panorama of celestial grandeur filled the viewport. A tall figure stood silhouetted against starlight. "Lord Rhix. This is the first of your guests."

"What are you called?" Deep and rich, the answering voice surprised me. Rhix, like Simish, spoke accented Sol Standard. He did not turn around.

"Gresh."

"Do you know who I am?"

"I'm afraid I don't."

"This is my domain. Here I deal out life, death, and business, sometimes in the same breath. You are part of a transaction, Gresh. There is no Remoliad Alliance here, no Sol Federation. There is only my law."

"I understand."

"Do you?" The deep voice held amused condescension. Rhix folded arms across his battle-armored chest, his expression still in shadow as he turned. "Remove your robe, please."

Beside me, Simish's anxiety grew the longer I waited. He nodded at me in encouragement. Finally, I pulled the garment over my head and handed it to my keeper.

"You seem reasonable, so I will ask— What are you?" Puzzlement played against my empathic nets. His question was offensive only in its phrasing. I sensed no malice.

"Human. I am a third-gender changeling."

"What is a changeling?"

"We can assume the secondary sexual characteristics of a male or female."

"The Nos thought you were malformed."

"Some of my own species see us in that light." I allowed my true feelings to color the statement.

Rhix moved to inspect me at a more intimate range. For the first time, I saw him clearly. Skin darker than mine, but not so deep as the reddish, earthy pigment of my father's. Fierce, high cheekbones and forehead resembled our Polynesian ancestry, as did the sable ringlets of hair. Beyond those passing familiarities, he had no external ear structures. Heavy-lidded eyes glinted without discernible sclera—bronze, dark, and inscrutable. He circled me in close proximity but did not touch me.

"The stunner burn is unfortunate but will heal." He pointed to the scar over my sternum. "I know a blade's mark when I see it. You were stabbed in the chest. How did it happen?"

"A private fight."

"What about?"

"Family honor. I deflowered his brother."

"Rape?"

I smirked. Couldn't help it. "Oh, no. He was most definitely a willing participant."

Eyes widened in appraisal. I stared back at him. Unlike the Nos, no impediments stood between my empathic senses and Rhix's emotional broadcast. I wasn't prepared for what I felt from him. The heat of lust from another human being is familiar, easy to deflect if not reciprocated. This surge of pheromonal activity bathed me in fire. Even in my weakened state, change hormones began to percolate in an unmistakable, feminine response. Involuntary. Unsettling. I tamped it down before it could culminate in any physical alterations.

His nostrils flared, head cocked as if listening. He drew back, and a wary, thoughtful expression took up residence on his hawk-like countenance. "You may dress."

Simish handed the robe back to me. As my head emerged from the cowl, Rhix asked, "What skills do you have?"

"Negotiation. I am—was—an officer in the Sol Fed Diplomatic Corps and Luna Militia. Briefly, an ambassador. I speak the Remoliad Standard and Zereid languages as well as Sol Fed's."

"Will they be looking for you?"

"I doubt it. I was judged unfit for duty." I lifted my chin defiantly.

"You disagree with their action?"

"No. They were right."

"Family?"

The spasm of pain destabilized my voice. "They died."

"I see." He went silent a moment. "You are remarkably composed for someone who was awakened from suspension in a Nos slave ship."

"I hadn't expected to wake up at all." I didn't avert my gaze from those challenging eyes. "I'll take my chances."

"Simish will be responsible for your well-being as you recover your strength." Rhix paused. "In reward for your cooperation, you may ask questions without consequence before you are dismissed."

"Is this the Shontavian Market? Why are we here?"

"You've heard of it."

"Yes. Rumors. Nothing concrete."

"I deal in favors and necessities, no matter how ugly they might seem. Everyone needs something." A bemused curve grew on his lips. "You and your companions are an offering of good faith, Gresh. A symbol of how far a new acquaintance is willing to go to obtain my assistance, but I have no idea what to do with you. For the moment, you are my guests here."

Seventeen

OUR ESCORT FELL in behind as Simish walked me back to the dormitory. I was confused. The Caligula-like reputation didn't seem to fit the mannered being I'd just met—yet the guard implied bloodshed in Eminence Odrik's meeting with Lord Rhix.

"You did well." Simish's pleasure glowed in my empathic nets.

"I'm not certain Dru and Kai can tolerate his inspection as easily. They were sexually abused during their captivity. It may seem threatening to them."

His face twitched. "I took the liberty of giving them something—without their knowledge, I'm afraid—but I wanted to spare them discomfort."

"Why did you give me a choice?"

"I am a good judge of personality; one of the reasons Lord Rhix keeps me on." Simish glanced my way. "I am sorry to learn about your family. How long ago?"

I had to do a calculation in my head. Even with my fictional suspension, the answer was the same. "It's been a little over a Sol year now."

As I spoke the words, I could hardly believe them. Was it possible? I could still taste his lips and remember the silken touch of her skin. My eyes grew hot. I missed them with sudden, sharp fierceness; Sida, and my Gresh, whose name I now wore like a shield.

"I wish your circumstances were different. Now you are here, and I will do what I can to make you comfortable while you recuperate from suspension. You are allowed access to the library and gallery—with an escort, of course."

"What about the Market?"

"I don't know why you'd want to go in there. It's not a civilized place."

"Simish, will you clarify something for me?" I dropped my voice. "Are we being groomed for someone else to—purchase?"

"I don't think he knows yet. He is not familiar with your attributes."

"What happened to the last people who occupied our rooms?"

Discomfort rose in Simish. He shot a glance at the guard several paces behind us. "It's far safer not to ask questions."

"If he's prone to killing his 'guests,' I'd rather know."

Simish licked his lips. "Only when they plot against him." The words were spoken in such a low whisper I couldn't be sure I caught it. We reached the door, and he placed his palm on the pad. "He can be generous, or he can be deadly. Listen, observe, and judge for yourself."

WHILE DRU AND Kai slept off the sedative Simish gave them, I prowled our common room with restless energy. I attempted some *zezjna* fundamentals but found my muscles still weak and unreliable when tested. Instead, I poked around and discovered controls that extended a door across the base of the dome. This feature had once been a hatch into the ship, but with extensive modifications. The door locked in place under the transparent window and sealed off the room. I still wasn't sure what provided such an unobstructed view of the stars. I returned the door to its hidden position and tossed a cushion up into the recess to test my theory.

The pillow sizzled with impressive ferocity. Ash drifted down like gray snow in the wake of smoking fluff and fabric. An energy shield. There were no power controls to be found in the seraglio. That meant it could be deactivated from somewhere besides this room—what an unnerving thought. The little palace revolt Simish mentioned must be a frequent occurrence to require a built-in consequence.

On the other hand, this former hatch was a direct exit if the energy emitters were somehow disrupted. *Potential escape route? Check.*

I assumed we were under surveillance, given the bank of holoscreens I'd glimpsed. But like a guilty kid hiding evidence, I stuffed the singed cushion beneath one of the lounges before Simish returned.

This time, he set the table in the communal area with a meal still suited to our convalescent stomachs, but mercifully not broth. Others of his species, so like him they had to be clones or relatives, arrived with armfuls of clothing they laid out on the cushioned surfaces. Simish gathered his flock at last and withdrew from the dormitory.

There were several items echoing Eurasian-based fashion favored by the third gender back in Sol Fed; long tunics with trousers or skirts beneath. I ended up with a mix of neutral and female, and a few close-fitting items I could sleep or work out in. I didn't allow myself to think on who might have worn them before me, or what had happened to them. I changed out of the robe into a knee-length tunic and leggings, a dark, smoky red banded by black nanosilk margins that adjusted the fit to my frame. Shoes were provided as well, stretchy slippers that accommodated my feet.

Kai wandered out of his bedroom with a yawn, drawn by the scent of the meal. "Jeeze, what hit me?" He fingered some of the expensive garments and whistled, then stopped and asked, head cocked, "Did he tell you to take your clothes off?"

"Ah. Yes."

"I was hoping I dreamed that. I guess he decided to keep us and not feed us to the monsters. So, are we going to be his..." Kai colored in embarrassment. "Whore seems like such a strong word, when my life might depend on it."

"Simish says Lord Rhix hasn't decided yet. He isn't sure what to make of us."

"I'm pretty sure he knew what to make of me." Dru padded out of her room, yawning. "He didn't touch, though. Clothes! Oh, these are beautiful." She picked up a blue gown and held the flowing material against her. "I could get used to this."

"Really? We're Sol Fed citizens. You're okay with being somebody's sex slave?" Kai arched eyebrows in disgust.

"He said we're his guests." Dru tossed her head.

"You believe that?"

"After what we just went through? I'll settle for not being chained up in a lab by species purity freaks. What do you think, Gresh?"

"I'll choose being a free citizen any day," I said.

Kai sat down at the table with me, reached for a slice of soft bread and eyed a platter in the center of the meal. "Is that real meat?"

"Some kind of roasted bird, I think."

"As long as it couldn't talk, I'm good." He seized a chunk and took a bite, eyes rolling up in pleasure. He groaned.

"Candy house?" I reminded.

"Don't care right now," he mumbled around the mouthful. "Hunger strike later. You have to try this."

"Survival first," I muttered to myself and pulled off some of the meat. Any reservation I might have had evaporated. The almost-forgotten alchemy of what happens when fire meets bird flesh and herbs melted over my tongue. I made an inarticulate, helpless noise of bliss and reached for more.

"Hey, save some for me." Dru plopped down next to us and dug in as well. "Oh. Oh! My god. This is amazing."

Kai pronounced, "We're doomed." Those were the last words spoken until the meal was consumed down to bone and crumb.

I FOUND SLEEP elusive there, too.

Even amid the increasing wonders of our seraglio, new food and entertainment items delivered with indulgent frequency each day, I was restless. It still felt too much like a cell when only a barrier of energy separated us from a purge of breathable atmosphere, without control of the power switch. I didn't mention that discovery to Dru or Kai.

Three nights into the mission, I decided I risked insanity if I didn't get out of those rooms. I wasn't learning anything new there. Despite the odd hour, I tested Simish's promise and asked our keepers outside if I could go for a walk.

I traveled in loops with my silent escort, a long track leading me past the security nave on each revolution. Four Ursetu mercenaries monitored the screens, helmets removed. I slowed my pace here. My guard thought I lingered too long and shifted his weapon. I took the hint, but not before I caught a glimpse and confirmed my suspicions of surveillance. The common area in our seraglio and our bedrooms were all represented in the flickering wall of light.

I counted mercenaries on my next round. One guard with me. One still at the door of our cushioned prison. Four in the security nave. The lift door to Rhix's private shuttle bay remained unguarded, within eyesight but still some distance away from the mercenary sentries.

At the end of the corridor furthest from the gallery loomed a set of reinforced blast doors, conspicuous in their practicality among the opulence. Two mercs stood before this entry as well. Melos mentioned high-level negotiations and entertainments took place behind barriers like these. The Market bays must be on the other side.

Each night, the number of guards remained constant. I learned something practical, at least.

My familiarity with the two changelings who shared the dormitory grew daily, but the forced intimacy of our captivity on the Nos ship relaxed here, and soon each of us had our own routine. Kai appeared more comfortable as male or neutral and only picked clothing that confirmed the sense. He was submissive to a fault, deferring to Dru or me rather than his own preference, but I liked him. When I increased efforts to regain my strength, something the diet of meat protein seemed to enhance quickly, it took little persuasion to get him to join me in workouts.

Dru identified as female in an almost defensive manner. The first few hours after we'd been yanked from suspension were the only time I ever saw her vulnerable, or in neutral gender. She preferred to supervise rather than join us when we worked out, and by observing her in turn, I learned more about her. She put on a front of a ditzy, shallow party girl, but underneath lay a mind that calculated everything before she spoke or acted.

I dozed in fitful spurts each night, time only delineated by a chronometer and the meals Simish brought. The fourth night in, I jerked awake in the darkness of my room.

Either I'd just heard the signal on my implant, or I was dreaming. Adrenaline spiked my pulse.

Nowhere in the seraglio was safe from the watchful bank of security surveillance, but I thought I could at least muffle my voice among the overstuffed lounges and cushions in the darkened common area. I got up and lay under the starry dome, barely breathing while I waited for the promised hourly repeat.

The hazy spindle of galaxies above revolved in slow measure as I stared up, arms folded behind my head. Rescue was coming. My heart raced.

Three tones in my skull. Excitement swept over me.

I rolled over and faced the back of the lounge as if to sleep, letting my finger tap the implant when I curled my arm over my face. "Inconceivable," I muttered.

"Miracle Max?" Sumner's voice sounded in my head. "You okay?"

"At the moment. I'm under surveillance. Hard to talk."

"I have your tracker signal. It's very clear. Are you near the outside?"

"There is an energy dome, a skylight, in Lord Rhix's residence. That's our quarters."

His voice returned after a few seconds, tight with relief. "I see it. Guards?"

"Two outside the door. Usually eight total. Heavy surveillance. The lift door to his private shuttle bay is not guarded. Blast doors at the end of the hall."

"Can you deactivate the dome?"

"No. It can only be sealed from here. I think it used to be a hatch."

"Make sure it stays open. It's a direct route to you we can work with. Are you in danger?"

"Not now. Tommi was right. They might be fattening us up for the next Market."

"How many people in there with you?"

"Only three of us." I swallowed. "One died on the Nos ship." Even whispering, my voice broke with guilt.

There was a long pause. "Damn. I'm sorry. The session closes in three days. You'll be out before then. I'll contact you again in a couple of hours. When we've set the plan, I'll relay the timeline."

"Understood."

"Keep everybody together. Sumner out."

No more than a couple of days. I could do this. Maybe my first mission would end better than it started. I closed my eyes and heaved a deep sigh, the sudden release of tension in my shoulders evidence of how tightly wound I'd been. Sleep hit me without preamble.

"Good morning, Gresh. It would be best if you return to your quarters for the next hour as we bring the ship into EM drive."

Disoriented at first, I sat up and rubbed my eyes. The meaning of his words penetrated my muddled brain. "We're leaving?" Panic threatened, an expanding core of ice in my chest. I fought to keep my expression from betraying my true thoughts.

"The Market is closing early. We must move on." Although Simish tried to hide his heightened anxiety, it buzzed against my mind, a match for my own. He crossed to the controls and unfurled the metal shielding over the dome.

The hatch sealed with a metallic wheeze and cut off my team's only direct route.

Simish turned with brisk movements. "I must prepare for the transition. You should too. Please go to your room, and lie down so you will be safe."

As if on cue, the sound of explosions sounded above us. The ship rocked with the unmistakable fire of ordinance against military grade shields. I'd been through enough low-caliber exercises in the militia to recognize it.

"What's happening?"

"Undoubtedly, someone dissatisfied with their terms. If they aren't careful, Lord Rhix will renegotiate."

The thud of mounted guns carried through the ceiling. A larger explosion and the resulting lurch caused things in the seraglio to rattle. "Ah. He settled the dispute in his favor."

I stood paralyzed, hoping what I'd heard did not mark the end of Sumner's *Thunder Child*. My mouth went dry.

Kai appeared in the door of his room, his eyes wide and wild. "What the hell?" Dru, pale and disheveled, also stumbled from her doorway.

"Go back to your beds, please. I suspect this transition will be hasty. You don't want to be standing up." Simish scuttled out of the room. I waved Kai and Dru back into their rooms and hurried to mine.

Three tones rang in my skull. I was torn between relief Sumner and his crew were still alive, and despair.

"Inconceivable!" The word fell from my lips like the curse it was.

Sumner's urgent voice said, "Dalí—"

And it faded. The Market ship already moved too fast for the limited range of the communicator. It was too late. I hoped the implanted tracker would let them find me again.

G-forces pushed my body into the mattress. I braced myself when a coarse vibration began to make its way through the walls and the bed. My teeth hummed, nerves complaining deep in the roots. By the time my insides threatened to become my outsides, the stomach-churning transition into exotic matter drive was a relief.

But it carried us away from any hope of immediate rescue.

Eighteen

WELL, FUCK. THAT didn't go as planned.

"How long until the next Market?" I asked while Simish laid out our breakfast the following day. Dru and Kai were still sleeping. I'd been up for hours after wrestling with my insomnia.

"A little more than thirty-five cycles," he replied. "This session is selective. Less rabble, and more personages of importance."

Over a month. My heart sank. "Will he sell us there?"

Simish stopped what he was doing. His heavy-lidded eyes softened in sympathy. "He still has not determined what will become of you. The truth is, he no longer deals in any living merchandise, including slaves, but this transaction was agreed upon before..." His abrupt halt made me wonder why he censored himself. "If he does decide you will be sold, you can at least be assured of civilization."

I smiled faintly. He meant to reassure me, genuine concern brushing against my empathic senses. "Thank you, Simish."

"He likes red."

Confused, I blinked at him. "What?"

"You said you did not expect to wake up after being stabbed. If you might wish to remain here...he likes the color red."

"Why are you telling me this?"

Simish glanced around and came closer. "I think he was intrigued. I put my money on you."

My jaw dropped, aghast. "You're betting on which of us he wants to sleep with?"

"Please don't take offense. We don't get many distractions here."

"I don't find any amusement in betting on rape."

"Rape?" He took a step back and shook his head vehemently. "You misunderstand me. With him, it is a business transaction. It would not be without your consent."

We were prisoners, despite the dubious "guest" status. Consent or not, it would be coercion at best. I couldn't conceal my revulsion for this idea. Troubled by my silence and dark countenance, Simish continued setting out the meal.

"I have distressed you. Truly, it is not an undesirable alternative. He can be kind in his own way."

I huffed in soft derision and wondered if the vanished concubines would agree. The more I thought about it, though, made me consider a calculated submission. I could ingratiate myself with the wrinkly little warden of our luxurious cell by winning his bet. A smattering of quid pro quo could go a long way. Almost five weeks stretched between today and any hope of my crewmates' return. The only thing I could do was look out for Dru and Kai until then, and if possible, spare them Rhix's "transactions"—by putting myself in the way of them.

SIMISH WASN'T JUST the name of our keeper—it designated his species. He and the half-dozen other servants who saw to our needs, and I presumed Rhix's as well, were a collective who shared the name Simish. Dru nicknamed them Happy, Sleepy, Dopey, Sneezy, Doc, Bashful, and Grumpy; a little unkind, perhaps, but the names were accurate. Each of them had definitive features and personality enough to determine who was who. Our original keeper remained Simish to me.

In the following days, it became clear that while Simish placed his money on me, Grumpy had hers on Dru. Kai seemed to be the long shot and resisted vehemently when pushed in the direction of femininity.

"I'm just not a girl," he protested when they left.

"None of us are girls, sweetie," Dru reminded him.

"I know, but...you and Gresh flow that way without a problem. It's not that I haven't been female for people, but it's not me. Why are they doing this?"

I sighed, and admitted with reluctance, "As I understand it, they placed bets on who Rhix wants to sleep with."

"Well, count me out. I don't want to be this guy's whore. I just want to go home." Kai's voice held a note of despair. "We need to get out of here."

"In case you haven't noticed, we're on a spaceship, and we're in EM drive. We don't even know what part of the galaxy we're in. Where are we going to go?" Dru shook her head at him. "We might just have to make the best of this."

"Oh, yeah? And what happens if he decides he doesn't like changeling pussy?"

She sneered. "Oh, *very* nice."

"Give me a break, Dru. You're not an innocent."

"I never said I was. Just because you wish you had a real one doesn't mean you need to be a dick."

"Let's not start taking it out on each other," I cautioned. "It's not going to help."

"Seriously, Gresh. What's going to happen to us?" Kai demanded.

I hesitated a moment before I answered. His emotions were already frayed. "Simish claims they don't deal in slavery anymore. Lord Rhix will decide what to do with us before the next Market, but it doesn't sound like he'll just let us go."

"Oh, god." Kai collapsed into the cushions. "I didn't sign up for any of this. I'm never going to see my home or my family again, am I?"

His despair flowed against my mind, heavy and slow. I sat down beside him as he buried his head in his hands and wept. Even Dru came and nestled into his other side, although her expression indicated her thoughts were elsewhere. We held him between us until he calmed.

"We'll do our best to stay together, whatever happens," I said finally. "Dru's more comfortable in female form, I'm neutral, and you prefer to be male. Maybe we can sell it that way—needing to be a unit, like Cthash siblings."

"You're neutral?" Kai's bitterness gave an edge to the words. "Gresh, have you looked in the mirror lately? You are definitely female right now, even without tits. You have been since the day we got inspected."

"He gives one hell of a pheromone buzz, doesn't he? Lord Rhix, I mean." Dru's eyes challenged me knowingly over Kai's back.

My body's involuntary response to Rhix still disconcerted me. I hadn't stopped to think that Dru or Kai experienced it as well. "You noticed, too?"

Dru's mouth curved in a smirk. "How could I miss it?"

"Apparently, I did." Kai sniffled. "But I don't swing that way."

"We'll come up with a way to stay together." I left my arm draped around him. On his other side, Dru's expression was still far away, even dreamy. Her attitude toward our captivity concerned me—people did desperate things when survival was at stake. Rhix's powerful pheromones had sent me reeling, and it could only complicate Dru's ability to see the situation for what it was, not knowing I was here to get them out. I wondered how the hell I could help Kai but made a silent vow to do everything in my power to get them home.

FUTILE ATTEMPTS AT sleep led me to pace the hallway with my silent, faceless guard. Behind the visor, I couldn't be sure what species he was. My empathic nets caught hints of boredom and condescension. When I spent too much time near the security alcove, he was quick to urge me forward with a jerk of the weapon he held loosely in front. The galleries, however, I was allowed to wander freely.

I wished I had someone to ask about the artifacts and works of art. Prominent, sealed cases contained the most fragile, some suspended in anti-grav vacuum due to their delicacy and possible origins.

I stared into one of these cases with fascination. Inside, a pulsing, opalescent mass of matter spun in slow revolutions, its shape in continuous flux.

"Do you know what this is?" I asked the guard in Remoliad Standard. My translator implant remained a secret weapon for now. The guard either did not understand or ignored my question and stared straight ahead. Friendly guys, mercenaries.

The blob took on forms that seemed to evoke strange spikes of emotion with each new pause, hypnotic and disconcerting. I put my fingertips against the case, and it strained toward me as if I were a magnet, its silvery heart flickering with the spectrum of blue, violet, and red.

"It is a psycho-reactive substance." The deep voice behind me spoke Sol Standard. I jerked my hand from the display. Rhix stood there.

No longer armored, he wore a long, black robe of nanosilk. My guard retreated to a position across the hall when Rhix joined me. "Living artwork, created by the mind of the beholder. What do you feel when you see it?"

"I'm not sure." I shook my head and attempted to sort out the emotions it conjured. "Wonder. Sadness."

"The artist was the last of their species. There will never be another piece like it." He moved to the opposite side and stared into the box. The shimmering mass inside swirled with fractal patterns as he traced a finger down the glass. "I value singularities."

"Your collection is impressive, but I have no idea what most of it is."

"Souvenirs. Trophies. The flattery of beings that wanted something in return. A few real treasures." He regarded me across the case. "Come. I will show you more of my favorites."

An enthusiastic tour of the gallery followed, led by someone with a deep appreciation for the subject of art. Rhix knew something about each piece, whether or not he deemed it special. Only a few times did his surprising command of Sol Standard fail to provide a word he wanted, and with our common knowledge of the Remoliad's standard tongue, we were able to find it. I reminded myself that despite his strange, aristocratic charm, this was someone reported to enjoy gladiatorial sport as punishment—and possibly flushing his concubines into the vacuum of space.

"May I ask when you learned to speak Sol Standard?" I ventured cautiously.

"There are no secrets if one speaks all the languages in his household." A hint of anger tangled in my empathic nets. "I have been learning the tongue since your species petitioned to join the Remoliad. It is clear I will deal with humanity on a regular basis."

"I heard spacers' talk on Zereid about the Market. I didn't know Sol Fed already had contact with it." Simish had warned me not to be too inquisitive, but I was in a position to find out more information. If I pushed the wrong button, I might find anger directed at me instead of curiosity. "May I ask questions, Lord Rhix?"

He appraised me. "You ask too many," he noted with dry indulgence. "Choose to play this game, and you alone are responsible for the answers. But you must answer my questions in return. Do you understand the consequences?"

"I believe so. Like Eminence Odrik?" Probably too blunt to ensure my continued health, but Rhix uttered a short laugh. His amusement played along the edges of my mind.

"The Eminence thought he could profit by selling something already promised to me. He allowed irreparable damage to one of you on board his ship. His greed and carelessness earned his reward, not his questions." He dismissed the guard with a flick of his hand. The mercenary moved to the next gallery immediately, still in sight but out of earshot. "Ask."

"You said we were part of a business transaction. Who offered human beings as collateral?"

"Your government."

That wasn't the answer I expected. A jolt shook my body and betrayed my surprise. Rhix let me absorb the information a moment.

"Now you will answer a question for me."

"Yes, of course."

"What happened during your inspection?" He moved closer to me. "Something changed. Your scent altered. Your heart beat faster."

"Change hormones. They prepare me for the physical adaptation of a gender. They're sometimes triggered by different emotional states of stress, or by sexual arousal."

"You did not seem frightened. Fear has its own scent."

Not frightened enough, anyway. My taste for dangerous liaisons did not seem to have diminished in the least. That's what I got for a season of living an ascetic's life with Gor. "I wasn't afraid."

The admission ignited Rhix's towering hunger and its effect on my personal chemistry. In an attempt to remain detached, I tried to dissect what washed over me, whether it was a murderous kind of rutting instinct or if it was basic, animal attraction, empathic or olfactory pheromones. This time, though, I allowed the slow physical changes to happen: the sliding pain of muscle against bone, the heat and ache in my swelling breast tissue, lips, and deep inside where the sensitive, nerve-filled areas prepared for internal rather than external stimulation.

He stared openly with appreciation, and his gaze lingered on the newly feminine form beneath my clothes. The hormone flood didn't end. I willed myself to reverse the changes, endured the tearing pain in my shoulders and arms as musculature shifted into a more masculine build. Rhix was not as enamored of this shape. The abatement of his interest allowed me to fall back into my neutral state. Trembling seized my muscles from the aftereffects of rapid transformation.

"Does it take a toll on you?"

"When I change too quickly. Usually it takes no effort, only the right stimulation."

"Your beauty is wasted in the masculine form." He studied me. "Our species must share a common ancestor. The Ursetu, the Nos, and dozens of others spring from a race which no longer exists, but spread its seed across the galaxy. We all reproduce in the same way, with varying levels of ritual. Our drive for the act can lead one to madness. My predecessor viewed it as an effective tool in negotiation. Was it one you used yourself?"

"Never in my work. My personal appetites and my profession are separate things."

"My drive to possess things of unique beauty sometimes overrides my better sense." He reached out and touched a strand of my hair. "What drives you, Gresh?"

I couldn't tell him the truth; right now, my body had no reservations about what it wanted, but my brain worked uncomfortably at the thought of the missing concubines. I didn't answer, and didn't flinch as he trailed his fingers down to graze the bare skin at my collarbone.

Those bronze eyes burned into mine. A slow smile grew in response to what he thought he saw there.

"We will talk again. And then, perhaps, we will negotiate."

He turned, black robes swirling about him as he crossed the gallery to his quarters. My guard resumed his post. Shaky in the post-hormonal flood, I retreated to the dormitory, where I fell into one of the deep chairs. My thoughts were chaotic. I breathed in slow measure, calling on Zereid meditative techniques to help order my mind.

Rhix claimed Sol Fed's government sanctioned this crime against its changeling citizens. I believed it more likely the Batterson empire had delusions of its own grandeur. But the President's position gave him claim to that authority. What they stood to gain, if it were so, remained a mystery.

Whether I would gain anything by playing a dangerous game of questions and pheromones with Rhix was uncertain. I had a few more weeks to stay alive and keep Dru and Kai safely with me, so Sumner could find us. My thumb traced the spot where a wedding ring once encircled my finger. I could try to gather more information about who bought the media bots used in the attack on Luna Terminal and avoid Rhix's bed.

Or not, on the last part.

Nineteen

DAYS STRETCHED INTO a second week aboard the floating market, and although we were treated with courtesy, it was still confinement. Dru seemed content to be pampered, and Kai remained miserably stoic. I needed an outlet for my restless energy or risked doing something really stupid.

"Simish, is there a gymnasium on board I can use?"

"Gymnasium?" He eyed me cautiously.

"For physical conditioning. Exercise."

"Ah. There is, but at the moment it would not be safe for you to go down to those decks." He gave me the side-eye. "Lord Rhix has a personal training area. I will ask if you might be allowed to use it. With appropriate supervision, of course."

The room was located opposite Rhix's private quarters. I whistled a Zereid expletive of wonder when I walked in. His obsessions ran to the collection of weapons as well as art. Blades hung on the walls, some in display cases and some clearly used in training. There were padded forms as well. Rhix must practice some form of martial arts. The equipment provided exactly what I needed for my own sessions.

I invited Kai to participate in the hope I could pull him out of his depression, but he declined. At least I now had something to do when sleep continued to elude me. My solitary workouts took place late at night under the eyes of my helmeted, armed guard dog, when it presented less risk of interrupting Rhix's use. I wasn't allowed access to any of the weapons, even the obvious, blunted training blades and staves. It directed and soothed some of my restless energy, but pressure still climbed, looking for my weakest point.

One night when I opened the door, I found Rhix already there.

Naked to the waist, he was magnificent and terrifying in a lethal dance of blade and grace, a rapid kata I assumed to be of Ursetu origin. Muscles gleamed beneath the sweat-slick umber planes of his back and shoulders, and as I watched, his scent reached me—sweat and hot skin, a hint of incense, all unmistakably male.

The tightening heat of tissues in my breasts and groin said, *Hey, I think we just found something stupid to do.*

No. Not smart. Once I crossed this line, there was no going back and no guarantee it would get me any useful information. I turned to leave.

"Gresh. You may stay."

Too late.

He replaced the blade in its rack. "You are a practitioner of *zezjna*, yes?"

"I am." I should have known the guards would mention it.

"How did you come to learn this?"

"My parents worked in the Embassy on Zereid. I grew up there. I studied with younglings my own age at a temple."

"This is not a skill the Zereid teach to just anyone." Rhix wiped the sweat from his body with a cloth. I forced myself not to stare.

"No. It's a philosophy of life as much as a martial art."

"A pacifist philosophy." He dismissed it with mild derision. "If you do not kill your enemy, they will come back and kill you. Foolish mercy."

"I take it you don't share their ideals."

"No. The Ursetu have never taught compassion as a desirable trait in combat." He studied me. "Do you follow this path of peace, Gresh?"

"I used to. Even though *zezjna* teaches mercy, it doesn't say I can't break someone's bones to keep from being killed. It's an effective defense."

"Show me this. I will not harm you. I am curious." He outweighed me by at least twenty kilos and stood a head taller. His confidence rained against my empathic nets as I led him to the mat, and when I turned my back on him, his arrogant dismissal increased. It might give me an advantage for the first few minutes. I took a deep breath and found the quiet place inside where I listened with all my senses.

"Whenever you're ready," I invited him.

He snorted. I knew when he made the decision to spring into forward motion. Turning before he could grab my shoulder, I gripped his arm instead, bent at the waist and let his own momentum carry him across my hip and over. He landed on his back with a surprised grunt.

The guard drew down on me. Rhix snarled something at him my implant translated as "Idiot!" and waved him out as he got up. The mercenary obeyed at once. Rhix's confidence was less prominent now in my heightened senses, replaced by mild irritation.

"How did you do that? You knew I was there without looking." He circled me.

"*Zezjna* relies on more than one sense."

"Again." He beckoned me.

I faced him this time and dropped into a stance. So did he, his eyes locked on mine. Once more, I sensed his intent a fraction of a second ahead of the punch, deflected the blow from his right hand and stepped in with my left leg. I went low, wrapped my arms around his calves and drove forward with my shoulders. He slammed to the mat again as I rolled sideways and free.

"You aren't taking control of your advantage," he accused, and kip-rolled to his feet. "Hit me."

"I wasn't sure I was allowed."

"I give you permission. But I will also take my hits when I see them." Heat glowed in those bronze eyes, something softer than aggression. This aroused him in other ways. Foreplay?

All right, then. Cross the line, or don't.

I took the offensive, gauging his strength, and found it equal to a human of similar size and build. I flowed around and beneath to sweep his legs. He spun away from the contact and swept me instead. I hit the mat and rolled over my shoulder back into a defensive stance.

The next exchange of blows was no longer a test on either of our parts. The forms he used were not familiar to me, but Zereid techniques are fluid and adaptable to the opponent. His concentration flagged with his growing frustration as I blocked every blow, but so did he. I finally drove a kick into his side, and he stumbled. I knew better than to apologize for my success and waited for him to retaliate.

He finally got in close. His fist hammered into my midsection and knocked the wind out of me. I bent over to catch my breath. When he moved in to finish the fight, I leaped on him, spun him down with a scissor hold and ended up sitting on his chest, my knuckles pressed into his trachea.

"Yield." I dug in a little harder.

Rhix stretched his arms out, palms up and to the sides in a gesture I took to mean surrender. I relaxed the pressure against his throat. He grabbed my wrists and rolled me over instantly, astride my thighs with my forearms pinned beneath his hands. We both panted, his mouth hovering above mine. The desire in his emotional broadcast and the flesh growing rigid between his legs left little to the imagination regarding his intent. My imagination had plenty of ideas of its own, anyway.

"You see what mercy delivers?" He eased his grip, hands sliding down my sweat-dampened skin. "What will you do?"

My body had a different sort of surrender in mind, change hormones boiling in my bloodstream, but my brain still functioned and temporarily kept me from following through.

"Negotiate." My voice was hoarse. I tucked in my upper arms before his fingers could accidentally discover the bump of the tracking device under my skin.

"What terms do you propose?" His arrogance was back. He held all the cards. Rhix humored me, nothing more.

"Privacy. No audience."

"There is no surveillance here or in my quarters." He gave up the first important bit of information without a fight. I wasn't too far down the rabbit hole not to realize it, but he was.

Rhix traced a hand slowly down the front of my formfitting shirt. Underneath, I was now female in all appearances. He found the hard peak of a nipple, and his thumb whispered a circular caress over the taut fabric. I shivered with pleasure. Damn, but his chemistry had a hold on my libido. My nails raked the slick fabric covering his buttocks and thighs. It was Rhix's turn to shudder; his fierce need broke against my empathic nets with a thrill of desire. I wondered how long it had been for him. The thought of the empty seraglio brought my lust down half a notch and allowed me to present my second term instead of fucking him right then and there.

"Autonomy. I'm not a prostitute."

"Agreed." Rhix's voice dropped into a register I felt in my chest. He stood and pulled me with him. "We will discuss my terms afterward."

Okay, so perhaps I wasn't thinking clearly. In hindsight, I should have negotiated his terms first.

Ursetu anatomy didn't prove to be much different from a human male's. Everything was in the right place as I freed his straining erection—heavy, warm, and hard—from the formfitting garment. His head rocked back with a sharp inhalation of breath as I wrapped my fingers around him.

"Take off your clothes." Rhix's hoarse voice carried rough command.

"Not yet." The blood-filled tissue of my mons swelled, aching with arousal and the pain of shifting pleasure centers. I wasn't quite ready. I went to my knees; my hands slid around to cup his buttocks. My lips brushed against the head of his penis. His agonized groan made me shiver, and I flicked my tongue against smooth ripples of rigid skin. His response to what I did sent hot, white sparks of pleasure through my empathic nets as I took him into my mouth. He gasped, knees threatening to buckle. His hands moved through my hair, tightening as I set up a slow, languorous rhythm and brought him to the brink more quickly than either of us wanted. Rhix pulled away, panting, our urgent hands stripping away the rest of our clothing.

His hand brushed my groin—fingers exploring the unfamiliar, smooth contours of my genitalia with a skillful touch—and sent fire streaking through me. I swayed, my hand gripping his arm to stay upright as his eyes burned into mine. I was more than ready now, the heat and slickness between my legs something he recognized.

He pulled me down to the mat. I pushed against his chest until he yielded to the demands of my need and lay back. I took him there on the floor, our bodies straining against each other in a more intimate form of sparring. Slippery flesh made way against delicious momentum, the sensation of his movement inside and against the swollen tissue of my mons a blinding pleasure. His hands gripped my hips with bruising force as I rode him, his eyes locked on mine until his body shuddered, a growl rising in his throat that built into a roar. My empathic senses filled with the electric scintillation of his climax; the intensity brought my own release in spasms, shaking me to the core as he bucked beneath me.

"You are a strange being, Gresh," he said breathlessly as we lay side by side on the mat and recovered our senses.

"How so?" As sex hangovers go, this one debilitated me. I could barely move, my muscles limp and spent.

"You could almost be an Ursetu female with your coloring and build, but for your eyes... They are like ash and smoke." He turned his head to look at me. "But you possess the heart of a volcano, a male's rage, and hunger."

"If you think the male of any species is more capable of rage and desire, you haven't met the right females."

His anger rose quickly and spilled over into my mind. His face, which had been soft and content in postcoital relaxation, hardened in expression. I'd said the wrong thing. Simish told me the concubines had plotted against him, but I'd forgotten, a misstep in the false afterglow of sex. He rolled and stood to retrieve his clothing. I sat up and dressed as well.

"Do not speak of our encounters or conversations to anyone else, neither Simish nor the others in the dormitory. What passes between us is a private transaction." He studied my face intently, brow furrowed. His loneliness caught me off guard, a stab of bitterness against my senses.

"I understand," I said. Flickers of other emotions played upon the edges of my unfurled empathic nets as I sought a glimmer of what his thoughts held. "Then we are agreed upon the terms?"

A hint of a smile finally tugged at the corners of his wide mouth. "You may come to my bed, or not, as you wish. I shall endeavor to make it worth your while."

Twenty

THE CONTRADICTION PRESENTED by my impressions of the Market's enigmatic lord and the cautionary tales told by Melos only continued to grow. Rhix went out of his way to have private conversations with my roommates one night. Dru returned from this meeting after an hour, with high color in her cheeks, a little starry-eyed. Kai left the room with Simish for his subsequent appointment, feet heavy as if he were walking to his doom. In her excitement, Dru missed his dread and discomfort and plopped down next to me on one of the lounges.

"He's fascinating."

"Be careful. He's dangerous, no matter how kind he seems."

"I can't believe that. He seems so nice." She sighed and made a gesture encompassing the lush furnishings around us. "I can see the luxury domes from the conveyor belt I take to the plant. My oldest sister works in one of the spaceport hotels at Olympus. She sneaked me into one of the penthouses once. It was like this."

"You know this place used to be a brothel, right?"

"I'm not stupid, Gresh." Her voice became brittle, and she swept the long fall of coppery hair away from her face in impatience. "But if it comes down to my survival, I'm not above being a sex toy if I get to live like this. My own room. Hot water baths. Not working in the processing plant until I drop is a big plus."

"You'd give up your freedom for a little luxury?"

"Like I'm free at home?" Her irritation rubbed against my empathic nets in abrasive swipes. "Don't judge me. I grew up in the tenements on Mars. You grew up on Luna, or somewhere posh, didn't you?"

"I lived on Luna. But I grew up off world." I frowned. "Why?"

"My shift was five twelve-hour days in the protein-processing plant. I got room and board, food and water allowances, a tiny little stipend of credits but nowhere to go except back to the plant every day, usually too tired to do anything but sleep on my days off. Slavery still exists in Sol Fed, even if we aren't bought and sold."

She stretched and got up, drifting back to her room. "And haven't you noticed nobody here cares that we're changeling, Gresh? If you didn't, you really were privileged."

She was right. I couldn't argue and conceded, spreading my hands.

Only fifteen minutes elapsed before Kai came back. He went directly to his room and didn't reappear. I knocked on the door of his quarters and found him curled into a fetal position on the bed.

"Are you all right? What happened?"

"He's not going to let us go." Kai took a deep, shaking breath. "I flat-out asked him, and he said no, he wouldn't do it. God, Gresh, I'm going to be a slave. I'll be sold. I can't do this." He trembled violently. I lay down next to him, settled against his back in an echo of the comfort offered on the Nos ship. "We're goddamned Sol Fed citizens," he said. "Do you think they're even looking for us?"

"Somebody is. I'm sure of it." I hugged him. The knowledge our own government delivered us to Rhix left sourness in my mouth.

"I'd rather die than be a slave." His despair gave an earnest sharpness to the words, and a chill rode the back of my neck.

"Don't give up, Kai. Please. I'm going to do my best to ensure we aren't separated. Together, we're stronger."

"Dru's got him in her sights. She's the only one of us who doesn't mind being here." Kai paused. "Or do you, too? You spend a lot of time out there."

"I don't want to be a slave, either."

"So what have you been doing with your nights, then?" The sarcastic edge to his voice accused me of lascivious things.

"Negotiating."

MY INSOMNIA DID not abate. I kept up my nocturnal workouts and vacillated between hoping for another "transaction" that might yield information, and scolding myself for letting my sexual appetite get the best of me. For several evenings, though, I didn't encounter Rhix, and a new, fine current of unease hung in the atmosphere outside the seraglio when I paced the halls a couple of nights later.

Rather than haunting my footsteps, only one visored guard monitored me from the surveillance nave down the hall, where a knot of mercenaries gathered. Tension lay thick in the corridor, a fog condensing in drops of dread on the web of my empathic nets.

The rest of the security detail clustered around the holo screens. With the Market closed, only a few glowed with activity. I'd presumed his hired soldiers lived in another area of the ship, and on my rounds, I caught a glimpse of what appeared to be the barracks, flickering in the holos.

On my second pass, the situation below decks unraveled. I stopped and stared as a brutal knife fight unfolded on the screen. The sentries didn't acknowledge me, their attention locked on the melee. The mob surrounding the combatants scattered as the gray bulk of a Shontavian blotted out our view of the brawl.

This electrified the guards to action. They herded me back to the dormitory with haste as all but three of the mercs scrambled for the blast doors. We weren't permitted to leave the seraglio for two nights. Simish and his fellows moved like ghosts, fear icing the mood as they tended to our needs.

Rhix's personal guards disappeared, conspicuous in their absence when I received permission to train again. Fewer sentries lurked the hall at night after the events in the mercenary quarters. More screens stayed lit in the alcove, and three mercs scanned the projections with grim vigilance. The undercurrent of tension mounted. I suspected dissent brewed among the subordinates and threatened the stability of Rhix's enterprise.

I had just begun my routine when Rhix stormed through the door of the training room and dismissed my guard. His face wore tight lines of rigid control.

"Spar with me, Gresh." He stripped off his body armor and the upper half of the skin-close garment beneath. We faced off across the mat. He exhibited more discipline than our previous engagement, despite his emotional state. Although my microseconds of empathic advantage spared me some painful contact, plenty landed. I left damage on him as well, but he fought with a single-minded focus as if his life depended upon it. This wasn't foreplay—more like combat, though we stopped short of blows that would end the fight. We finished the workout spent, bleeding, and bruised.

Rhix touched a split above my left eye, and warmth trickled down my cheek. "Have Simish treat this. It may scar otherwise."

"I don't mind a few more scars."

He gave a short laugh and prodded his own lower lip, twice its normal size. My knuckles, the mechanism of injury, bore the marks of his teeth. "Strange, that I am reduced to training with you rather than my mercenaries. At least you are a challenge to me. Do you fight with any weapons?"

"I had basic instruction with knives and staves in the militia." Ziggy's crash refresher course might come in handy, after all.

"We will start with those tomorrow night." We regarded each other for a moment in silence. His blood was up despite his fatigue; lust and anger competed for dominance in his emotional broadcast. My change hormones simmered in anticipatory response until Rhix nodded at me in stiff courtesy. "I'll send Simish to you."

I winced as I stretched. I'd need time to recuperate, unless Simish had something more than the magic salve he'd given me for the stunner burn. I hurt to the bone. Rhix and I seemed well matched in martial skills, but weapons presented a new game. I wondered if he trained me for concubine or bodyguard, with the others missing in action.

Kai sat up reading in the common area when I returned. He did a double take. "Jesus, Gresh. Rough sex?"

"Training."

"So you beat yourself up." Kai's mouth twisted. "Nice trick."

I shrugged, pretty sure it fell under Rhix's do-not-talk-about rules, and erred on the side of caution. Simish arrived a few seconds later, a medical kit in his hands, and spared me from having to come up with an answer. He hustled me into my quarters, fussed over my contusions, and inspected the cut above my eye.

"Was he angry with you?"

I stifled a growl as he probed. "No. He wanted to spar, so we did." Simish cleaned the laceration with something from his kit. The liquid had a fierce antiseptic sting and an odor that shriveled my nasal passages and made me cough. I spoke in a whisper as he leaned in to inspect his work. "I need to ask questions."

"I told you it isn't safe," he murmured back.

"I won the bet for you, didn't I?"

His sure hands stilled. After a moment of silence, he turned his body and pretended to clean the wound again. "What do you want to know?"

His movement placed his back between the surveillance system's watchful eye and me, blocking out our conversation. "Why is he training with me? Doesn't he trust his mercenaries?" I asked, the words only a breath.

Simish pressed his lips together. "Not long ago, he was one of them. Of course, he doesn't trust them."

I struggled to ensure my expression remained neutral. "How long has he been in charge?"

"One hundred and fifty cycles. Some do not agree with the changes he has made. Others would overthrow him. The Shontavians, in particular, are not fond of his rules, and it gives the rest excuse to be disobedient."

"Who would replace him?"

"One gains the title by killing the current Lord Rhix. Please do not ask me any more of these questions. They cannot lead to anything but grief." Simish's fear pulsed against my senses, and his deft hands trembled a little in their task.

"I'm aware something's wrong. Can I help him?"

He pressed the edges of the cut together and sealed the wound with a dermal accelerant. "I don't see how. But if you could, we Simish would be grateful. Our Lord Rhix may possess a volatile temper, but he is less a barbarian than the others. Things are much more pleasant when one's family isn't being fed to the Shontavians."

"How many of you are there?"

"We seven are all that remain. They engineered us in lots of twelve until Lord Rhix destroyed the incubators. There will be no more."

"I'm sorry."

"Not for the incubators, I hope."

"No. For you and your family."

Simple gratitude blossomed against my empathic nets. He massaged the purpling areas around my left eye, ribs, and jaw with an unguent. "The bruises will last another day, but this will help them fade quickly."

"Thank you, Simish."

"I am here to serve you, Gresh." He gave me a little bow.

Twenty-one days remained until the next session opened. Forever— and at the same time, not long enough—to win confidence and perhaps some large favors. Rhix's personal code appeared to revolve on a system of quid pro quo.

But as things happened, an opportunity to influence him presented itself the following night. I didn't even have to negotiate.

Twenty-One

OUR SESSION BEGAN with training knives, blunted copies of the ornate, one-edged daggers displayed on the wall. Rhix's blade skills held more confirmation that I did not want to piss him off—he was clearly a killing machine in his former role of hired soldier. The serpentine Ursetu style he began to teach me proved challenging. Early in, he dismissed my visored escort to train with me in private.

"No. Hold the weapon so..." He flipped it in my hand. "The upward stroke delivers the damage. You must be able to change the weapon's direction in midstrike. In this position, it protects your forearm."

"Like this?" I telegraphed the movement, and he grunted in approval.

"Better. Again. More speed."

I made grazing contact with his skin this time, but he blocked my arm, trapped it over his chest and brought me down. The side of my face smacked the mat. Ligaments protested the awkward angle of my shoulder joint, but the cold kiss of his knife against my throat concerned me more. "You drew blood, but you would be dead now."

Rhix let me up, and I rubbed my bicep, rolling the socket.

"Can you continue?"

"Yes." My upper body strength was better in male form, but I didn't know how he would react to me in that guise. He responded more positively to my feminine side—and it, to him. I wanted to keep the trust going, and use it when I could to get information.

"Pull the beast's fangs to diminish its threat. Your lead hand is your shield. Use it to deflect and block. Control your opponent's arm and disable them."

Empathic senses helped in minimal capacity here. It gave me half a second of advantage in blocking, but the follow-through with my own weapon remained clumsy compared to the viper's grace Rhix possessed. His edgeless knife raked across my abdomen. In a real fight, I would have been eviscerated.

"No. Control it! Do not let go until you disarm me or take me to the ground."

Gritting my teeth, I prepared, senses open and waiting for his attack. This time, I trapped his arm, forced it upwards and stepped in close. The knife moved against his throat.

"Yes. Again."

The room echoed with the sound of our breathing, metallic clatter of weapons, solid convergence of flesh and mat as he threw me down to the floor. My offensive hand was paralyzed by his grip as he knelt above me; the point of his weapon hung over my throat and advanced slowly even with his wrist trapped in my left hand.

"Yield," I gasped, "or I might hurt you."

"You think so?"

I pushed my knee firmly against the sensitive organs between his legs. Rhix grunted in surprise.

"Conceded." He rose, extending a hand to help me roll to my feet and continued. "I warned you about mercy."

"Does that mean you want me to crush your *raho* next time?"

"No," he said hastily. "Simply, do not hesitate to employ your advantages, whether you are armed or naked."

"Naked?" My thoughts swan dived into innuendo.

"Without a blade." Judged by the speed with which his awakening pheromones circulated through my olfactory system, our minds occupied the same gutter. "Your form needs work. There is an exercise that will help familiarize you with the transitions."

His dagger blurred into an arc as he performed another lightning-paced kata, the knife's edge changing directions almost quicker than my eye could follow. The formfitting garments we trained in disguised nothing; his body's agile movement, the play of muscle beneath skin, and his chemical shortcut to my sex drive had my pulse racing before he turned back to me, his breathing accelerated from martial effort.

"Like this." Rhix repeated the first series in slow motion, and I mirrored him.

"Yes. Again, but let your body counterbalance the strike." He moved behind me and controlled my speed, his correction of my technique more sensual than any of my militia instructors would have tolerated. "Widen your stance. Your center is here." Hands drifted to rest at my hips, breath close to my ear. "Until you know the form, the movement is slow. A dance with death." His hips rocked with mine, thighs pressed against me, the nudge of hardening flesh impossible to miss.

Arousal kindled warmth everywhere in my body. Always ready to do more stupid things.

Pretense of training fell away. I pressed back against him, yielding to the hand exploring the contour of my ribs, up to the swelling of my breast, which rose to meet his touch. A sound of approval vibrated deep in his throat. His other hand still enveloped mine, gripping the training blade, and Rhix brought it up, guiding me to brush the flat edge over a tightening nipple. My breath caught in an appreciative gasp. His other hand slid over the tight fabric covering my abdomen, and down.

The transition state between neutral and female had only begun, my mons prominent as the tissue beneath prepared to shift inside. My free hand interrupted the movement before his fingertips brushed the protuberant area. He persisted despite my resistance. The hesitant, featherlight touch as he discovered the engorged flesh wrested a groan of pleasure from me. I guided his hand to trace the area in a gentle circle. Instead of pulling away, he continued to explore, the surge against my backside a positive response. On the hilt of the knife, our fingers intertwined.

Gunfire.

It brought us up short and to attention, thoughts of foreplay extinguished by the cold rush of danger.

The guard's abrupt return, with his sidearm drawn, dangling loosely in his hand, confirmed something was seriously wrong.

"What is happening?" Rhix barked in Ursetu. The guard didn't reply.

The hair crawled on the back of my neck as a wave of excitement and fear from the mercenary assaulted my senses. His gun came up.

He took aim on Rhix. I didn't think, didn't hesitate, and threw the training knife. It bounced off his armored head, and the blast went wide, enough time for Rhix to move. The merc swiveled the weapon to me, the whine of a projectile burning past my ear.

Rhix's body collided with our attacker's as another shot passed through my side in a scorching track below the ribs. They crashed to the floor. Pain took me to a knee, my hand pressed against the torn flesh. But Rhix was losing ground with his assailant, who knelt astride him now and pounded savage blows to his throat and jaw. I staggered back to my feet and seized the first edged weapon at hand: a short sword from the wall.

When the traitorous guard raised a fist to strike again, I stood behind him. I caught his arm and twisted it back. The visored face looked up in surprise, and the blade's point slipped easily between the line of his neck and chest plates.

He gurgled. Arterial spray washed me in crimson. In my head, I felt the mercenary's panic, his desperation to breathe through blood-filled lungs, pain. My breath and pulse twinned their pace with his, struggling to pump blood and oxygen to a place it could no longer reach. Terror faded into black as he died. There was nothing else.

I heaved the twitching body off Rhix and stood over him, streaked in gore, the sword still in my hand. He stared at me in wary expectation. For a moment I wondered a bit hysterically what would happen if I did kill him. My brain fired in wild, disjointed thoughts. Would I become Lord Rhix? I could order them to steer this behemoth of a ship toward home. I just killed one person. Another wouldn't be difficult.

Shock. Recognition came as a spasm of pain gripped me. The blade fell from nerveless fingers and stuck point first in the mat. I clutched my side and sank down, my back sliding against the wall.

Rhix stripped the visor off the assassin and stared down at the blank, dead face. "I can no longer tell my friends from my enemies. How badly are you wounded?"

I couldn't take my eyes off the Ursetu mercenary I killed. Blood spread in a widening circle and crept closer to me. My lips were cold and numb, preventing me from answering. A hormone flood threatened to sweep me away in fight-or-flight instinct as muscles slid beneath my skin.

"Gresh." His hand seized my chin and forced me to meet his eyes. The umber planes of his fierce cheekbones were decorated with rubies, glistening scarlet cabochons that swam in and out of focus. My head finally made the connection he was spattered with the blood of his intended assassin. "Your first kill is always the most difficult. There may be others waiting outside. Can you still fight?"

Bronze eyes demanded an answer. I took an experimental breath. It didn't hurt to inhale or exhale. He extended a hand, and I gripped his wrist, rose to my feet before the scarlet pool reached me. The burning in my flank stayed the same either way.

"I can fight." My voice broke, ragged in my own ears as I picked up the grisly blade. "Do your mercenaries frequently try to kill you?"

"Of late, in between each Market."

"Why?"

Collecting the sidearm from the floor, he checked the magazine. "They view me as weak. I retired some of the more barbaric practices my predecessor allowed to go unchecked in favor of good business."

"Can you trust any of them?"

"Most. Evidently not some of my Ursetu brothers." He nudged the dead body with his foot. "I never suspected he was the one trying to replace me."

Voices sounded outside.

A grim glance passed between us. He offered me the gun instead and took the bloody short sword. I moved to one side of the door, Rhix the other, and we waited.

All senses unfurled in my attempt to determine how many gathered out there. If any Nos lurked, I wouldn't know it. Overwhelmingly, a scrabble of concern and panic assaulted my mind from a source I did recognize. A tremulous voice called out, tones muffled through the port,

"Lord Rhix? Gresh?"

"Simish," I mouthed. His mouth tightened.

"Has he betrayed me, too?"

"I don't think so," I whispered back, and raised my voice. "Who's out there with you?"

"Three members of the family. There is a dead guard on the floor here, and the others have neutralized four more mercenaries in the hallway. I believe it is safe to come out."

I sensed no coercion or deception and hoped I was right. "Let me go first to be certain it's secure."

"Watch yourself."

"I'm coming out." With the gun gripped in my right hand, I thumbed the portal release and cleared the doorway as it slid open, sweeping the weapon left to right. Simish and three of his siblings jumped back in horror at my bloody face, my gore-streaked clothing. The guard who usually accompanied me lay sprawled in the corridor, a hole in the middle of his chest plate.

"Lord Rhix...is he still living?" Simish pleaded.

In answer I stepped aside and gave a curt nod to Rhix. Still clutching the gruesome blade, he grabbed the dead mercenary by the back of his armor and dragged him through the door, leaving a red trail behind him.

Down the hall near Rhix's quarters, guards held mercenaries in the sights of their pulse rifles. The three captives knelt in grim submission, hands behind their heads. Another corpse defiled the thick carpets, a smoking gap in his helmet.

To these subdued men, Rhix dragged the body of their leader and heaved it into them. They toppled and fell. My translator sounded a beat behind his furious words as he roared in Ursetu, "It is over. Take this refuse below decks, and let the Shontavians have it, since they value sentient meat so highly. Tell the rest of your discontented brothers to pick someone to speak for them. This mutiny ends now!"

His basso voice echoed from the walls. The captured mercenaries stared at me in horror, covered head to foot in their leader's blood and my own. I glared back from beneath clotted strands of hair with hooded eyes. Their intimidation could only give Rhix a better chance to avert more assassination plots. Once they were gone, I was going to pass out.

Still brandishing the bloody sword, he jerked his head for me to follow and stalked to the door of his own quarters, the ever-attentive Simish trotting at our heels. We passed through the portal before I staggered. Rhix caught me in his free arm and helped me sit on a bench.

Droopy features tight with concern, Simish eased the nasty shirt over my head and examined the wound in my side. "It appears superficial, but still bleeding. I will need a medical kit."

"I have one." Rhix disappeared into another room.

"Why did they shoot you?" Simish muttered.

"I threw a knife at the guy's head." A groan escaped me as the hormone cascade allowed my anatomy to slip back into more neutral arrangement. The oblique muscles damaged by the projectile shrieked as shock and adrenaline subsided.

"Is Lord Rhix unharmed?"

"As far as I can tell."

"You saved his life." His deep-set eyes stared up at me with a new expression. I'd earned his gratitude, and a little hero worship.

Rhix returned with the medical kit and knelt in front of me as his servant cleansed the wound. "My first thought is to herd them all into space without life support, but I need them." Rhix's eyes burned into mine. "They know you killed Essek, not I. All one must do is look at you."

My breath hitched, and I stifled a shout into a growl as Simish's finger probed inside the projectile's track. "I'm not going to tell anyone you didn't."

"It does not penetrate the abdominal cavity, but Gresh needs attention in the infirmary, not here," Simish told Rhix. He injected a subdermal painkiller, and the complaint of the raw nerve endings in my side subsided to a dull roar.

"I do not believe Gresh should go below decks. Especially now."

Simish rose. "There are things I need to close this wound and prevent infection. I will be back in a moment." He hurried away.

Rhix gave me a beaker of potent liquor. "Drink this."

The liquid burned all the way to my stomach. "Do you ever get used to killing?" I asked dully.

He knew what I meant. "Death should never be easy to deliver. If I must kill them, I should be able to look them in the eye. It is why I prefer to fight at close quarter. At the end of a gun it is anonymous and cowardly."

The bombing that killed my family represented an act of cowardice, to be sure. But those deaths were quick. The mercenary's prolonged agony still clung to my empathic nets, sticky and sour, like bile.

It didn't bother me as much as I thought it should.

Twenty-Two

SIMISH RETURNED WITH a larger medical kit. He flooded my side with antiseptic and my breath emerged in short gasps. Tears burned my eyes as the stuff sizzled its way along raw flesh. He sutured my side with deft efficiency. A hypospray of antibiotic followed, the wound sealed beneath a layer of the dermal accelerant.

Rhix supported me as we went to one of his inner rooms, where I discarded the rest of my bloody clothes. Standing under the warm embrace of running water proved less painful than the vibration of the cleanser, but gore adhered in stubborn clots to my hair and skin. In a surprisingly gentle manner, Rhix helped me scrub the mercenary's blood away, silent all the while, grim and thoughtful. An attempt to discern his emotional state only left me guessing, too mentally fatigued to pursue further.

Happy to dress in anything not soaked with congealed body fluids, I didn't protest the flimsy nightwear my efficient little keeper brought, and I eased into the white robe. "Did anyone check on Dru and Kai?" I asked Simish.

"The weapons fire alarmed them, but I assured them all is well. They asked after you. I told them you are not badly damaged."

Exhaustion increased the weight of my eyelids. "I should go back to the dormitory and sleep."

"Stay here tonight." Rhix reappeared, dressed in the close-fitting undergarments his body armor would encase. "I must choose a new captain of my guard and discuss security arrangements."

"Are you sure it's safe now?"

"Essek is dead. These malcontents will not regroup themselves quickly." He snapped on leg and arm sheaths of the composite plating, and Simish went to assist him with the rest. "I must appear among them and not cower behind a concubine."

"You're welcome." My sarcasm will backfire one day. Simish's head came up at my tone and he stared at me with fear. Rhix's voice rumbled with irritation.

"I did not say I am not grateful. You must understand there are complicated levels to this enterprise."

"Let me help you negotiate with them."

"Your presence there would be more of a distraction. I employ no female mercenaries for a reason."

"I'm not female." My voice dropped to the midrange I normally used, instead of the alto I adopted for his benefit. Startled by the reminder, Rhix's head came up sharply. "Put me in a visor, and it's impossible to tell me from one of your bodyguards." An idea reoccurred. Straightening, I tried not to wince as I spoke in my male register. "After tonight, I could be your bodyguard." The privilege might give me more access to other parts of the ship instead of being restricted to the private residence. More chances to learn information about the Sol Fed deal, perhaps.

Rhix's eyes narrowed with calculation. "I will think on this idea. Tonight, you must rest."

MY DREAMS WERE not as traumatic as I feared they would be after my first kill. Kiran Singh was right—I could be a cold bastard when I needed to.

Rhix's bed took up half the room, enormous and comfortable, and my body protested leaving. I had no idea how long I slept, but the analgesic Simish gave me wore off during that time. Climbing out in stiff movements, I surveyed my environment. A hatch dominated the ceiling, recessed like the dome of the seraglio. Perhaps another energy window lay above. The scent of incense I noted on Rhix's skin clung more prominently here, its source an altar in the corner of the bedroom.

Expecting some fierce warrior god of the lower caste, I contemplated the gentle goddess figure that occupied the place of reverence instead. Offerings of gems and wilted, alien flowers were strewn at her feet. A purposeful, dark smear stained the delicate stone toes. Dried blood. I wondered whose.

His quarters were sizable, but spartan compared to the opulence of the galleries and the seraglio. The outer room held a desk, a bench, and a rack of weapons and composite armor. Beside a second set of the protective suit he'd donned last night, a more ornate piece hung there. The breastplate shone with inlaid patterns of bright metal wire, its function obviously ceremonial, though functional.

In the silence of his rooms, I realized I was alone. No Simish. Rhix had not returned, and yet here I stood in front of a rack of unsecured weapons, without surveillance. More privileges were earned last night. Not too many, however. The palm scanner blinked in disapproval when I tried to exit Rhix's quarters.

With furtive haste, I went back and rifled through his desk. The data well I found powered up at my touch. Ursetu glyphs filled the screen in crowded graffiti, a language I didn't read or speak, but the device itself I knew. Kua technology ranked the best in the galaxy. The toggle for languages provided an option for Remoliad Standard, replacing the symbols with an alphabet I could comprehend.

Transactions. Account numbers, transfers, and notations of merchandise. The amount of galactic credit here staggered me. This page listed information regarding what had been sold or purchased at the last session. I flicked the screen up and the dates stretched farther back. I kept going until the date displayed read more than six hundred cycles past the first entry, thousands of transactions and payments recorded in the data well.

This. I needed this to find out who purchased the media bots. My pulse sped up, and pain drummed in my side. I returned to the original page, reset the language and replaced the device exactly where I'd found it.

Clothes and a tube of the analgesic salve waited for me in the lavatory. I applied the numbing agent, grateful for Simish and his efficiency. Movement became less torturous.

A tray of food and a steaming, self-warming vessel occupied the desk when I came back. Rhix glanced up as he unstrapped the leg pieces of his armor. "Good. You are awake."

"How is the mood below decks?"

"Better than I expected, but with complications I did not foresee." He stripped off the gauntlets and vambraces. "As I feared, rumor has spread naming you the instrument of Essek's death. They believe you are something strange. The Ursetu guards are not certain you are mortal." A smile grew on his wide mouth, the first real one I'd seen from him. "They think you are a *dali*."

The syllables held different inflection than my name, but to hear it on his lips startled me nonetheless. "What?"

"A demon of..." Creases appeared on his forehead. "I do not know your word. In my language, and in the Remoliad tongue, it means repayment of wrongs done to you."

"A vengeance demon?" Never knew I was so scary. "I'm flattered. I think." My laugh cut short with a stabbing reminder from my sutures.

He waved toward the food. "Sit and eat. There is enough for both of us." He finished removing his armor. "What frightens them more is the possibility you own my soul." The smile faded; gravity replaced amusement. "Do you understand what a life debt is, Gresh?"

I shook my head. I had context for a few galactic customs but suspected it might mean something different for him.

"To place one's self in harm's way and protect the life of another is sacred to the goddess. It is an act she values above all else. I must honor you in my own lifetime, or I will never walk beside her in the next." A surge of pious devotion for the goddess, soft, tender, and passionate, startled me as it brushed against my senses. "I owe you my life, and I will protect yours. There are no others in the galaxy who hold such a claim on me." He pulled off his boots. "The fact my mercenaries think you are a demon amuses me and works to my advantage. The stories say as long as a *dali* owns my soul, I will be invincible until it chooses to collect the debt. There will be no trouble from the Ursetu, or from any others as long as their greed is satisfied. But it is clear I will be forced to make an example of those who came to kill me."

"How?"

"In the arena." His grim pronouncement echoed the angry resignation in his emotional output. "I have had no contests since I took power. It is not something I wanted to perpetuate, but they betrayed me. I cannot let them go unpunished. They will face my Shontavians."

Not a contest I wanted to witness. "How many are in your service?"

"Only two. Enough to bring down this ship, if they wished. You know about them; yes?"

"Other than their reputation for eating enemies? Very little. I know they are bred for war, but your planet hasn't been in any conflict for centuries."

"The ruling caste have been suppliers of engineered life forms for more than a thousand years." He drew up a second chair and joined me at the desk. "It is still a profitable enterprise in some parts of the galaxy, but not for me. First—I find it reprehensible, and I refuse to support the trade as my predecessors did. Second—the cost of keeping merchandise healthy matches the price. The poor conditions my forerunners allowed kept the Shontavians fed, but left little to sell. Since I no longer deal in the slave trade, there is no resource for sentient prey other than the arena."

"If you're no longer involved in slave trade, why am I here?"

"You ask too many questions." His lips made a thin, compressed line, but amusement lifted one corner. "The transaction happened before my time. It would have been fulfilled at the next Market."

"What changed?"

"Less than half of what they promised arrived. These clients are unreliable. I considered terminating the agreement, but I will give them a chance to make it right."

"By stealing more people like me from their homes and families?" My fist clenched under the desk where he couldn't see it.

"This was not my doing, but, no. The price will be steeper now in credits, rather than in combination with merchandise. The transaction is void if they refuse. I considered returning you to them, but I believe you will be better treated here than in their hands."

He had a point. "You can't just free us?"

"No." He frowned. "You are part of a transaction that has not been fulfilled yet, and technically, you do not belong to me, but to the Market. If I were to release you, rather than profit from your sale, my mercenaries will never trust me. Simish told you how short a time ago I took control."

"I hope you didn't punish him for telling me. He's grateful to you for changing the way his family is treated. Any consequences belong to me."

"Your actions earned the right to ask questions." His eyes met mine briefly as he poured himself a cup of dark, aromatic tea. "Ask me what you feel you need to know, not my servants. I will decide if I answer."

I wanted to learn more about who initiated the Sol Fed agreement bringing the changelings here, but sensed he expected me to ask something else first. I phrased the question carefully. "Will you tell me what happened to the concubines?"

"Are you certain you want to know?" His nostrils flared, body taut and guarded.

"Yes."

Rhix's hand curled around the cup, knuckles whitening. "Two conspired with a mercenary who tried to take my place. They gained my trust, claiming gratitude for my having done away with the traditions of my predecessor. Then they attempted to murder me as I slept. I killed them both with my bare hands." His emotions spilled against me in a melange of anger and shame. "Others, I injured during questioning. When they recovered, I sold them all to the first bidder, two sessions ago. I would not have them serve me after I abused them in such a manner. It would be fertile ground for more treachery. I am not kind, Gresh. I am a dangerous man without control of his passions. It is the reason I am here, now, and not a member of the ruling caste on Ursetu. One cannot abuse his subjects and expect them to follow."

"You truly are royalty?" The clues were there—the urbane polish, his deep appreciation and knowledge of art, and his practice of intricate blade and sword techniques all spoke of another life beyond mercenary service. "I thought Lord Rhix might be an honorary rank."

"For most, it is. For me, it is the abdication of a title I do not deserve." He drained the tea. "I will meet with those who speak for the mercenaries in a few hours. I have thought about your offer to assist in negotiations and will welcome your advice. I am far too angry yet to be objective. Perhaps it is best."

"It will help if I know what their demands are before we begin. We can predetermine your strategy. What are you willing to concede?"

"I will concede nothing."

"Then your negotiations are over before they start."

He frowned into the dregs of his tea. "They want a larger share of the profit."

"Is this a profitable enterprise?"

He snorted. "My head would be safer on my shoulders if it was not."

"Are you willing to invest in it to be certain it remains so?" I poured him another cup and filled my own.

"Every transaction I make is an investment."

"So are your mercenaries. What do they do?"

"They protect my goods. They persuade those who would disrupt business to leave while they still breathe. They guard me—at least, those who are not trying to kill me."

"I would consider your loyal troops indispensable. How many are in your employment, and what are their species?"

"I employ sixty at a time. Half are Ursetu. The rest are Nos and a scattering of others."

"A larger share of the take is negotiable. They will undoubtedly demand something higher than you are willing to give, but it's only a starting point. I assume the amount varies with each Market, based on your profit. Is it the only way they are compensated for their service?"

"Yes. It has always been done this way."

I sipped my tea, bitter enough to make me grimace. "You've already changed many things. This is a business. I would advise you to offer them a stipend. Regular wages."

"Pay them wages?" His voice started out in a tone of protest and became thoughtful.

"It doesn't need to be high; only what their share would be for an average take. Offer them a small percentage above their pay, based on profit for each session. A bonus. It might give them more interest in maintaining order so business is not interrupted." I decided to fish for some information. "The last Market closed early, according to Simish."

"The Nos allowed some of their brethren to get out of hand. My ship was fired upon."

Relieved to hear he hadn't suspected the pending rescue mission, I suggested, "Any you can't trust or who refuse your terms will be given notice their services are no longer under contract. Put out a subspace message you will hire more at the next session. The new recruits can be hired under different terms, if you wish, but those who are loyal and stay can earn the option for a percentage."

"You have been thinking about this more than a few hours."

"No. It's standard Sol Fed business negotiation. We're not in the habit of killing disgruntled workers or executing our employer. What about the Shontavians? Will you offer them the same terms?"

"They are not motivated by profit. Their loyalty is bought with blood and sentient meat."

The term "sentient meat" made me wonder if the creatures did not possess some kind of rudimentary empathy. The implications were horrific, to say the least. I didn't want to think about it. "Can they be negotiated with?"

"They understand if I hold their leash, they must obey me. But they need motivation to do so without resistance."

"What motivates them?"

"Things not easily delivered." Rhix's expression darkened. "They were created for war, and they are restless. They are not indestructible, but almost impossible to kill. These two served at least three of my predecessors."

"You may need to consider whether keeping them in your employment is necessary."

"It would not be the Shontavian Market without their presence." He sat back. "The fear they instill is part of the draw for many, and one of the ways in which order is kept."

"How could you stop them if they decided to leave?"

"The decision has been bred out of them for centuries."

"They have no choice but to stay, and they are denied the only thing for which they were created. It's a disaster waiting to happen." I paused. "Let me negotiate with them as well."

"Negotiation is impossible. They are not engineered for reason, only violence."

"Allow me to try." Ensuring he remained in charge might increase the chance of Dru, Kai, and me staying together until Sumner and the team extracted us.

"I believe it will be a futile exercise." Rhix shrugged. "We shall see how my mercenaries react to these terms. If you are as skilled as you say in this art of negotiation, I will consider it."

Twenty-Three

THE SUMMIT PROVED more successful than Rhix expected. Although I attended, he didn't need much help. Armed with my suggestions, most of the mercenaries agreed to his terms. When Rhix transmitted a subspace invitation to the upcoming Market, in their presence, he included code that invited mercenaries for hire. A few of the holdouts reconsidered immediately.

Others who spurned the contract watched me too suspiciously for comfort. They knew who I was, even visored and faceless like the rest of Rhix's bodyguards. My senses recoiled against the unease and raw animosity emanating from the group. This kind of notoriety, I didn't need.

After the meeting, I returned to the dormitory for a set of clothes. Rhix wanted to go over the financial aspects of the agreement.

Kai and Dru sat in the common area when I entered. They stared with uncertainty at my anonymous armor until I removed the helmet and grinned at them. "It's me."

"Gresh!" Dru jumped up. "We thought you were dead or something."

"Not dead. A little worse for the wear, maybe." Sore and tired, I wanted nothing more than a hot bath and more of the painkillers Simish hoarded.

"What the hell happened last night?"

"I shouldn't talk about it here." I nodded at Kai, strangely silent and subdued as Dru's rapid-fire questions continued.

"Simish said—well, he really didn't say anything, but he said you were hurt. We heard guns."

"I'm fine."

"They won't let us out of this room at all."

Not surprising. Simish and his family had been working to clean blood and brains off the expensive carpets. "It should be sorted out soon."

"So where did you sleep last night?" Kai's voice fell flat on my ears.

"Kai, Gresh probably slept in the infirmary." Dru defended me.

"Yeah, right. That's why Simish took lingerie with him."

"What are you saying?" Dru rounded on him. "You think Gresh got shot just to sleep with Rhix?"

"No, I'm saying for all the big talk about sticking together, Gresh sure seems to be doing everything possible to get on Rhix's good side."

Not in the underhanded manner he insinuated. "I'm not."

"Please." Kai snorted. "You're turning female, and Simish sneaks you out every night to 'train.'" He waved his hands to form sarcastic quotation marks around the word. "I know what's going on."

"Gresh?" Dru turned to me.

"No, I was in Rhix's quarters last night," I admitted. Her face fell. "But he wasn't there. Do I look like I've been having sex?" My fist knocked at the composite breastplate.

"So you're making yourself indispensable in other ways besides fucking." Kai's monotone did not carry the despair his emotional broadcast did. "You know exactly what you're doing. You're making sure you aren't sold."

Dru watched me, doubt creeping into her expression.

"You have to believe me." I spoke softly, directly to Kai. "I am doing everything I can to make sure we stay together. If Rhix trusts me, I might be able to negotiate a position for us here, rather than any of us get sold. It's not home. It's not Sol Fed, but it could be so much worse."

"Right. Negotiating." His despondency rained against my mind, his suspicions stronger than his belief in me. I couldn't tell them my real agenda. Not under surveillance, and not yet. To raise their hope seemed crueler than the appearance I might be a self-serving asshole. When I said nothing, he turned and went to his room. The door closed behind him.

With a deep breath, I appealed, "Dru?"

"Kai trusts you. I guess I do, too. He's really depressed today." She shook her head. "He's right, though; I can't figure you out. One second, you're this protective older brother, and the next you're chasing after Lord Rhix like he's your first schoolgirl crush. Can you blame Kai for being confused?"

In the process of gaining Rhix's confidence, I hadn't stopped to think how it looked to Dru and Kai. I'd fractured a more important trust.

TWO DAYS LATER, I met the Shontavians.

Through the blast doors and into the bowels of the ship, in visored battle helmet and armor, I walked behind Rhix, flanked by his surviving personal guards. A pulse rifle completed my charade, but the magazine remained empty. He trusted me, but not yet enough to give me a live weapon.

The silent honeycomb of the Market, three stories of cold, silent catwalks, platforms, and bays, echoed with our footsteps.

The two upper bays rose in dark, cavernous emptiness, but behind grated security screens humming with energy, the lower bay held Armageddon.

Racks of weapons from all over the galaxy crowded the secured alcoves, enough to equip one of the colonies' militias with some of the most terrifying firepower available. Cradles of missiles and torpedoes lay arranged in a sobering display. A second bay remained closed, the heavy, shielded door marked with the galactic symbol for radiation.

Wonderful.

A service lift took us down to the shuttle bays and the barracks beneath the Market. Off-duty mercenaries assessed us with varying expressions of interest, sullen or curious. Rhix wore no visor, his identity proclaimed in arrogant confidence. This end of the barracks seemed dense with bodies, the soldiers clustered together in deference to the two large humanoids at the far end.

The Shontavians sat on benches in the gloomy curve of the ship's outer hull. Two smooth, gray heads raised and regarded us with glittering black eyes.

"Lord." The guttural voice of the largest spoke Ursetu.

"Ouros." Rhix greeted it.

A brush of my mind against the Shontavian's confirmed my suspicions: they possessed at least an empathic sense, if not telepathic. The engineered creature's head swiveled to me at once, one of its four arms coming up to point at my chest.

"Who." Nightmare teeth bared in what appeared at first glance to be a threatening display, its head lifted. I realized Ouros scented the air, tasted it. "Not masters. Not Nos."

Rhix's brow creased as he glanced at me. "Human," he said.

Childlike curiosity accompanied the brush of its mind against mine. Ouros stood, a small mountain coming to its feet, and stared at me. The other one rose as well, and the guards tightened around Rhix. I stood my ground as the Shontavians approached and kept the rifle, not useful for anything but a club, pointed at the ground.

So far they didn't want to eat me, but I wondered what they did want. They circled around me, filtered my scent through mouths full of pointy teeth. I pushed my discomfort down into the recesses of my mind. Rhix's mounting concern overwhelmed what I sensed from the Shontavians, but what I parsed didn't seem threatening. Yet.

Two minds probed my empathic nets with simplistic fascination. I raised the visor. They weaved around me in curiosity, almost like a dance, or a pack of predators circling their prey.

"You. Not like Nos or Ursetu."

The translation from the helmet parroted what Ouros said, but I couldn't reply. "I don't speak your language." My regret touched them. Ouros cocked its head.

"Gresh wishes to help you reach a new agreement with me." Rhix took his cue from me when I didn't panic. "The mercenaries agreed to a new contract. I would also learn what you want in exchange for your continued service."

"More meat. More fight." Ouros grunted. Boredom and restless energy vibrated from its aura; something else these creatures and I shared in common. Left with no outlet, nothing positive could result.

"You know I will not promise this. You received meat yesterday."

"Dead." Its disappointment chilled me a little. They liked their food alive and screaming.

"What else do you want?"

"Out of ship."

"What would you do outside the ship?"

"See stars." Ouros's gruff voice held near-reverence.

"Have they ever been planetside?" I asked.

"They were engineered in an orbiting facility. To place them on any civilized world outside combat is to court disaster."

"How long has it been since they saw stars?"

Once my question was relayed to Ouros, the creature held up two of its hands, five digits spread wide. "As many lords."

"Ten lords?" Rhix's mouth hung open for a brief second. "More than one hundred years. I did not realize you served on board so long, Ouros."

"No more dark. Stars." Its eyes glinted. "And profit."

"What would you do with profit?"

"Others get. We want too." Intelligence lay behind the fearsome visage; I suspected their speech centers lacked development in their engineering, but the brain behind the broken words worked quickly, if simply.

"To profit, I agree. I will require time to think on the other terms."

Ouros made a gesture and led the other back to the benches. He seemed content for now. The Shontavians continued to study me. Ouros gave me an empathic nudge, aware I listened underneath. In respect, I inclined my head. Rhix beckoned me to join him, and I lowered the visor. The guards parted to allow me to walk beside him and took up the front and the rear once more.

Once we entered the lift, Rhix turned to me. "What happened back there?"

"I'm not sure. They haven't met a human before?"

"No. I have not seen Shontavians do that with any but their own kind." Approval warmed his expression. "You were not frightened."

I shrugged. "More interested than afraid."

Rhix said nothing else until the blast doors of his private residence closed behind us. His guards escorted us to his quarters, where he barked a dismissal.

Once inside, I discarded my helmet. "Is there anywhere on board they could see the stars?"

Rhix began to remove his armor. "To give them access to viewports, I must allow entrance to critical areas. A precedent like this may have repercussions I cannot predict."

"Conceded." I released the tabs holding my breast and back plate together and pulled it off, wincing. My right side still complained with certain movements.

"Their wish to go outside is not what puzzles me." One foot up on the bench, the sharp snap of clips punctuated his speech. "They never wanted a share of the profit before."

"What do you think they will do with credits?" I unfastened the vambraces and sat down to unstrap the shin and thigh plates.

"I could not guess, but their demands are more reasonable than I anticipated." Rhix put the last of the protective gear in storage and stretched. The formfitting garment only accentuated the powerful physique underneath. I couldn't help but appreciate the view. Almost a week after our "transaction," memories of the primal encounter made me shiver, and he caught me staring.

Heat flooded between us in a molten torrent. The hair on the back of my neck stirred. I wore the same kind of skintight foundation he did; nothing concealed the engorgement of my pectoral and groin tissues. Whatever pheromones he produced catalyzed every hormonal instinct urging my body toward the female form. The black material of his underarmor tented as well. He knelt in front of me.

"I thought to let you heal." His voice gained rough edges.

"I'm tougher than I look."

Fingertips brushed my inner thighs. "I will try to be gentle."

"We don't have to be." My voice fell from the lighter, higher range I adopted for him. The huskiness seemed to inflame him all the more.

"You don't know..." A growl rumbled deep in his throat. Hands tightened on my hips and pulled me astride him with slow, irresistible demand. My inflamed mons registered the swelling knot between his legs, and low in my body, a deep contraction took my breath away. The blood-filled tissue of my external erection brushed against his, and bronze eyes widened. An answering surge against me proved he remained more intrigued than put off.

With careful hands, Rhix peeled the shirt from my upper body. His mouth traveled over skin rendered deliciously hypersensitive by desire, my muscles taut and quivering. I gasped when he took a nipple into his mouth, the faint spice of incense from his tight curls carried with my sharp inhalation. His lips continued their skillful work, and my tongue teased the ridge of his aural canal. The groan against my chest told me Ursetu ears possessed the all the sensitivity of a human's. Breath ragged, he pulled back.

"I cannot control myself if you do that."

"I can't promise I won't."

"You test me. I do not want to hurt you." In one fluid motion, he stood, his arms beneath my buttocks as he carried me with him to the bed. "Not this time, at least."

His uniquely inspirational pheromones booted up my changeling chemistry every damn time, almost like being under the influence of a drug, except my head remained separate from the actions of my body. Cold. Calculating how long before he fell asleep once he lay there, sticky, spent, and happy from recreational bliss, so I could go paw through his data well again.

It bothered me more than killing the mercenary. How fucked up was that?

Twenty-Four

KAI PRETENDED THE accusatory conversation had never taken place. I took my cues from him as we tried to play the Ferian equivalent of chess.

"Who is this again?" His finger tapped the fanged creature in the point of the diamond-shaped board.

"Your pride alpha."

"So he can go anywhere but the white spaces."

"Not unless you want me to attack him. White is my pride's territory."

"Okay." He shifted the piece down into the delta of the playing field.

I picked up the den-mother and plopped it in front of six smaller pieces. "Protecting the cubs."

"The nipples on that thing are a little disconcerting."

"Ferians find it sexy."

"What's the sand in the middle of the board for?"

"Not sure. Maybe that's where they shit."

He snorted. "That's racist."

"You think I'm kidding. They do poop rituals. Have you ever met a Ferian?"

"Once, coming in on a government shuttle. I had to lint roll the passenger compartment afterward to get the fur off the seats."

We both wheezed in guilty laughter. Kai moved another piece on the board. I pondered my next strategy and tried to decide if my scout could kidnap any of his cubs, when he said quietly, "I'm sorry. You know I don't think you're trying to fuck us over, right?"

"I hope so. I'm not."

"Bashful keeps telling me I'm going to be sold if Lord Rhix can't find a reason to keep me."

"I haven't heard anything like that." I glanced at him. "He doesn't seem in a hurry to get rid of us."

"Not you. So you're, what, a guard now?"

"When it's convenient, anyway."

"Something else happened when you got shot, didn't it? Simish and the others are practically kissing your feet."

"I kind of...prevented an assassination," I murmured, and advanced the scout into a position to take his cubs.

His eyes widened. "Whose?" Kai whispered.

"I'm not supposed to talk about it." Staring at him, I raised an eyebrow. He got it.

"No shit?" Kai moved his pride alpha and decimated my offensive attempt. "Wow. You might not be trying to make yourself indispensable, but it is happening."

My conscience would not allow me to remain silent. The first time we sparred again after the attempted mutiny, I broached the subject with Rhix.

"May I ask what's going to happen to us at the Market?" I held the padded form steady as he punched and kicked full-strength.

"Us?"

"The three of us. Dru, Kai, and me."

Sinking a flurry of punches into the dummy, he frowned. "I still have not found a solution for this. If I do not return them to the Sol Fed petitioners, I will have to sell them, if not this Market, then the next, unless I find a way they can contribute to my enterprise."

"They're my friends. I hoped there might be some way the three of us can stay together."

He beckoned me to the mat. Until we completed a pass of blows, Rhix didn't answer. "Is this important to you?"

"Human beings are social animals. We need our own kind to be comfortable, and I'm worried about Kai. I don't think he'll survive being sold."

"Simish assures me he is in good health."

"Physically, but it isn't what I meant. They were abused. It leaves emotional damage that doesn't show."

"You think he would kill himself?"

"I'm afraid he might try."

Blocking his next volley, I ducked under a roundhouse before making my own advance and landed a hard punch to his midsection.

Rhix eyed me as he rubbed the area. "What about the other one?"

"Dru's a survivor. She'll do whatever it takes."

"Why are you concerned about them?"

"If they're sold, there won't be anyone to look out for them."

"You're so certain I have decided to keep you?" He attacked. I brought him down. My back hit the floor with my forearm locked across his throat, legs wrapped around his thighs.

"Not certain," I grunted. "But I think I proved I'm useful." I held him until he yielded and slapped the mat.

"Useful." He agreed with a rumble as he climbed to his feet. "Perhaps not indispensable."

"Oh?" I glared up at him with insolence from beneath hooded eyes. "Is there anyone else on board the ship who can make you scream, or was last night a common occurrence?"

His gaze smoldered. "I think Dru could with training, if you truly wish her to stay."

"Oh, I'm not teaching her to do *that*."

He chuckled and grew sober. "This is a business. I cannot keep on "friends" who eat my food and do nothing to strengthen my enterprise, Gresh. But..." he hesitated. "Prominent clients meet with me here in the gallery, rather than on the Market floor. The Sol Fed party will be among the first. I plan to have you attend this meeting."

My head came up, too quickly in my interest, as Rhix went on, "I will ask Simish to train Kai and Dru to serve in various capacities during these negotiations. I will not sell them at this session if they prove useful. I cannot promise anything beyond that until my position is more secure."

"Thank you." He pulled me to my feet. We continued sparring sans conversation.

His intent to have me attend the meeting presented a chance to learn more about the Sol Fed transaction, and his concession regarding my friends held the best outcome I could hope for at the moment. I hoped Dru and Kai would cooperate. Success would mean another month's grace for Sumner to find us should he not reach this Market in time. The possibility he wouldn't meant another month of sparring with Rhix in arenas of sex and martial arts. One was a harmless pastime. The other could be dangerous if I lost control of the situation.

I wasn't sure which was harmless. If I couldn't figure it out, Sumner had better be waiting for my ass on the other side.

I TOLD KAI and Dru human beings would be among Rhix's clients settling deals in the gallery, and he wanted us to make them welcome. The news energized Kai briefly, and he sat up straight.

"Do you think they can help us? If we tell them we're being held against our will, they could alert somebody back in Sol Fed or help us escape."

I hated to kill that spark of hope. "These people aren't the kind you want to rescue us."

"Why not?"

"They're the ones who sent us here."

His jaw dropped and shut without a sound several times, finally terminated in a hysterical "What?"

"What the fuck?" Dru was incensed. "He wants us to wait on them?"

"Maybe not them, specifically. He said there would be several clients meeting with him."

"They're coming here." Kai's voice was suddenly cold as space, his eyes blank and frightening. "The motherfuckers who stole my life from me are coming here. And they get to leave, but we don't."

"I'm afraid so. If we did leave with them, I doubt we'd make it back home." I knelt in front of them. "I was able to get Lord Rhix to agree he won't sell us at this Market if we can earn our keep, so to speak. The alternative is the three of us separated and unable to look out for each other. It isn't perfect, but this is the only idea I've got."

"He really is going to sell us?" Dru gulped. "I thought he said we were his guests."

"It's just a fancy word for prisoners, Dru." Kai's arms crossed defensively in front of his chest. "I told you so. Nice guy, huh?"

I shook my head. "Believe me, he's the best option we have. His predecessors used sex slaves as a bargaining chip. He won't allow us to be used that way. All bets are off if someone replaces him."

"When do they get here?" Kai was calm and resigned on the outside, but black despair simmered against my empathic nets.

"A couple of days." I shifted. "Kai, what are you thinking?"

"Nothing. I can't do anything about it, can I? I'll do this, if it means staying together." He looked askance at our roommate. "Dru?"

"Yeah. Yeah, I guess." She swept her hair back. "I can't swear I won't spit in their faces, though."

Kai and Dru absorbed the etiquette in which Simish instructed them. Droopy proved to be an expert mixologist, and Kai used Dru and me to test his newly learned concoctions of exotic liqueurs served in delicate crystal beakers. We all went to bed shit-faced at the end of the lessons, but Kai appeared to have his niche in this bizarre situation. He broadcast a sense of relief I didn't like, as if he'd finally found an answer. I knew it wasn't bartending. I would need to keep an eye on him.

INSOMNIA ENTERTAINED ME in the common room two nights later, my hair still wet from a postencounter bath in Rhix's quarters. The almost imperceptible shatter of glass reached my ears. A terrible wave of despair, triumph, and fear assaulted the fringes of my mind. I leapt from the couch and slapped in frantic haste at the door controls of Kai's room.

He slashed his wrists in vertical lines with a razor of crystal, fragments of a beaker somehow hidden after Dopey's drink-mixing lessons. Wresting the glass from his lacerated fingers, I held him trapped in my arms. He bled on me and fought bitterly as I tried to stem the flow.

"Let me die! Goddamn you, Gresh, let me die!"

"I can't do that, Kai."

He collapsed against me and cursed in between hoarse, braying sobs. Kai's hopelessness poured over me, numbing my empathic nets with its weight. I wept with him.

Mercifully, he missed the arteries, but not for lack of trying. The guards arrived within seconds; Simish flew in close behind the sentries, medical kit in hand. He examined the gaping wounds, his layered features grim, and rushed Kai to the infirmary. I was left to deal with Dru, hysterical at the sight of our friend whose wrenching pleas to be allowed to die continued as they carried him from the room. A tumultuous empathic wave comprised of rage and fear, suppressed so long by Dru's psychological defenses, slammed against me in a blistering paroxysm. It wasn't just Kai's suicide attempt she railed against; it was our captivity, the betrayal by our own race. She rained blows on my head and hands, the only safe target in range.

At last, I grasped her forearms and forced her to sit down. Kai's blood made scarlet handprints on her pale skin. I let her scream wordlessly at me until she collapsed and sobbed against the cushions of the lounge. While she cried I changed my clothes and washed my crimson hands. Second time in a week, covered in somebody else's blood. It was getting old.

I brought a warm cloth back to where Dru lay and started to gently wash the handprints off her skin. She slapped at me and grabbed the cloth.

"I can do it myself." She scrubbed her arms until they were nearly as red as the blood she removed. "I didn't ask you to take care of me, Gresh, and neither did Kai. Who appointed you our babysitter?"

Her bitterness made me recoil. "No one. I'm only trying to keep us together."

"You're doing a great job." Dru's swollen eyes met mine. "But you're trying too hard to protect us."

"What do you mean?"

"It's obvious what Kai wants."

This, I couldn't let rest. "So I'm supposed to let him commit suicide?"

"What's going to happen if we get sold? Best-case scenario, we're slaves; the last thing he wants to be. Worst case, he gets raped and abused all over again. What's the kinder thing to do?"

I closed my eyes and sighed harshly. She had an ugly point, whether I liked it or not. If they were sold before Sumner found me again, where would they end up? How would we find them? Head in hands, I dropped to the couch. Dru sat down beside me. A wave of pity came from her.

"You're not responsible for us. You're not some kind of knight coming to save us. You're a victim, just like we are."

She thought it was my way of coping with our captivity—except, I was here to rescue them. That was the point of the whole goddamned mission. But I was exhausted and so tired of this masquerade.

My eyes were wet when I raised my head. She patted my shoulder.

"I appreciate what you're trying to do." She rose and wandered back toward her door, her voice dull. "Get some rest. They'll take care of Kai."

Tweny-Five

THE SHIP'S TRANSITION out of dark space woke me from thin sleep—and dreams I preferred not to remember anyway.

When I came out of my room, the airlock was rolled back from the energy dome to reveal the fire of stars and nebulae. The view still made me pause in admiration. Simish bustled around the table as he laid out breakfast.

"How is Kai?" I asked immediately.

"He is doing well. We had to sedate him and give him blood replacements, but the vessels are repaired, and the wounds closed. One of the tendons was cut. It will take time for his hand to regain movement, but it will heal."

"Can I see him, please?"

"Later, perhaps, when we are certain he will not try to harm himself again. The Sol Fed contingency arrived early at the rendezvous point and requested to meet with Lord Rhix as soon as possible. He wants you to attend this meeting as one of his bodyguards. Because you are a native speaker of the language, you will greet them in the private shuttle bay. You'll carry a live weapon this time."

"How do the rest of the guards feel about this?"

"You saved Lord Rhix's life. The Ursetu will follow his lead. The others saw you with the Shontavians. They will not dare to disagree."

Somehow, I'd cursed myself with notoriety again. I needed to stop.

A shift of light in the common area marked a change in view, and I glanced up at the energy window. The face of a dark planetoid blotted out the distant galaxies. A single, irregular asteroid swam by through the sea of stars, closer to the ship than the planet below. My heart pounded, breath catching in my throat. I knew this satellite, its disproportionate, hourglass shape, and what dwarf planet's gravitational fist held it in orbit.

Sedna.

The distal edge of Sol's own system, thirteen billion miles from the sun in a sector still uninhabited and unmonitored.

Almost all the way back to the Fed.

I KEPT BUGGING Simish until he allowed me to see Kai in the infirmary. He agreed at last to take me there before I joined Rhix's guards. With my hair tied back into a warrior's topknot to keep it under the helmet, I followed him to the blast doors. All the screens in the security alcove glowed again. Mercenaries scanned them with new focus—it seemed having a personal financial stake in the Market's profits changed a few attitudes among the troops.

The three-story vault where the Market would take place swarmed with activity, platforms above me transformed and crowded with stalls set up by merchants invited to take part. I had learned Rhix demanded a heavy share of their revenues for the privilege of participation. Judged by the number of credits generated at each session, those terms remained more than profitable. The majority of them appeared to be selling arms, but areas boasted luxury items, no doubt "liberated" from their rightful owners, in seductive displays of avarice. We passed a curtained alcove through which drifted a scent I recognized from the Labyrinth: spicy, sweet, and beguiling.

Invisible hooks sank into my brain, craving the promised oblivion even months after my last hit. Illegal vapes were being sold and consumed here by early customers among the vendors. Rhix's soldiers patrolled this area with vigilance.

We took the lift down to the crew decks. The medical bay adjoined the barracks. Though most of the mercs already attended their Market duties, I was glad to be safely anonymous behind the visored armor until we reached our destination.

Bashful sat at the screens reflecting Kai's vital signs, and I watched Kai for a minute before he realized I was there. Pale patches of dermal accelerant covered his inner forearms, and his drawn features wore haunted, hollow shadows. I removed the headgear and articulated gloves and put them on a work surface.

"Can I talk to him alone for a few minutes, please?" The siblings moved to the opposite side of the room and gave us a semblance of privacy. Kai managed to meet my eyes, his acknowledgement little more than a blink and shift of his chin. I couldn't tell if he still wanted to die, but he held confused resentment toward me. I understood that. "Are they treating you okay down here?"

"I guess." He rolled his head away from me. "The drugs are good, at any rate."

"I'm sorry, Kai."

"What for?"

"For not realizing sooner you were in so much pain. I should have recognized it." I took a deep breath. "You remember when I told you I got knifed in the Labyrinth? You asked me if I had a death wish. Well, that's exactly what it was."

"You were trying to get killed?" Sharpened, his gaze returned to me. "Why?"

"My wife, husband, and unborn child, they..." I passed a hand over my trembling mouth. It never got any easier to say. "I watched them die in the Luna Terminal bombing."

"Jesus." Kai pulled himself up on one elbow, stricken. "How do you survive something like that?"

"I didn't. I just took six months longer to die. I didn't have the guts or the energy to do it myself, so I looked for somebody else to do it for me. I didn't expect to wake up after. The fact I did must mean something. I got so busy doing what I thought I had to do to keep us all together, I didn't pay enough attention."

"I didn't want you to." He lay back and folded his arms over his stomach. "What's with the armor again?"

"The Sol Fed party is about to arrive." A quick eyes-only survey of the medical bay didn't turn up any watchful cameras or microphones, but it didn't mean they weren't there. My lips almost touched his ear when I leaned in. "Please. Give me some time. I swear I'll get you home."

"How?" he breathed.

"Trust me. But you have to promise to stay alive, no matter what happens to you. I'll tell you more when it's safe. Promise me."

Kai considered it silently for a moment. "All right."

Simish beckoned me. "Gresh, we must go."

"Coming." I touched Kai's forehead. "I'll talk to you when you get back to the dormitory. We need to work out together."

"Yeah, right. Funny."

I was serious. No surveillance cameras peeped on the training room. If I told him hope remained, maybe it would be enough.

When I went back to the desk to pick up my helmet, an unexpected opportunity waited there. Beside the data well Bashful used to record Kai's vital signs, a couple of holo cards lay scattered on top of the workstation. I glanced at the door. Bashful and Simish spoke to each other about Kai's condition, their attention on each other. Palming one of the cards as I picked up my gear was easy. The card nestled in the hollow of my hand as I pulled on the glove.

CHYDRI, THE NEW head of Rhix's guard, wasn't sure how to treat me— Rhix's rules, which forbid the mercenaries to speak to his concubines, contradicted this situation. He finally decided that when I was in armor, the rules didn't apply.

"I have been ordered to give you a loaded weapon. Do you know how to use them?"

"I served in the Lunar Militia, Captain. I'm not a stranger to weapons." His sidearm caught my attention, and I gestured at the gun. "I qualified with a Sivad Mark III, but it didn't have a pulse component."

"No. I modified it myself." His suspicion ebbed by micrometers. Chydri drew the weapon and held it like a proud father so I could examine it.

We found our footing then. Though he still regarded me with mild bewilderment, he gave me a loaded sidearm and briefed me on what to say to the Sol Fed party. My palm print was registered for security.

A squad of mercenaries joined us—and Ouros. Even beneath my visor, the Shontavian identified me, and we exchanged mental nudges. In one set of his four massive arms, he carried what appeared to be a small cannon. Whoever came to the meeting might lose control of their bodily functions when they saw Ouros. I'd almost forgotten how much more fearsome the Shontavians looked in battle armor.

The airlock warning klaxons brayed a throaty alarm as the bay repressurized. I only half listened to Chydri as he gave orders and craned my neck to peer through the narrow window. The small, intersystem shuttle which had landed there lacked any government insignia, but I couldn't imagine them advertising they dealt with the Shontavian

Market. When the doors opened at last, the mercenaries took position, weapons held loosely but ready to aim. Ouros moved slowly to stand beside me, and the rest of the mercs stared. Either I gained a new comrade in arms, or it sensed my heightened state of anxiety and wondered what was up.

Two men advanced with caution down the ramp. They held themselves like bodyguards. When none of us moved, one turned back to the open doorway, and with a curt jerk of his head invited their party to advance.

Three people disembarked—a silver-haired Eurasian man dressed in an expensive suit. I didn't know him either. The other seemed vaguely familiar, though I couldn't think why. As the third person ducked out the squat door of the shuttle, my breath caught. Well...I guess I should have known.

Jon Batterson.

Ribbons of scarlet rage threatened my vision. My chest ached with the memory of a cold blade driving through my ribs. I forced myself to regain calm as Ouros shifted next to me, sensing my mood change. Batterson deserved a bullet through his skull for each of the changelings he'd stolen from their lives. An extra one for Aja, who had died in my arms. But if I killed him now, my cover would evaporate before Sumner found us again. Probably my life, too.

Chydri's head turned, and I realized he waited for me. I moved forward and keyed the external microphone. I spoke in the deeper tones of my male voice, but adopted a hint of Rhix's Ursetu accent to camouflage my human status. It was doubtful Batterson would recognize anything about me with the visor. It still paid to be cautious. Anger gave an edge to my speech and provided further dissemblance. "You are in the private residence of Lord Rhix. Weapons are not allowed here. Are any of you armed?"

"Do we look like we're armed?" Batterson's voice held the boredom of entitled impatience. Underneath his bluster, a tinge of fear iced my empathic nets. Liar.

"Check his right leg for a knife." I said privately over the helmet com. He drew the blade from a boot sheath in the Labyrinth, I remembered.

"Search them." Chydri waved two of the mercs forward as the rest of us shifted arms to a ready position. Small weapons were confiscated from the bodyguards. The mercenary patting down Jon removed the blade from his boot sheath and handed it to his commanding officer. In the swarm of pat downs, I felt smug and congratulated myself. I earned points with Rhix's captain and got to make Batterson squirm. Bonus.

"Not armed?" I questioned softly.

"I forgot I had it." Batterson shrugged. "Forgive me."

Chydri jerked his head at me.

"Gentlemen, if you will follow us, please." The motion of my weapon's muzzle directed them. The group began to move to the lift. Chydri looked past my shoulder and stiffened.

"You. Back in formation," he ordered in Ursetu.

Ouros had taken steps forward with me as if it meant to get on the lift as well. It swayed, the cannon cradled in its arms, eyes riveted on Jon Batterson.

Twenty-Six

"I SAID, GET back in formation." Chydri's hands tightened on his weapon. The other guards, uneasy now, started to sight their weapons in jerky movements.

Ouros moaned quietly and looked to me as if waiting for some kind of instruction. Its expressionless face told me nothing. Against my mind, a broadcast of hunger gnawed, eager anticipation of prey. It wanted Batterson, lured by the sharp scent of his fear.

I gave it an empathic nudge of disapproval, and Ouros fell back with the other mercenaries, who gave the Shontavian a generous berth. Chydri herded the group into the lift with haste. I followed, my eyes never leaving the gray bulk hovering reluctantly outside.

The door closed between Ouros and me. I took a deep breath through my nose, and exhaled in slow increments. I measured my voice and found it steady. "Lord Rhix will meet you in the gallery conference room."

"Excellent. We have much to discuss," the Eurasian man said.

"If I remember, when we negotiated before, he was drunk," Batterson noted with a derisive sneer.

"You'll find him a different man." The pun evaded the guests, but after the heightened tension of the last minutes, Chydri and the guards snickered over the coms as the translation came through. Low humor held galactic appreciation. Who knew?

In Rhix's negotiation chamber the energy window looked out onto the dark face of Sedna, defined by a curving diadem of stars visible above the northern hemisphere. Now in front of this impressive backdrop, an empty throne-like chair sat at the head of a long table. Chydri motioned me to take up position to the left of the window. The Sol Fed bodyguards, stripped of their weapons, stood behind Batterson and the other two men.

"I will tell him you're ready." The last two mercenaries arranged themselves outside the door as the captain exited.

"What's this?" The elder of the three waved at the throne in derision. "He thinks he's royal now?"

"Then he and Batterson have something in common, don't they?" the other man smirked. Jon glared at him.

"Shut your mouth, Hyatt, or I'll shut it for you."

"Enough." The older man frowned at both of them. "We agreed our mutual goals are what is important. We can't waste time on this."

Rhix strode through the door, proud and arrogant in his ceremonial armor. Ursetu royalty, indeed. He had experience making an entrance that commanded attention. The three men stared at him as he took his place at the head of the table. Captain Chydri took an attentive stance on his right.

"Welcome, gentlemen."

"You aren't Lord Rhix." Batterson eyed him.

"At least, not the one we first dealt with." The silver-haired man corrected Batterson quickly. "Are you his heir, sir?"

"I am his successor. Be assured I am familiar with your previous transaction. I did attend, though you would not remember me. I am eager to learn what you feel is so important we must meet before the Market begins."

"We didn't hear from you." Batterson, another alpha male like Rhix, sat forward in his seat, fists clenched on the table. "Did we waste our time and money?"

"I did not receive what we agreed upon. In fact, I received none of the additional hardware and less than half of the living merchandise promised. They are...unusual. I am not even certain a market exists for them."

"Our understanding was the previous Lord Rhix wanted exotics."

"I am not my predecessor...Mr. Tanaka, isn't it?"

"Yes."

"I made changes to this enterprise after my succession. All further transactions will be in the form of galactic credits or hardware, not living merchandise."

"Will you do business with us, or not?" The last man spoke. "We're working against a deadline, and my time is limited."

"I do not know who you are." Rhix narrowed his eyes. "You were not present for the initial negotiation."

"Edward Hyatt, Sol Fed Senate." That's why I recognized him; the head of the goddamned Senate!

"I heard Remoliad membership is imminent," Rhix said. "I assume this coincides with your deadline."

"It will pass under the terms the diplomatic team hammered out." Hyatt's mouth took on a petulant sneer.

Go, Mom. She'd done her job well and pissed off the isolationists.

"You do not seem pleased with this outcome." Rhix didn't miss his tone either.

"Too many conditions inhibit our growth as a galactic presence."

Jon curled his lip. "We don't need the Remoliad. We've been just fine on our own without alien interference."

"But you are eager to do business with *this* alien." Rhix sat back. "Remind me why you are here, Mr. Batterson."

"I represent the board of Batterson Robotics." Jon shifted in his seat, annoyed. "We built the enhanced media tech you received. I also procured the living merchandise requested by the other Rhix, at steep personal cost, I might add. I was led to believe it would be an ongoing enterprise."

"Strange that the Nos possessed accurate knowledge of what ships they traveled upon." Rhix's mouth lifted in a sardonic smile. "They intercepted both shipments meant to ensure good faith. Tell me, Mr. Batterson, how do you think they discovered the location of the containers?"

"We think it was a spy." Jon's answer, rehearsed and casual, fell flat. A wave of his anxiety reached me even though his expression remained neutral. "We were at war with them, after all."

I couldn't see Rhix's face from my vantage point, but mockery dripped from his vocal expression. "That engineered spat hardly counted as a war."

Tanaka and Hyatt exchanged troubled glances as Rhix continued, "I learned about the pact. I am sometimes paid with information, and in order to save his remaining limbs, Eminence Odrik of the Nos confessed to me his part in the so-called 'war' with Sol Fed."

Batterson began to sweat. His dread pounded against my empathic nets, almost drowned by my own disbelief. Rhix continued, "An agreement with one clan of Nos pirates to harry the trade routes does not constitute war with the entire Conglomerate. If it did, nothing would be left of your climate domes but shards among the bodies." He studied them in their uneasiness. "What did you hope to accomplish with that weak effort?"

"We meant to prove to our citizens we could handle a conflict on our own, and reduce support for Remoliad negotiations. The conflict did not play out as we hoped. Once we started firing back, the Nos lost their eagerness to help us. An expensive lesson in galactic duplicity." Hyatt folded his arms over his chest. "Can we get down to our business, sir?"

"What do you want from me?"

"We need assets we cannot come by in our system without undue questions." Hyatt removed a small data device from his pocket and slid it across the table to Rhix. "You will find our specifications and accounts here."

Rhix viewed the information on Hyatt's PDD with a cursory eye. "How soon do you need it?"

"We would prefer to leave with our new assets."

"Of course." Rhix kept the device. "One of the items is a specialty in which I do not deal often. I will not keep it on my ship. You are in luck; I will meet with another client today who should be able to provide the very thing you seek."

"We brought more of the enhanced media tech if you are interested in a trade, but in terms of payment, I presume you have nothing against galactic credits of varying origin—anonymous, of course. Our approval will be required before transfer."

"I shall think on the media technology. There does not seem to be a demand. Others do not share your species' fascination with drama and sensationalism. The credits will be adequate."

Batterson leaned forward, his eyes narrowed. "If there's no market, how did the original hardware we provided find its way back to Sol Fed? I didn't expect to have it used against us."

My breath stopped. *Luna Terminal.* My chest tightened as I waited for Rhix's answer.

"I would need to research the transaction. It, too, took place before my time. Frankly, I do not have the inclination to do so. My services are confidential, and a violation of trust would be detrimental to business. I am certain you understand." He stood, and everyone at the table followed suit.

"Until tomorrow, gentlemen. My guards will see you back to your shuttle."

"Will that thing still be out there?" Batterson asked. Rhix's brow furrowed in dark amusement.

"Do you mean my Shontavian? As long as you do business with me in good faith, you have nothing to fear. It only has a taste for cowards and oathbreakers." Rhix held Batterson's gaze for a moment before he inclined his head to Tanaka and Hyatt. He swept from the room.

"Please." I motioned with one hand to the door. The two guards outside fell in with the captain and me.

As I thumbed the lift call, Senator Hyatt turned to me. "How did you and your master learn to speak Sol Standard?"

"He thinks it important to understand the languages of business." I shaped the words to preserve my adopted accent.

"Has he treated the merchandise we sent him well?" Tanaka asked.

As if you care, asshole. "Three are alive and healthy."

"There were four in each shipment." Batterson interjected. "What happened to the fourth?"

"One died aboard the Nos ship."

"Do you know them? Are any of them named Dalí?" A spike of violent emotion accompanied his naming me, knotted up in hate and jealous rage.

I turned to regard Jon, glad for the concealing visor. "I do not know that name."

Tanaka shrugged. "If one is dead, perhaps the problem sorted itself out."

"This isn't the time to talk about it." If Hyatt's voice were any colder, his words would have shattered like ice against the elevator walls.

Ouros still lurked in the bay with the rest of the mercenaries, but it didn't approach again. Chydri returned all confiscated personal weapons to the bodyguards, and the Sol Fed party hustled into the shuttle.

As we retreated through the airlock doors and klaxons blared their warnings of depressurization, Chydri's head kept turning to me. His unease pulsed against my empathic nets.

"Did I do something wrong, Captain Chydri?"

The delay for translation let me gauge his body language, tight and controlled. "The human said they are looking for a *dali*. What did he mean?"

The troops shifted as his statement came over the com. Helmets swiveled toward me.

"It's someone's name." I'd forgotten the Ursetu vengeance demon shared almost identical syllables. "That's all. There are a few names in the Sol Fed tongue pronounced the same way."

My explanation did nothing to reassure him. I had no idea if the impression the mercs held of me could be useful, or if it made me a target.

The shuttle departed, and the mercenaries broke ranks in casual groups. Ouros and I were avoided as if we were equally frightening. When the Shontavian shuffled up to me once again, the rest retreated to a safe distance in case it decided to eat me. I lifted the visor of my helmet. The engineered creature cocked its head and repeated the strange, weaving dance from the barracks. Its mind touched mine in submission. The overwhelming sense it apologized to me for its earlier behavior left me confounded. I brushed its mind with a neutral touch. What the hell was happening? I didn't want to do the wrong thing.

Ouros seemed satisfied and lumbered off toward the armory. Chydri held out a hand and motioned for my weapon. I surrendered it as the lift returned to the bay.

"Simish is waiting upstairs. You are dismissed."

They all stared as I got on the platform alone. I stifled the urge to shout *boo!* at them as the door closed.

It left about twenty seconds to indulge myself in a brain meltdown, and I sagged against the wall.

My mind raced with the implications of the last hour's conversation. Fury ran through my veins. Impotent frustration crashed down upon shoulders faltering with the weight of a mission I'd been ridiculously certain I could handle. What an idiot. What a goddamned idiot. Sumner's faith in me was poorly placed, and this had turned into one huge storm of fucked-up. Jon Batterson knew I infiltrated the shipment, if not that I'd been standing next to him. There was no way to know if Tella Sharp was a traitor or gave up the information under duress. I might only have about twenty-four hours of cover left, with no sign of rescue.

Shit. I had a lot to do.

The lift's motion slowed. I took one last deep breath, removed the helmet, and faked an outward composure by the time Simish's droopy little mug appeared. My pulse still raced, and the knot of tension in my chest refused to dissipate.

"Lord Rhix is overseeing Market preparations and does not require your presence now. You are free to do whatever you like until this evening. He will call for you to join him in his chambers then. Your palm print is approved for permission to enter and exit his quarters, the dormitory, and the training room."

We had no other escort, just me and my little butler/medic. I took it as another mark of my growing privileges; though it was possible the other guards were busy keeping order as the Market set up. Only one sentry maintained his place outside the seraglio. The door to Rhix's quarters was unguarded. Simish let me in. He helped me divest myself of the armor. I left the holo card concealed in my glove where I could retrieve it later.

"You will be pleased to know Kai is returning to the dormitory tonight. He seems to be in better spirits since you visited him and promises he will not try to harm himself again." Simish's face fell. "I must tell you...Kai's specifications were listed among the items available at this Market. Lord Rhix is not one to risk losing an asset before sale."

"No. Of course not." I closed my eyes in weary resignation. Damn. This day just kept getting better.

Twenty-Seven

KAI RETURNED TO the seraglio, pale and quiet, under the care of Bashful. I wasn't able to speak with him before Rhix called me to his quarters. I found him at his desk, still wearing his ceremonial armor as he pored over the data device from Hyatt.

"Your friends are greedy."

"They are definitely not my friends."

"You hold a grudge against them for your presence here?" Rhix didn't look up.

Since I'd chosen to be here, I couldn't say that, exactly. "I resent their view of people like me as less than human." I chose my next words carefully. "Will you tell me what they want?"

He considered a moment and held out the device so I could see. The notations on the list sent chills up my spine.

Enough arms and explosives to arm a small strike force. Masks to filter toxins.

Chemical weapons.

"How can you condone the sale of merchandise like that?" Heat bloomed in my face as fury threatened.

Rhix set the PDD aside. "The majority of Market transactions are with murderers and thieves. Once the items leave, how they are used no longer concerns me."

His nonchalant dismissal of moral culpability disappointed me. I'm not sure what I expected. "Those men aren't what they present themselves to be. This is no federal transaction. They're extremists."

"I do not care who they are. What matters is if they can afford my services." He stood. "You need to think more like a mercenary, not a diplomat."

I fought to compose myself. If I lost my temper, I might never learn more about the transaction or who bought the explosive media bots. The answer was here in the data well. "I'd be of less use to you if I did."

"True. I enjoy our negotiations far more than I should." Rhix began to remove his formal armor piece by piece. More complicated than his standard battle gear, he struggled with it. Finally, I moved to help him detach the pauldrons.

"I cannot continue in this manner," he said. "If you are to be my bodyguard, you cannot be in my bed, and if you are my concubine, I cannot treat you as I would one of my mercenaries. There are unique advantages to each. I must decide which is the more beneficial relationship."

"Compare the advantages. What do I offer your other bodyguards can't?"

"A fearless training partner who is not a potential rival. One who proved they will do what is necessary to protect my life." He ducked out of the breast and back plates, and I set them on the rack as he unsnapped the arm sheaths. "You are an intelligent officer, who can perform tasks requiring a more gentle approach than brute force. A skilled advisor and negotiator."

Easy to guess where this conversation was going. His desire was already on the rise and started the chemical reaction between us that had nothing to do with reason or intelligence. My continued ire gave arousal a shimmering edge of danger. "And as a concubine?"

"A fearless lover, both rival and partner in the pursuit of pleasure. One who responds to the demanding hand or gentle caress with equal passion." His voice dropped to a whisper as fathomless as the face of the planet outside, bronze eyes hooded. "A skilled negotiator of things spoken only skin to skin in the dark."

Damn. Heat flooded through my body. "This kind of poetry doesn't happen without forethought."

"Can I not be a poet and a mercenary?"

"Can I not be a concubine and your bodyguard?"

"No. It would not be appropriate for one person to be both—for *you* to be both and hold my life and my pleasure in your hands." He turned away moodily as he stripped off his upper garment. "Your nature confuses my mercenaries. They do not know if you are male or female."

It confused *him*. I knew that look. "Ah, but I'm neither." Kneeling, I gazed up at him. "I'm a demon; a *dali*. Remember?"

His breath started to come faster as I unfastened the thigh plates and greaves of his armor. Pulling them away slowly, I let my hands linger too long in sensitive places before my fingers slipped under the waist of his pants and eased them down.

"Will you claim my soul?" he rasped.

"You don't have one. Neither do I."

"Then show me your claws and teeth, demon. I am not afraid of you."

Stars outside burned with the same cold, bitter fire I harbored in my core as he pulled me into his bed. My anger lent this encounter an aura of violence, and I took him at his word, inflicting pain whenever I could. The fusion of desire and rage kept me from surrendering completely, genitalia caught in the midpoint between masculine and feminine, my external erection an iron-hard reminder to Rhix of my changeling nature. We struggled against each other, my nails tearing the skin of his back, teeth sinking into the muscle of his shoulder as he drove himself into me. The pressure of his pelvis against mine brought me to climax in a violent spasm, a cry torn from my throat even I could not distinguish between rapture and fury.

The anger abated as my pulse slowed, poured out in sex and left in the bloody furrows I'd made on his skin. Rhix didn't unsheathe himself from me; his eyes locked with mine, and he moved again in a slow, sensual rhythm. His mounting pleasure sent tingling shocks through my empathic nets; the unique, intoxicating mix of pheromones exuding from his effort-dampened skin a new addiction for me. I didn't fight my body's response but wrapped arms and legs around him and rode the building waves.

When three tones sounded in my skull, my gasp and widened eyes were interpreted as appreciation. Rhix's tempo inside me became more urgent, and I gave myself up to the shattering intensity of his climax. I didn't care if Sumner or whoever monitored the other end of the call got an earful of his roaring orgasm. I was having another of my own. I figured they knew I was alive, anyway.

"You are not tired?" His voice slurred, thick with sleep as I sat up.

"I want to check on Kai. He's back in the dormitory."

"Gresh, you know I cannot keep him here."

"No. Simish told me."

"I found a buyer."

"So quickly?" My breath caught in a laugh of despair. Not now, not with his rescue so close.

"He will be well treated, if it is any consolation."

"How long?"

"The Market opens tomorrow. They will leave as soon as the transaction goes through."

"Let me break the news to him."

He was silent a moment. "Do you think that's wise?"

"Better than being hauled away without warning." An edge crept into my voice.

"You may tell him. Call for Simish if he needs to be sedated." An enormous yawn shook him, and he turned over with a wince and a curse. The crimson tracks of my nails and teeth stood out like abstract artwork against his dark skin. "Perhaps I cannot keep a concubine who would leave me wounded like this."

It brought half a smile to my lips. "Do you want me to treat them?"

"No. These I will wear for the memory, *dali*." His eyes burned into mine and slowly disappeared under heavy lids.

I padded out of Rhix's bedchamber and retrieved my clothes from the front room.

Hyatt's data device still lay on the desk. The screen came alive at my touch, displaying two account numbers and balances of galactic credits higher than I would ever see in a lifetime. Below was the deadly wish list.

Sol Fed had no real enemies. The Nos weren't truly at war with us; Senator Hyatt admitted it. The target for these weapons could only be something within the solar system.

An act of domestic terror.

Innocent lives were at risk. The storms in my mind seethed like the chaos of Jupiter's atmosphere, the deaths of Gresh and Rasida and our child still a gaping, open wound that bled me dry. I couldn't let it happen.

It took only a few minutes to retrieve the holo card from my glove and make a copy of the data on Hyatt's device. I pulled Rhix's data well out of the desk and downloaded the transaction records to the card.

Rhix still breathed in slow, deep cadence, dead to the world, when I crossed to his door and checked. To sleep so soundly after his former lovers tried to kill him proved how he trusted me. And technically, I was about to betray him.

I slipped into the lavatory to run a bath. Hoping the sound of running water would cover my hushed voice, I tapped the implant.

"Inconceivable."

"Is this Buttercup or Miracle Max?" Relieved laughter filled Tommi's voice with music, even through the translation.

"Buttercup."

"And what have you been doing?"

"Oh, you know. Making friends. Influencing people." I glanced at the door. "Who else is on?"

"Only me and Ozzie. The Man in Black and Fezzik might be listening but they can't talk now."

"You may have an ROUS on board. My cover is at risk."

"Yeah. About that? Lots of things to tell but no time. We won't be able to give you much notice."

"Understood. There's something more. A Sol Fed contingency is purchasing arms and chemical weapons here at the Market. I suspect another terrorist attack. I have a holo card in a Kua handheld. Is there any way you can link with it and download remotely?"

"You don't start small, do you? I can piggyback a data stream on your com, but it's not fast. We can't talk while it's downloading."

"What's the frequency?"

I plugged the numbers Tommi gave me into the device. "I'm getting a signal," she said. "Go."

The data crawled through the link in small chunks. First to complete was Hyatt's wish list and accounts. The larger file began to transmit at a ridiculous, glacial pace. By the time the bathwater shut off automatically to avoid flooding the lavatory, it still hadn't completed.

"Gresh?" Rhix's sleepy voice called.

Come on, come on. Statistics oozed through bit by bit. Sol Standard text glared from the screen. My fingers hovered over the switch to abort the transmission if necessary.

"Gresh?" Rhix stirred in the bedroom.

"Got it." Tommi's voice said briskly. "We received a warning we're too close to the ship. Ozzie needs to move out of range. The Man in Black or Fezzik will contact you. Leave your com on. Over and out."

An unexpected, fine tremor seized me, born of anticipation and dread. I shucked out of my robe and hid the data well underneath. I sank into the bath without a splash, submersing myself entirely. When I came up for air, Rhix stood in the doorway.

"Are you all right? You did not answer."

"Fine. I'm sorry. I didn't hear you." I smoothed my dripping hair back.

"You're shivering."

"Change hormones," I lied. It sounded glib to my own ears, and I tempered it with a slow smile. "That was a rather intense session tonight. I'm just coming down."

"I agree." He rolled his shoulders. "Are you still angry with me?"

"Not anymore." There were other things on my mind now.

"Can you forgive me for selling Kai?" His question caught me by surprise.

"The chance he'll be well treated doesn't make it any different. He'll never see his home or his family again."

"What about you?"

"What about me?"

"You seem content enough to stay. Almost as if you wish to be here." Too close. Far too close.

"I enjoy your company. It has been a long time since I had someone I could call friend. I understand you did not choose to come here, but I can still offer you a choice. I owe you my life. It would be wrong not to let you decide whether to remain in my bed as a lover, or at my side as a friend and bodyguard. I can give you this much freedom, at least."

Words deserted me. His emotional state was in flux. Sincerity, yes. Hope. And the beginning of something I never expected.

"I ask you to think on it." He turned away and went back to the bedroom.

Guilt is a weird thing. Especially when I knew what awaited me if Rhix discovered what I was doing.

When I got out of the bath, I replaced the data device in the desk and hid the holo card back in the glove of my armor. Before I left, I found Rhix's medical kit. I took a scalpel, topical anesthetic, antiseptic, and dermal accelerant and folded them into a towel before stowing the box back in its place. Draped around my neck, the small bulge stayed concealed beneath my damp hair as I let myself out. All I needed was to be alone with Kai for ten minutes in the training room. If everything went to hell, I meant to give him a chance to make it back.

Even if I didn't.

Twenty-Eight

"JESUS, GRESH, ARE you crazy?" Kai complained the entire way down the hall. "It's the middle of the fucking night. Normal people sleep. You don't, but I do."

"These exercises are important. You might not regain use of your hand if you don't start now." This was for the benefit of the surveillance cameras in the hallway, and for Simish, as bewildered as Kai at the moment. The towel still rested around my neck, the small weight of the stolen items reassuring.

Once inside, I led Kai to the mat. "Here. Take a seat." Cross-legged and huffing, he let me ease him to the floor. Our keeper hovered nearby, and I beckoned him to join me at the door.

"Can I talk with him in private?"

"He is not cleared to be alone, as you are. It would not be proper."

"Please." My voice fell to a whisper. "Rhix told me he's been sold and gave me permission to tell him. I need to break this to him gently."

With a glance of trepidation at the blades lining the walls, Simish capitulated. "Do not let him near the weapons. Call if you require assistance."

I thumbed the inside lock and turned back to Kai. After a second's debate, I turned off my implant. The team wouldn't be happy with what I planned, but I didn't have a better idea.

"What kind of exercise is so important?" He yawned as I sat down and faced him.

"We don't have much time. Keep your voice down." The towel unrolled as I pulled it off my neck, spilling the scalpel and medical supplies.

Instantly alert when he saw them, Kai sputtered, "What is this?"

"Shut up and listen. I brought you here because there aren't any surveillance cameras." Stripping off my shirt, I smeared numbing gel on the skin over my personal tracker. "You don't remember me from the lab because I wasn't in it. The shipment was infiltrated en route to the Market and they put me inside. This is a rescue mission."

"Wha-what?"

"The other four changelings and the one I replaced are safe on Zereid. Listen, and don't react yet, Kai. You were sold. The transaction will go through early today, and you'll leave with the buyer."

Color drained from his face as I lifted the scalpel, took a deep breath, and found the small bump in my armpit. The cold blade sliced flesh, a stifled hiss forced its way through my lips. Kai's eyes bulged.

"Gresh, what the fuck?"

"Quiet!" The fingertip-sized dome squeezed out of the incision as I sank my teeth into my lower lip to keep from crying out. I rinsed it and the surgical instrument with a vial of antiseptic. "Take off your shirt and raise your arm."

To his credit, Kai complied. "What are you? Some kind of spy?"

"Something like that." The underside of Kai's left arm got a swab of numbing gel. "We were supposed to be rescued at the last Market, but the session closed early because of mutiny."

"Holy shit." Kai's eyes darted over my face. "You really were trying to keep us together."

"Hold still. This will hurt, no matter what. I'm sorry." I made a small incision under Kai's arm with the scalpel. Face red with the effort not to cry out, he held his breath when I pushed the tracker underneath his skin. "This will let my team keep tabs on you when you leave the ship, so they can pick you up later." Antiseptic flooded the area as I compressed the vial, and Kai gasped with high-pitched stridor. One inner edge of the absorbent material wiped away the trickle of blood and disinfectant, and I sealed the cut with a dermal patch and more numbing gel. I handed him his tunic.

"Put this back on. Fast."

He pulled it with clumsy haste over his head, encumbered by the splint. My own blood scrubbed away by the cloth, I tortured myself with the remainder of the antiseptic and dermal accelerant before I replaced my shirt. The scalpel and refuse of the other items I rolled back into the towel, the bloody edge inside. The astringent pong was too strong to put it back around my neck at the moment. I would need to get rid of the evidence.

"You can't say a word about this, not even to Dru. Everywhere else in the ship is monitored."

"But..."

"Listen to me. Rhix thinks you'll be well treated. Swear to me you won't try to kill yourself again, no matter what happens. I just gave you my personal tracker. I'm not wasting it on a corpse. You fucking promise you will stay alive."

"I-I promise. But if you gave me yours, how—"

"I'll figure it out later. Remember—don't say anything outside this room and don't draw attention to it. That's your ticket home."

Kai's face crumpled, and he started to cry. Relief and terror mingled into an emulsion and battered me with its blunt edges. I put my forehead against his, one arm draped over his shoulder.

"You survived more outrage than most people will suffer in a lifetime, Kai. You're stronger than you think. Just a little longer, I swear."

"I'm going home?" Kai swiped at his eyes.

"I don't know about Sol Fed yet. It might be Zereid with the others until we can guarantee your safety. There are some extremely powerful figures behind this. They won't want the story to get out."

"What about Dru? She wants to be here."

"I may not give her a choice. She's in over her head and doesn't realize it."

"Lord Rhix. Christ. He'll feed you to the Shontavians if he finds out."

"Probably." I pushed the thought away. "Let's wrap this up before Simish figures out I locked the door. Do you think you can keep it together?"

He took a shuddering breath. "Yeah, I can do this. How long do you think, before I'm rescued?"

"Not sure. It will happen. Believe me."

We returned to the seraglio. Kai's expression, though I recognized the relief in it, remained shell-shocked, and our nervous keeper decided to give him a sedative. While Simish saw to his patient, I went into my own quarters and lay down. The contraband items ended up rolled tightly and stuffed under the pillows, my nose still full of the reek of antiseptic. After the rough sex, Tommi's call, and my debut as a surgeon, I short-circuited and crashed.

When I woke, Kai was gone.

THE SERAGLIO ECHOED with new emptiness. Staring up through the energy window into the stars, I hoped I hadn't failed him. Dru curled up near me, lost in her own thoughts. We didn't talk, but I sensed she was more unnerved by this development than she let on.

"Dalí?" Tommi's voice came urgently into my head. "If you can't talk, cough once."

Surprise made it easy to feign an attack of a dry throat.

"Right. Your signal shows you're boarding another ship out here in orbit. Are you? One cough for yes, two for no."

I hacked twice.

"Did you take your tracker out?" Exasperation carried over the translator. "Damn it. You're as bad as Sumner. You gave it to one of the changelings, didn't you?"

Good guess. Dru asked in concern when I coughed once again, "Gresh, are you sick?"

"No, a dry throat, I think," I croaked.

Tommi spoke so fast I could hardly catch what she said. "Sumner's inside. Keep the implant on. We're working out a plan to take you together within the next twenty-four hours, but you should tell them so they don't fight us if we have to take you separately. Contact you soon. Tommi out."

I already played the training room card with Kai. That left Rhix's quarters. I needed an excuse for taking Dru there alone.

"Let's go for a walk." I held my hand out. Dru stared at me dully for a second.

"A walk?"

"Yeah. Come on."

With a reluctant, feline stretch, Dru unwound herself from the cushions and took my hand. I pressed my palm to the scanner. The heavy door hissed aside, and Dru raised her eyebrows.

"That's new. When did you get to do that?"

"Last night." I turned us down the hall to pass the security nave first. There was only one guard in the hallway near the seraglio, but some distance away from us. Three ranged themselves in front of the blast doors. Four monitored business in the now-open Market, the bank of holo screens flickering with action. We moved in a casual arc back toward the gallery, and I asked Dru quietly, "Are you okay?"

"I guess. Maybe. No." The admission came with reluctance. "I've been thinking about it too much. It made me wonder. Kai got sold so fast, how long do I have? You're safe, obviously."

"I'm walking on very thin ice. One mistake, and I'm dead." I jerked my chin at the camera eye as we passed. "We're under constant surveillance."

"I figured."

I linked my arm through hers and leaned closer. "So how do you feel about group sex?"

"What?" She gave a tremulous laugh.

"Let's go to Rhix's quarters. No cameras. I need to talk to you, even for a minute. I don't think they'll let us stay, but we can't be overheard. If we're found, we'll tell them we're waiting for him to come back, so we can do him together."

"What if Rhix comes back? I'm not really into ménage à trois." Dru looked askance at me. I shrugged.

"Neither am I, but I doubt anyone will believe you're going to work out with me, so the training room isn't an option."

"Don't be mean." Dru studied me with a frown. "What's so important? Anyway, we can't get in."

"He gave me a key." I waggled my fingers at her.

We reached the end of the gallery and turned back. I angled us deliberately so we would pass in front of the entrance to Rhix's rooms. Dru bit her lip and glanced down the hall at the guards a couple of times. They weren't paying a lot of attention to us, accustomed to my pacing.

"Don't look guilty. Act excited."

She grinned with forced glee and bounced a little as the scanner read my palm print. The door slid aside, and I led her in, making sure my own smile held a hint of wickedness as we entered.

His quarters were deserted. I couldn't sense anyone's emotional output but Dru's, an edge of fear, tinged with bewilderment.

"Bedroom." I pulled her with me. We sat on the acreage of Rhix's mattress before the vista of the energy window. It was more like the traffic control berth on Rosetta Station now. Ships buzzed around the Market like metallic wasps, drawn by the sticky promise of what lay inside. "Dru, we're about to be rescued."

Her jaw dropped. "Rescued?"

"My team is going to take you even if I'm not there. I don't have any idea who's coming, so you need to be ready for anybody. Nos, Cthash, Andari, human...any of the above. The rest of the changelings are safe. We intercepted the first shipment, and Akia Parker told me what was happening after he woke up. I infiltrated this shipment to find out where you were going and set up a rescue."

"Gresh." Dru's hands went over her mouth. "I don't know if I want to go back to the Fed."

"You don't have to. The rest are on Zereid, or they were when I joined you and Kai in suspension. But we're on Sol Fed's doorstep. Anywhere you're free to make your own choices will be better."

"Will it?" She swayed a little on the bed, and I steadied her. "How will I recognize your team?"

"Have you ever seen *The Princess Bride*?"

"You mean the drinking game?" Confusion edged her voice.

"Close enough. Just say, 'Inconceivable'. If they quote something back at you, they're part of the team."

Dru's eyes were round, her complexion blotchy with shock and fear. "What about Kai?"

"I gave him a tracker. They know where he is. We'll bring him back."

"Gresh?" Simish's voice came from the front room. Dru jumped, her nerves heightened, and her expression couldn't be mistaken for anything but guilt.

"Relax," I hissed. My admiration for her rose another notch as she stretched out on the bed and arranged her body in a sensual pose. I raised my voice. "In here, Simish."

His craggy little face peered around the door. "What are you doing?"

"We thought we might offer Lord Rhix some distraction from business." I exchanged a suggestive glance with Dru, who giggled nervously.

Simish's mouth twitched. "He is quite busy at the moment, I fear. He is beginning to finalize early transactions." He gave a little bow to Dru. "I am sorry, but I need to speak with Gresh regarding business. May I escort you back to the dormitory?"

"I can find my own way." She rose in a convincing show of reluctance. "The guard will let me back in, I'm sure." Shepherded out of Rhix's bedroom, Dru glanced back at me, and I nodded encouragement.

Simish scolded me when he came back, quivering with indignation. "Gresh, your privileges do not extend to granting access to others without permission. Precedent forbids this. His former concubines..."

Oh, shit. I groaned in genuine dismay and mentally kicked my own ass. "Simish, I didn't think about that. I'm sorry. It won't happen again. We only wanted to..." I made a gesture to the bed. "To please him."

"Perhaps later, when he knows Dru well enough to trust her and decides she can stay." Mollified, Simish got back to business. "He will not need your presence in the conference room, but he would like you to speak with the crew of their ship as the merchandise is brought aboard. Instructions vital for proper transportation of a certain item are required to minimize the risks. The vessel is in his private bay. If you will put on your armor, we will go at once."

"Yes, of course."

I retrieved the skintight foundation for the armor from the rack and retreated to the lavatory to change. When I returned to the outer room, my mouth went dry. Simish had Hyatt's handheld and Rhix's Kua data device. The Kua was powered up, and I could see from my vantage point that it still displayed Remoliad Standard rather than Ursetu glyphs.

I didn't switch the language option back when I downloaded the data or clear the frequency numbers Tommi gave me. Fuck.

Twenty-Nine

SIMISH STARED AT it blankly for a moment. He said nothing but tapped in a command and new data displayed. He synced the two devices. I kept my head down, hoped my dark-tan complexion didn't leach to match my mother's pale Scottish genetics, and strapped on the thigh plates and boots with intense concentration until he came back with Hyatt's device. On the screen, my native language spelled out the ugly shopping list.

"These are specifications to store the chemical weapon safely aboard their vessel. You may open it one time in their presence to verify the material is within. It will be sealed in a crate and must not be opened again while they are inside the Market. Improper handling could be disastrous." He handed me the PDD when I came upright. I saw what the final purchase entailed, and my breath stopped again.

The Andari called it *arsha'an*. Silent death.

Remoliad treaties banned what the Sol Fed contingency purchased from Rhix's source in warfare against any oxygen-breathing race. A small amount released into the carbon dioxide scrubbers every ship, climate dome, and space station had by necessity of ventilation changed the composition of breathable oxygen into an airborne poison. Anyone inside the enclosed environment would never know what hit them.

We already knew it was an effective chemical weapon against humanity. Our own aerosolized compound was developed long before we had regular contact with the galactics. Millions of people died during the last war on Earth. The population of entire cities dropped in their tracks at jobs, around the table at dinner, their desks at school. We unleashed this horror on ourselves.

"Are you all right?" Simish noted my sickened expression when he handed me a sidearm from Rhix's private armory. I stood and attached the holster to the magnet in the outer thigh plate with a sharp click.

"No. I'm not all right," I admitted. The knot in my throat strangled me. I hoped Tommi or Sumner was listening. "The Sol Fed contingency bought *arsha'an* toxin? This..." My voice broke in revulsion. "This is a tool for mass murder."

"It is best not to dwell on it," he murmured as he helped me lift the chest and back plate over my head.

"How is that possible?"

He snapped the connections at my waist and armpits. "The same way Lord Rhix thinks of it. Merchandise. Nothing more."

I pulled the helmet on, glad to mask my expression of disgust with the visor. Used to my constant questions, my silence troubled Simish. My keeper had to trot to keep up with me as I strode angrily to the lift doors. He was right to be concerned. The red, volcanic pool I held inside boiled with enough pressure to do something incredibly stupid.

"The Ursetu who will transfer the item is waiting below in the bay. Mr. Tanaka will inspect the purchases while the financial aspects of the deal are closed. Captain Chydri will contact you on the helmet com when it is time to load the crates."

I nodded in curt acknowledgement. Simish swayed toward me as if he wanted to follow but thought better of it. He stood with furrowed brow, uncertain, and watched me. I corrected my rigid stance and raised an open hand in a gesture of acquiescence. I would do what was expected. I had no other option at the moment. He relaxed minutely before the door closed between us.

In Rhix's private bay, two other small vessels sandwiched the Sol Fed ship. The first was a Nos shuttle, similar to what had transported Kai, Dru, and me to the Market. Its doors were not yet open. The other was Ursetu, sleek and expensive. The waiting crew bristled with armor and exchanged uneasy stares with the human officers of the other craft, hovering near their cargo door.

No one was openly armed besides the octet of Rhix's troops. One of the bio-engineered creatures presided over a standing gun array; not Ouros, but the other Shontavian, which never spoke in my presence. Four more soldiers manned a floater pallet stacked with crates. One of the mercenaries fell in beside me—to guard me or keep an eye on me; I wasn't sure which. He gave me a nod, his weapon held ready but pointed down. He had to be one of the Nos who served Rhix. I felt nothing from him, while the cool suspicion of the Ursetu mercs scraped down my empathic nets as I passed them.

The engineered creature's head swiveled to me. Its open mouth sifted the air. I nudged the Shontavian's mind experimentally and got an interested response. Its telepathic sense invaded my head more bluntly than Ouros had done, my disquiet laid bare to its curious probe. The combination of my negative emotions toward the Sol Fed party, or perhaps only Batterson's nervous fear, might have spiked Ouros's mild aggression the previous day. A repeat performance with a canister of lethal toxin in the immediate vicinity? Phenomenally bad idea. I took a deep breath, seeking calm, and willed my outward aura to change.

Tanaka descended the ramp of the Sol Fed ship, and I met him at the bottom. Keying the external communicator, I resumed the fictional accent I used before. "Mr. Tanaka. Is your crew prepared to receive the cargo?"

"It is. How long before the transaction is finalized? They have been meeting with Lord Rhix an inordinately long time for financial approval."

"I expect to be notified at any moment." Immediately, in fact; Captain Chydri's brusque voice came over the com in my helmet, his words echoed by the translator.

"Proceed with the transfer." The signal was amplified by the external com. Tanaka pulled a small PDD out of his pocket and fiddled with it.

"Acknowledged." I signaled the floater pallet with a crisp motion and then beckoned the waiting Ursetu. "We are ready."

The Ursetu smuggler, a female dressed in dark armor, brought a small case forward. Another rolled a shipping container toward us. Rhix's mercs piloted the floater to the Sol Fed ship's cargo door and began to load other crates of varying sizes into Tanaka's ship.

"You have the item?" I asked the Ursetu in Remoliad Standard.

"I do." Her hard, golden eyes flicked over Tanaka as his attention remained on the device in his hand. "This human is the buyer?" She spoke the same language I did.

"He is here to inspect the merchandise and receive instruction on its handling."

"I will be sure to use small words." She smirked. My own mouth twitched, even though the visor concealed my face.

Tanaka's expression changed as I glanced at him. He waggled the PDD at me. "Voice translation program. I am well aware of what she said."

"He's listening," I informed her.

"Then he may survive his purchase." The smuggler placed her burden gingerly atop the container and opened it with slow care. A transparent canister lay cradled in shock-resistant pads. Red mist swirled, like blood in water, a scarlet ebb and flow of invisible currents as particles shifted within the tube. The hair on the back of my neck crawled. Standing this close to something so deadly unnerved me. My visored watchdog took a few steps back, like it would help if everything went wrong.

"This button deploys the chemical." She indicated a blinking red indentation on the top. "Once depressed, it begins a countdown in atomic time. One hundred and twenty revolutions before the vacuum seal is broken and the toxin is released."

"Is there a way to abort the release if needed?" Tanaka asked. I translated.

She pointed to another depression, glowing blue-white. "This will blink once the countdown begins. Depress both switches together to stop the timer and prevent it from opening."

The smuggler closed the case, activated the external clamps, and then nestled it into the larger crate's padding. The container was locked, the draconian hiss of an airtight gasket sealing death inside.

The Ursetu dealers took their leave of us in a rather abrupt manner—relieved to be rid of the stuff, I thought. I regarded Tanaka, who wore an odd expression as he studied his PDD. Something surprised him. It sparked against my empathic nets.

"Do not open this case again until your vessel leaves the Market. Is that clear, sir?"

"I have no intention."

"The specifications for all your purchases have been downloaded to this device." I gave him Hyatt's handheld. He juggled the two for a moment before slipping his own tech into a pocket.

The ramp of the Nos shuttle startled us both with the bang and whine of hydraulics. Metal gangplanks extended in preparation for its crew to disembark. Tanaka's lips tightened. His body language and the discomfort sliding down my empathic nets echoed the rigid expression. Bad blood remained between the Nos and these conspirators even if skirmishes no longer took place.

"I need to see the rest. I want to be sure we have the toxin masks." He turned away and hurried toward his ship. I followed him.

The last crate rolled up the ramp, steadied by two mercenaries to avoid jarring the chemical within. My personal guard stayed at the bottom with Tanaka's crew, the tension between them thick enough to breathe into my lungs. With the container secured by a net and strapped to the floor to prevent movement, the mercs scurried out of the cargo hold.

I shoved impatiently through more nets hanging from the ceiling and opened one of the long, flat crates. Twelve brand-new Sivad pulse rifles gleamed in deadly array against protective insulation. There were four of these containers—enough to arm a platoon of mercenaries. More cases held ammunition and grenades. The final crate revealed stacks of toxin masks with empty, dark lenses, oval black filters like open mouths. A sarcophagus full of hollow, screaming skulls. Some of the ruined cities on Earth looked like that after the war.

Fuck. I had to do something.

One more crate stood at the back—an upright, unmarked container behind all the rest, as if it had been on board prior to delivery of the merchandise. I went to it. A green blinking light on the pad gave an indication of its unlocked status. "This is not one of ours."

"No, Lord Rhix refused our hardware," Tanaka said distractedly as he checked the contents of the crates against their original list on the data device. The door gapped open, and I caught a shadowed glimpse of blank camera eyes glittering in the partial light.

Media bots. More than half a year passed since I'd seen one, and I still wanted to smash them.

"Does everything appear to be to your satisfaction?" Clipped monotone dulled my voice, syllables falling in impuissant despair.

"Yes. Close the cases. The crew has no need to know." He had his own handheld out again, busy with something.

I did as he asked and pushed my way back through the nets in my path, like a cluster of thick vines. My brain spun in useless circles as it tried to think of some way, any way, I could prevent them from leaving with a cargo hold full of death. If I didn't get out of this enclosed space with Tanaka so temptingly near, the psychic trauma of killing would almost be worth it.

My helmet burped static before Chydri's voice came over the com. "Lord Rhix is in transit to the bay. All hands be prepared to receive the Nos party. High risk. Chydri out."

Rhix expected trouble? Outside the shuttle, mercenaries began to move calmly toward the lift doors, weapons shifting to ready positions.

"If you do not require anything else, I must return to my post." I had one boot on the ramp when his casual remark arrested my movement.

"You confused it with the accent, but you speak Remoliad Standard the same way you always have, Ambassador Tamareia. It's a one hundred percent match. My translator program runs in tandem with voice recognition software."

A trail of synaptic frost went down my spine. I remained silent. If I said anything, the software in my helmet would kick in, and I'd out myself to the mercenaries waiting below. All I could do was turn my head and listen. My ears pounded with the rush of my pulse, his words far away and faint over the sound of my own heart.

"I should tell Batterson it's you. It's driving him insane, not knowing for certain you're here. He's a vicious little bastard, more than a bit obsessed with retribution after his wife confessed she slept with you. It might be amusing to tell Jon and Lord Rhix at the same time, and see which one kills you first."

Thirty

THE VISOR STILL concealed my identity. Tanaka might have a match on voice software, but he hadn't seen my face. Frozen for a moment on the ramp, my hand twitched and drifted toward the sidearm until I arrested the instinct. I turned away and shaped the careful imitation of Rhix's clipped Sol Standard.

"I think you mistake me for another, Mr. Tanaka."

"My apologies." Condescension left a cloying residue in my empathic nets. This wasn't fooling him.

Rhix exited the lift between Hyatt and Batterson, Captain Chydri a step behind him. The human bodyguards brought up the rear. Market soldiers folded into position to escort them. I descended the ramp and moved toward the approaching party. They passed the boxy shuttle docked in the front of the bay, where six black-armored pirates now waited at the end of the gangplank.

Jon Batterson passed the cluster of Nos, and his head ducked down and away from the sullen group of pale-eyed aliens. I recognized the movement, a dissemblance I performed many times to avoid the facial recognition software of his company's media bots. Jon didn't want to be seen, but he couldn't hide. Like my father once pointed out, Batterson was built like the ass-end of a freighter and stood above everyone else in the bay except Rhix.

One of the pale-eyed pirates lurched forward. "Oathbreaker!"

Batterson jerked as if struck and assumed a defensive stance. His bodyguards belatedly stumbled in front of him as half of the unfriendly party surged in their direction.

In the back of my mind, a wave of eager aggression thumped against my empathic nets. The Shontavian swiveled its mounted guns toward the fight, all four appendages gripping the handles.

Mercenaries raised weapons and surrounded their employer in a protective circle, Batterson and his escorts left to fend for themselves.

Hyatt moved to stand behind his host. Smart man. Rhix's troops, myself among them, rushed the area. I released my sidearm from its clip and trained my sights on the pirate brawling with Jon. Bodies closely entangled, I didn't have a clear shot on either. Did I care which one I hit?

"Oligarch! Control your party, or I will order my mercenaries to fire." Rhix shouted in Nos. The command rolled over the din of the fray, the mechanical voice of the helmet's translation program echoed by my implant.

The gold-torqued officer gaped up into the muzzle of the sidearm I'd drawn down on him and relinquished his hold on Jon's coat as Rhix's mercenaries pulled them apart. Crimson stained his mouth where Batterson landed a lucky punch. Both panted, red-faced, Batterson's teeth bared in a snarl. Mercs hauled the Oligarch's guards off their Sol Fed counterparts as Tanaka hurried from the ship, drawn by the commotion.

"This human cannot be trusted," the officer growled. "He is an oathbreaker and a swindler. I accuse him of cheating me."

"What is he saying?" Batterson demanded as he came to his feet.

Rhix regarded him coolly. "Gresh." His eyes traveled around the armored mercs in the bay, looking for me. I stepped forward as he beckoned. "Translate for my guests."

My sidearm secured, I repeated the Eminence's accusation in Sol Standard. While Rhix questioned the pirates in their own language, I relayed the words a beat behind the mechanical voice in my helmet.

"In what way did he cheat you?"

"Living merchandise and hardware promised by this human in return for our services. He told us what passenger vessel to find them on." The Oligarch sneered at Jon and spat bright blood on the floor. "When Eminence Yarol boarded the vessel, nothing happened as that oathbreaker said it would. Troops waited for us. The ship threatened us with the same remote explosives we were meant to receive."

Huh. Gor and I hardly constituted troops. The rest was fairly accurate.

Almost before I finished translating, Jon refuted it. "I have no idea what you're talking about."

"Which of you is truthful?" Rhix mused softly and turned back to the Oligarch. "Mr. Batterson told me yesterday he holds a spy responsible for the interception of my goods. Are you the spy?"

"Your goods?" The Nos gulped. "No, I acted in faith! This human promised me unique living merchandise, sure to fetch a high price, in return for my clan's cooperation in our trade routes. A standard verbal contract conducted over subspace within their own system. We communicated more than once."

"I don't know anything about this," Batterson insisted.

Jon was a bad liar. Sweat rolled off his forehead, and he blinked rapidly. His guilt and fear ricocheted off my empathic senses.

If I could feel it, so did the Shontavian.

A soft, impatient moan came from its throat. It left its guns and swayed toward Batterson.

The group took a collective step backward. The Oligarch scrambled up the ramp of his ship. My empathic nets spread like a shield, I moved between the Shontavian and Jon to broadcast a wall of disapproval. The creature did not want to be distracted from the slippery feel of Batterson's near panic and hissed at me, unhappy. Wordless resentment assaulted my mind as it stubbornly held in place, teeth bared.

"Take them back to the conference room under guard," Rhix instructed Chydri. The mercenaries circled the Sol Fed party and began to herd them in urgent haste toward the lift.

"Don't touch me!" Jon snarled while he flung off mercenary hands and received close attention from the business end of their pulse rifles. "I demand—"

A savage gesture from Rhix cut him off, bronze eyes riveted on the Shontavian. "Get him out of here."

The mercs hustled them into the elevator. The beast raised its head, watching the lift as it rose into the upper decks and moaned again. Black, gleaming eyes returned to me, and I got hammered with a telepathic blast of hunger and irritation. One hand reached out and shoved me backward, hard enough to make me stumble. Rhix steadied me as the Shontavian glared.

"Go back to the barracks and await my orders," he barked at the hulking gray figure.

For a moment, it appeared it would defy him. Then it turned with a snort and lumbered past the gun array. Like a petulant child, it pushed the heavily armored base sideways in a grind of metal and leaping sparks. Rhix's breath went out in a rush as it disappeared.

The remainder of the mercenaries stood in a broken crescent around us. Their attention toward me held the sharpness of fear. My strangeness unnerved them, the *dali* who changed sexes at will and faced down monsters.

"Where is the toxin?" Rhix asked me.

"Secured in their cargo bay." My eyes still followed the Shontavian's departure as it disappeared into the bowels of the ship. Tanaka could strip me of my cover at any moment, and the mercs would need no excuse to turn on me. If I didn't dampen the apprehension from my own empathic broadcast, so would the Shontavian.

"I have questions for the Oligarch before I speak to Mr. Batterson. Bring the Sol Fed crew until I decide what to do with them." Rhix's voice hardened as he motioned me to follow his orders, and he strode to the ramp of the Nos ship with his personal escorts. I signaled two mercenaries to accompany me. We cleared the Sol Fed vessel of four startled officers in the upper compartment. All the while, my thoughts kept returning to what lay under my feet in the cargo hold. Time grew short. There wasn't much I could do. The guards escorted them toward the lift, but I lagged behind and waved them on.

"Take them up. I want to make sure nobody is hiding below."

Once they moved on, I took off my helmet. I dumped it on top of one of the cases and hurried to the crate holding the media bots, wrenching the door open.

"Inconceivable!" I muttered. "Somebody, please tell me you're listening."

"Buttercup." The sibilant voice over the com belonged to Ozzie. "I was about to contact you."

"I've been identified by one of the Sol Fed party. My cover is disintegrating."

Ozzie swore in five languages. "The boss is inside the Market. He can hear you. He knows where Dru is. Where are you?"

"In Rhix's private shuttle bay, cargo hold of the Sol Fed ship. I'm in armor. It's the only thing that's kept them guessing so far. Did you receive the message about their purchase?"

"We did. Silent death." A guttural vocalization followed, a uniquely Cthash way of expressing disgust. "We're working on that, too."

"I still don't know what they're planning." I seized a media bot from the rack and pressed the power switch. Blue light swelled in the lens, and the robot hovered in place. "I'm setting up two cameras. Standard broadcast frequency. Record them and don't stop monitoring. For the moment, the Sol Fed party is under house arrest, but I don't think they'll hesitate to turn me in as a bargaining chip." With the camera eye aimed toward the container holding the toxin, I pressed the scan button. Red grids enveloped the area and the white light blinked, indicating a target registered.

"Get Dru out whenever you can. She's expecting you."

"Hold tight. We're not giving up on you. Keep your implant on."

I camouflaged the media bot in one of the hanging nets. "Voice programming," I said hoarsely. The view screen lit up, waiting for a command. "Continuous video and audio broadcast and recording. Wide angle of subject."

"Acknowledged," the prim robotic voice replied. I repeated the power-up with a second bot and closed the crate.

Climbing the ladder from the cargo bay to the crew compartment with the media bot hovering over my head sucked, but I made it. The luxury vessel, probably registered to Batterson Robotics or Hyatt's hydroponics company, had twelve enclosed sleeping berths lining one side. Comfortable jump seats and worktops occupied the opposite side of the aisle. I checked each berth until I found an unused compartment midcabin and stowed the bot inside.

"Voice programming. Parabolic microphone. No video. Continuous broadcast and recording." As soon as it registered the command, I shut the door and descended the ladder hastily. I shoved the helmet back on seconds before a mercenary came up the ramp. He asked a terse question in Ursetu.

"Lord Rhix is looking for you. Why aren't you answering your com?"

"I apologize. The helmet was off so I could see the crate better. It hasn't been tampered with."

"You said you were looking for more crew."

"I did."

Suspicion played in each line of his body and emotional output. He finally waved me off the ship. "He is waiting. Move."

At the bottom of the Nos shuttle ramp, my escort in tow, I couldn't help but notice the tension level was not what I expected. In fact, Rhix and the Oligarch conversed easily, no conflict evident in the meeting.

"The misunderstanding between our clan and the Market is resolved? Are we free to trade and sell here again?"

"Yes. I now possess hard evidence to conclude the matter." A holo card lay between Rhix's gloved fingers. "Thank you for your cooperation, Oligarch."

"Will he face punishment?"

Rhix's countenance clouded against the Oligarch's eager question. "I hoped to run my enterprise differently than my predecessors. But my hand may already be forced in this."

"I will look forward to the entertainment." The Oligarch grinned unpleasantly.

Turning away, Rhix reached out with one hand and motioned me to follow him to the lift, waving off my escort. The doors shut, and I raised my visor. "The confrontation was a setup?" His devious streak blindsided me.

He grunted. "I knew Mr. Batterson was responsible for giving the Nos the location of the goods. Eminence Odrik proved eager to share the information after I parted him from his left arm. I gave them a chance to redeem themselves." His expression held a strange mix of satisfaction and regret, echoed wordlessly in my empathic nets as he regarded the slim piece of tech in his hand.

"What's on the holo card?"

"Proof of the conspiracy, they said. I believe Batterson's partners will not rise to his defense. Senator Hyatt and Mr. Tanaka appear to need him for his credits and little else."

"What's going to happen to Batterson?" A sense of dread rotated in the pit of my stomach.

"If I do not punish those who betray me, I lose control. You saw firsthand what occurs when they think me weak." A pause, and a sigh of resignation. "He will fight for his freedom in the arena."

I despised the son of a bitch, but not enough for him to get eaten alive. After what I saw in the shuttle bay, once the Shontavians fixated on something, it was hard to get them off. I couldn't imagine them in the arena with free reign to follow through on their instincts.

The hard outline of smuggled data still pressed against my palm. Sweat trickled down the back of my neck as I lowered the visor. Unless Sumner and the Brute Squad came up with a miracle, the countdown on my own appointment with the arena started fifteen minutes ago.

Thirty-One

IN THE GALLERY, the fearful Sol Fed crew and Batterson's bodyguards knelt in submission, their hands clasped on top of their heads. Captain Chydri jerked his head to the door of the conference room. Rhix swept through the portal, his pace slow and predatory. To hide the tremor in my hands, I locked them behind my back and took an at-ease stance in front of the energy window.

Surrounded by Rhix's guards, the prisoners sat in varied attitudes at the table—Batterson hyperattentive to everything, Tanaka suspiciously relaxed and inscrutable. Indignant fury vibrated the senator's body, and he leapt to his feet.

"Release us at once. I am head of the Sol Fed Senate. This is our sovereign territory, and you cannot hold us without counsel..."

"Sit down." The command rumbled through the room as Rhix dropped into the ornate chair at the table's head. Half a dozen pulse rifles were trained in Hyatt's direction until he complied. "I would enjoy hearing you attempt to explain to your authorities why you have a hold full of black market weapons and a volatile toxin, Senator. You tried to pay the Nos with the same merchandise promised to me and reneged on the bargain when they attempted to collect. This transaction could be your last."

"There was no agreement," Hyatt sneered. "You received your credits, and the price was extortionate to begin with. You lost nothing in this deal, sir."

The holo card flashed between Rhix's thumb and forefinger. "Shall we watch this together?" He slid the data into a slot on the table's surface. A recording of Batterson's head popped up to hover over the surface. Its mouth moved without sound, fast-forward. Opposite him, the talking head of the Oligarch babbled back. Translation software spelled out the conversation between them in bilingual text.

"What did you do?" Acid dripped from Hyatt's voice as he turned to Jon. The Senator's outrage, forged in fear, held no hint of contrivance. On the other side of Batterson, Tanaka's hand started to cover his mouth, and he swallowed hard. Not so smug any more.

"I made a contingency plan. We never received confirmation our offer was accepted, and the Nos were willing to take those abominations off my hands as payment for the raids. They were going to sell them here. Lord Rhix would receive a share either way."

"You admit you offered them the same merchandise promised to the Market." Arms folded over his chest, Rhix scanned him with the eyes of a raptor, waiting for a misstep.

"Think carefully before you answer, Jon," Tanaka advised and passed a hand over his pallid forehead.

"He can't do anything. I'm a Sol Fed citizen."

"That means nothing here, you entitled little bastard," the politician spat. "You've worked yourself into a corner, but you are not taking us down with you."

Eyes shifting back and forth between Tanaka and Hyatt, Jon's mouth took on a twist of loathing. "Fuck you. Fuck you both. I preserved the NPM's interests!"

Rhix shook his head when neither of them spoke in his defense, just as he'd predicted. "I am afraid you stand alone, Mr. Batterson."

"You said sometimes you get paid with information. I'll tell you something important." Jon sat up straight. "You might have a spy on board."

"The same one who told the Nos where to find the merchandise, undoubtedly." An imperious wave dismissed his statement.

"No, the shipment you received was infiltrated," Jon blurted. Across the table, Tanaka narrowed his eyes and sat forward, trying to catch Jon's attention. His expression said, *Stop talking, you idiot.* Oblivious, Jon continued, "A changeling named Tamareia posed as one of the living merchandise."

"How did you discover this?" Rhix's measured voice held a warning everyone but Batterson recognized.

"My wife. Ex-wife." Batterson's lip curled. "She's the doctor who put them into suspension. Someone attached to the Remoliad tracked her down and threatened to press charges unless she put Tamareia under for the mission."

"You had knowledge the shipment was infiltrated...by the Remoliad." Frigid, controlled patience stiffened Rhix's voice. "Two days, we met in negotiation, and you did not warn me until now, Mr. Batterson?"

"Tamareia is the one who intercepted the crates on the *Bedia*." Oblivious to the chasm yawning under his feet, Batterson jabbed a finger at the holo recording. "There. That's Dalí Tamareia."

Oh. Fuck. Me.

The flickering clip of a report gleaned from one of the Sol Fed media outlets played. A small image, partly obstructed by the cables concealing the camera, of Gor and me fighting the boarding party in the *Bedia's* cargo hold. Too far away to see my features clearly, but what we did showed clear enough. *Zezjna*. Taking down pirates, one by one.

Rhix's fist clenched until his knuckles turned pale beneath his dark skin.

He recognized my movements even at the clip's accelerated speed. He knew. Too much flak from Jon, Hyatt, and Tanaka bombarding my empathic nets made it impossible to tell which particular flavor of anger-infused shock belonged to Rhix.

"You did not warn me, Mr. Batterson." Deceptively mild, Rhix repeated his accusation. Across the table, Tanaka shook his head minutely at Hyatt, whose face had gone still with apprehension. They, too, were aware I infiltrated the shipment. Tanaka held proof in his PDD. He faced more jeopardy than Jon if discovered.

Rhix stood. "Captain Chydri. Take Mr. Batterson to a cell. The others will wait on their ship under guard. No transmissions in or out. Send Simish to me."

"Sir, what about—"

"Do as I said!" Rhix's fury crackled in a lightning burst against my mind, the acrid sting of betrayal carried on a searing wave. I was screwed. Already figured as much. A strange calm settled over me.

Chydri swept his arm. The mercs moved, and Jon lurched from his seat. White showed around the irises of his eyes, nostrils flared. "I am not going anywhere until I see counsel. Under galactic statutes—"

"Your species is not protected by Remoliad statutes yet. You cannot have this both ways, Mr. Batterson. We keep our own laws in the Market. Tradition dictates your sentence, not me. The arena has been unused for some time. I regret it will be opened for you."

Batterson roared. Chairs toppled in his wake. The guards subdued him, but they had to stun him in the end, his body convulsed by the neuro shock. Hyatt and Tanaka went quietly after that.

Only Rhix and I were left in the room. To remove my helmet and meet his eyes took an act of will.

Rage and bloodlust, I could work with. I could let the violence roll off my senses like the deflection of a physical attack. Unprepared for emotional pain, the impact created an involuntary response in me. An obverse of our sexual chemistry, silent death in its own way—of hope, of trust. Something I couldn't deflect. It seeped in around the edges, through gaps left by loss in my own heart, and lay bitter against my tongue.

My sidearm detached from the thigh plate with deliberate, slow movements. I gripped it by the muzzle and placed the weapon on the table. Waited for him to speak, to attack me, demand answers. Try to kill me. But he didn't. The hum of the energy window behind me made my eardrums shiver in the silence.

Simish arrived. Rhix finally spoke, leaning on fists knotted against the table. He did not raise his head, and I had to strain to hear.

"I will deal with you later. Simish, take Gresh to the dormitory. Search it. All privileges are revoked." He stalked out of the room.

In dismay, Simish blinked, but motioned to me. A mercenary fell in behind us.

Dru was sitting on one of the lounges and jumped up when she saw me. "Gresh! Did you—" She stopped short, her eyes round with fear and surprise to see me held at the end of a rifle. The guard made a savage gesture for her to sit near me, and we were both covered in his sights as our keeper searched my room.

The bloody towel, the scalpel and refuse of my emergency surgery on Kai still rolled inside did not take long for him to find, led by the smell of antiseptic. Simish motioned for me to remove the armor under the guard's vigilant eyes. I clumsily palmed the holo card as I pulled the gloves off, but he spotted the motion. Fearful eyes searched mine; shoulders slumped when he read my resignation. I'd betrayed him, too. He said nothing, but held out his hand. I surrendered the card.

Simish and his siblings took the armor and contraband away. The sentry moved outside the door.

"Gresh?" Dru whispered through colorless lips. "What's going on?" I didn't answer. The less she knew, the better. I might have endangered her by taking her to Rhix's quarters.

I dressed with calculation and chose a tunic and pants, not Rhix's favorite shade of red, but a silvery gray. The physical adaptations I made for him disappeared in sharp complaints of tissue, bone, and muscle. They continued to ache long after, like bruises beneath the skin.

Dru still waited in the common area. She opened her mouth to speak but jumped instead as the abrupt wail of klaxons shrieked inside the seraglio and the corridor outside.

"What is it?" Dru cried, her hands over her ears.

"I don't know." I glanced up at the dome and prayed we wouldn't experience the sudden roar of decompression.

Something moved overhead in the transparent field—a small ship, less than a dozen yards above the energy window. It grew larger... Proximity alarms. The raucous noise screamed warnings of a collision.

Three tones in my skull, barely audible over the external cacophony. "This is it, Buttercup!" Ozzie's voice said triumphantly. "Sumner set off a bug that has alerts going off all over the ship. They won't know where to look first. Melos is coming in. Get away from the dome. He's going to mag lock on the hull and fry the emitter on the shield. He'll drop a harness."

"Come on! We need to move!" I pulled Dru with me, and we huddled together inside the door of my room.

Lights in the seraglio stuttered above our heads as the metallic *thunk* of a magnetic airlock connected with the ship's hull. A spitting arc of power rode the air and brought the hair on my arms to attention. Sparks showered down into the cushioned furnishings below the dome.

A cable dropped, the straps of a harness pooled at its end.

"Go!" I shoved Dru toward the gear and helped her into the loops, peering up into the tube of the magnetic lock. Melos stared down at me, his yellow hair caught in a nimbus of static around his head. He beckoned urgently for haste. "Dalí, we must hurry!" His words sounded over my implant, voice drowned out by the vibration of the small ship's engines, the bray of the klaxons.

"Hold on, Dru." The last strap tightened around her. "Take her up!"

She clutched the cable with both hands. The recoil spun Dru up into the tube. Melos hauled her aboard and stripped the harness from her body, prepared to drop the line back to me.

A warning shot from a pulse rifle burned past my thigh and eviscerated a cushion in an explosion of stuffing. A mercenary stood in the doorway, his sights trained on me. I surrendered, my hands rising.

Two more guards arrived. One swung the butt of his weapon at me. It connected with the side of my head, and I went down. My vision spiraled in and out of focus as the other soldier pointed his muzzle upwards.

"Gresh!" Dru's scream echoed down the tube, cut off abruptly when the hatch on Melos' ship banged into place. The whine of engines built up.

"Close it, or we all die!" I shouted over the howling. "I won't resist."

A guard punched his gloved fist into the emergency release. The door slammed across the overhead port. With a shudder and groan of metal, the mag lock disengaged from the hull a second behind the port's final seal. The engines of Melos' ship fired and rattled everything in the room.

Abrupt silence filled my ringing ears when the klaxons' wail ceased. The hollow, black muzzles of two pulse rifles followed me as I stood. Mercenaries shouted at me in Ursetu, a stream of liquid syllables untranslated in my head. I touched the back of my ear, hot and sticky with blood. The once smooth bump of my implant com read like jagged Braille beneath my fingertips.

Thirty-Two

HOURS PASSED AFTER Dru's rescue. I suspected the Market was thrown into chaos with the diversion Sumner unleashed. A single guard, augmented by two of Simish's less chatty siblings, held me at gunpoint even in the lavatory. His eager animosity spiked against my senses each time I moved. He only needed a reason to shoot me. I kept my activity to a minimum and stayed in the common area. My eyes closed, I remembered the tang of Zereid's atmosphere, the softness of rain on my upturned face. The attempt at meditation failed to win much peace.

"Lord Rhix requests you join him in the training room." Simish's voice, a bleak whisper, let me know my time was up.

The sharp talons of my companion's fear sent a shiver through empathic nets already spread to catch a hint of what lay ahead.

"I'm sorry, Simish." My voice was pitched for his ears alone. He gazed up at me, huge eyes swimming, and didn't say anything but raised his hand and gripped my arm as he led me down the corridor. To the guards it gave the appearance he ensured I did not try to run. The difference was in the touch; gentle, and meant to comfort. His fear was for me.

The door slid open to reveal Rhix inside, his back to us, armor discarded on the floor. He wore only the snug garment beneath. A sword gleamed in his hand—the same one with which I'd killed his mutinous rival.

"Leave us," he snapped without turning around. The guards obeyed immediately. Simish gave one last squeeze on my arm before he fled. The port closed behind them with finality. I waited.

"Your full name."

"Dalí Tamareia."

His head went up at the sound of my natural voice. "You truly are named for a demon, then."

"No. Salvador Dalí was an artist—a painter. My mother is an admirer of his work."

"What did he paint?"

"He was celebrated for an art form called surrealism."

"I do not recognize this term. Define it."

"A blurring of the line between dreams and reality."

His breath went out in a soft *hah*, as if he laughed at a private joke. "We never sparred with swords. Do you know how to handle a blade of this size?"

"No. I've only ever seen sword fighting in holo vids."

"Then perhaps it is time you learned." He turned and tossed the weapon to me. I managed to catch the hilt and avoid severing my fingers. Rhix took another from the wall. "It is a different strategy. Still close enough to be personal, but far enough away for one to remain detached from the fight."

Methodical and completely in control of himself, Rhix's calm unnerved me more than any other reaction I'd anticipated.

"These are the strikes." Without advancing, he telegraphed them for me. "The blocks." Again, he ran through them in half time. "Show me."

I mirrored them with my own weapon.

"Mr. Batterson will not return to Sol Fed. The penalty for oathbreakers and those who betray me is the same. The Shontavians will be pleased." He raised his blade. "Attack."

Cold sweat began to bead on my forehead, but I advanced. He blocked my offensive easily, still too calm, as if he'd reached the eye of a hurricane. The other side of the storm I'd only glimpsed before still seethed behind his veneer of control.

"You are overreaching. Step in."

I did and changed the order of my strikes. Rhix made a sound of approval.

"Good. Now, defend." He advanced. His blade whistled toward my head. I parried clumsily but deflected the blow, barely able to bring the edge around to block the next. Listening underneath to sense where he might strike gave me no advantage, too inexperienced, and Rhix a master. The point of his sword sliced a burning arc across my chest. Cloth parted with a hiss. A line of blood trembled against my skin.

Rhix paced around me. I wondered what he waited for and tried to keep his weapon in my sight. "What about Tanaka and Hyatt? Do they get to go home with their new toys?"

His mouth set in a grim mien. "They are still in my custody and retain all their limbs for now."

I managed to delay their departure, at least. I hoped it gave the team time to warn somebody in Sol Fed.

A shift of stance alerted me to his attack. The clash shuddered through my bones as I parried his strike—too late. Metal bit into my left shoulder. A growl of pain escaped, and I pressed my retaliation with fatalistic certainty this would be my last advance. Swords crossed and slid down to the guard on the hilt. Rhix trapped my forearm and dragged me in.

His fist crashed into my jaw and spun me face-first into the floor, the taste of blood heavy in my mouth. The blade whistled toward my head as I flipped over. I frantically batted it aside with mine. His outstretched arm provided a point I could grab, and I pulled him off balance, planted my foot in his midsection to throw him over onto his side.

He hit the mat with a resounding smack. We both came back to our feet minus the blades. My first attack landed a fist squarely in his teeth. There was no return after that. Rhix came at me with a berserker's rage. Blood and sweat obscured my vision. My *zezjna* skills and senses wouldn't be enough. I had nowhere to go.

The air went out of my lungs as he brought me down to the mat. His hands closed around my throat, thumbs in my windpipe. Sight began to dim. My fingers scrabbled against the slick material on his forearms. His eyes bored into mine, but just as muscles began to fail my command and that soft gray veil thickened to black, he released me and rolled to the side with a roar of frustration.

Air rushed back into my lungs with a spasmodic gasp. Fire burned in my trachea, and I drew in deep gasps, racked with coughing.

"I should break your neck." Rhix's voice rasped in weak defeat. His emotions assaulted my empathic nets with far more bitterness than fury. "I thought perhaps you were my friend. Now I find you are no better than the whores who plotted to kill me in my sleep. What were you to accomplish here?"

He waited until I could answer. It took effort and fucking hurt to speak. "I infiltrated the shipment to find out where the changelings were being sold and learn who's behind it. Rescue them if I could."

"How did you communicate with them? Are there more on board my ship?"

"No. I had a tracker, and a short-range implant. I cut out the tracker and gave it to Kai last night."

"Do you spy for your government? Were you to prevent this arms transaction?"

"Didn't know about that until yesterday." A convulsive swallow brought tears of pain to my eyes. "I resigned my commission months ago as an expatriate. I don't work for Sol Fed."

"For the Remoliad?"

"No."

"You will not tell me to whom you would report?"

I shook my head in a negative motion. Ow.

"That was not your only mission here. Why did you steal transaction records?"

"Personal reasons. I wanted to find out who bought Batterson's media bots from the Market and shipped them back to Sol Fed. They were used in the explosion that killed my family." Blood stung in my eyes.

Rhix grunted. "A mission of vengeance. Perhaps your mother named you well. You complicated my position, Dalí." I couldn't tell if he spoke my real name, or called me demon. "The holo card found in your possession contained sensitive information. Your accomplice stole Dru from the Market. My mercenaries are demanding your execution. The unrest will begin again if they think me lenient."

"Then punish me in a way they can't ignore. Let it serve as a warning."

"Still negotiating in my favor, even to the end." Rhix laughed hollowly. "It will leave an impression." He spat blood on the floor. "I cannot kill you. I believe the goddess will never allow me to walk with her in the next world if I did. Answer this question with truth, if there is any honor in you." His lips thinned. "Did I—did our transactions—mean nothing to you? Was it a calculated use of my weakness?"

"It was my own weakness."

"Explain."

"I wanted you." My breath caught as I said it. Those bronze eyes darted to mine.

"Then we are both foolish." His expression seemed to soften for a moment. "I cannot see any way to spare you the arena, but I will give you a chance to save yourself."

I pulled up into a sitting position and listened.

"You and Batterson will be mid-Market entertainment. The fight begins hand to hand but progresses to a weapon of my choice. The winner faces Ouros for their freedom."

My eyes shut in defeat for a moment. When I opened them, Rhix watched me.

"I saw you with the Shontavians. There is a kinship there I do not understand. I do not think Ouros will kill you. I will declare you the victor if that happens."

This was giving me a chance to survive and appease his goddess? It was a long shot. "Thank you."

"You can defeat Batterson. He is a coward."

I didn't know if I could take a life again. I didn't need Jon dying in my head. Some things just don't wash out.

Rhix climbed to his feet. "This taught me a valuable lesson, Gresh." He paused. "Dalí. I will no longer blur the line between dreams and reality. I can trust no one."

"I hurt you. I'm sorry." Even though my body shrieked I should just stay down, I rose to face him. "But you're wrong. The most loyal friend you could wish for is Simish. There's no duplicity in him."

"Simish is not the kind of companion I had begun to hope you could be."

I didn't want to feel that die in my head, either.

"There is one last thing. You cannot walk out of this room, or my mercenaries will see I am being lenient. Simish will make certain you're ready for the arena."

I looked up to see his fist traveling at light speed, then stars in the blackness of space. My final thought as I hit the floor was that Ouros would like the view.

Thirty-Three

MY CELL BUTTED up to Batterson's. I listened to him shout about his rights as a Sol Fed citizen and how his father would make them pay; blah, blah, blah. A semipermanent headache and a permanent state of pissed off helped me maintain a high level of hormonal activity. If he kept this up, I might not have any trouble killing him after all.

The brig, a much warmer environment than the Nos ship's metal cell, still proved a far cry from the comforts of the seraglio. Driven by my restless nature, I employed a routine of calisthenics to keep my muscles from losing strength in the cramped environment. On my most bulked-up days, I can only be called wiry—my sexless physique just doesn't have that kind of anatomy. My training with Rhix earned a lean, hard tone, and I would need all of it against Batterson's chemically enhanced frame.

Twice a day, a period delineated by an automatic plunge into darkness, Simish came in with armed escort and wordlessly treated my injuries with his unguents and salves. I didn't complicate his position by speaking to him, but his sadness and worry flitted across my mind and answered what I wanted to know. He injected boneset into the jaw Rhix's parting blow refractured, but several teeth still wiggled against my probing tongue. The thick, liquid supplements dispensed each day didn't require any chewing.

Simish offered painkillers, but I declined. I didn't know when they'd come for us and didn't want to be impaired.

On the fourth day, the cell opened to reveal Captain Chydri and three other guards, visored and faceless, rifles held ready. My hands were restrained in a set of cuffs. Chydri barked something in Ursetu and the motion of his sidearm told me I should follow. Down the corridor, Batterson hunched sullenly between another trio of guards.

The roar of voices assaulted my ears as we went through the blast doors. The Market bay overflowed with beings from all over the galaxy—

I even caught a glimpse of a patchy, scarred, blue Zereid as she leaned over a rail to watch us. The bay's central shaft teemed with spectators who jeered and shouted as Batterson and I got paraded through the lowest level to an open lift.

Jon sneered at me from his place between the guards. Sweat dotted his forehead. "I hear I get to kill you again, freak." He leaned forward. "I'm coming for you."

"That's what Tella Sharp said." I favored him with a thin smile. "And your brother."

A really dick thing to say, but worth the price. His lunge for me almost earned a couple of the mercenaries a tumble off the lift before they forced us to our knees. Bellows of approval from the watching mass of pirates and smugglers rose in crescendo at the high tension between us. The lift lurched down into position on the midlevel and they yanked us up. More troops formed a ring around us as we marched down the crowded catwalk to part of the ship I hadn't been in before.

The multi-species throng streamed in behind us, pushed and shoved their way into the tiered stands of a circular arena. Booths at the back of each quadrant took bets. The odds had to be heavily in favor of Batterson once the crowd laid eyes on us.

My guards pulled me to one side. Jon Batterson's went to the opposite sector. Harsh, blinding lights shone on a metal floor stained and scarred with the marks of previous contests. A humming energy cage separated the spectators from the combatants. The door through which we'd come ranked the only gap wider than a few centimeters. On the outer circumference, a heavy, reinforced door at the end of a caged tunnel remained closed.

One of the mercs fumbled at the release of my cuffs and raised his visor impatiently to get a better view. Chydri hissed an order, something in Nos. The merc replied in the same language.

The voice. I knew it, and my head came up. Ocean-colored eyes stared at me as the restraints parted.

"They're out," Sumner muttered in Sol Standard.

They're out. He meant Dru and Kai. His gaze fixed on mine for a split second.

Damned null. I couldn't sense what else he might be trying to tell me with the glance. He lowered the visor, but not before I read the grim sorrow in his eyes, the helpless anger in his face.

I gave him a shrug as I rubbed my wrists. *I understand.* No rescue this time. So, this was it, then—a glorious end to my very first undercover mission. It was up to me.

I was probably fucked.

The guards exited the combat area. Shouts rose to a fevered pitch as the energy cage thrummed into full power and cut off any escape. If Rhix attended, I couldn't see him against the shimmer of the bars and the white-hot lights.

I walked to the center of the arena under the glare. Batterson decided to meet me. He hated me, but fear rolled off him like a cold wind. Until he opened his mouth, I almost felt sorry for him.

"Ready to die, freak?"

"Your vocabulary still needs improvement." I shook my head in mock disappointment.

He rushed me, crouched low to take me down. I pivoted, my elbow in his abdomen, and threw him over. He didn't let go, his sheer momentum carrying us both to the floor, rolling me into the metal. Batterson reared back to punch. My thumb jabbed into the corner of his eye. He howled in pain, and I planted a foot in the hollow of his hip and thigh and pushed. His hold broke; I slid and rolled out of his grasp.

Blinking and cursing, Jon suckered me with the next blow. I blocked the fist headed for my jaw with a forearm, but his left drove into my stomach. I folded, all breath exiting my lungs. The arena tilted as he lifted me bodily and threw me sideways. Static snapped in the air as I arrested my slide only a foot from the sizzling energy barrier.

Something clattered to the floor not far from my head, and roars erupted. A slender, Ursetu dagger laid there, the blade twenty centimeters long and honed to a razor's edge. We'd reached the second phase of combat.

Batterson saw the weapon at the same time and threw himself over me even as I reached for it. The knife skittered out of reach of my fingers as we clawed over the pitted floor. I finally grasped the hilt and slashed desperately across his forearm.

He bellowed in rage and rolled away. Scrambling up, I flipped the blade in my hand like Rhix had taught me and took up a stance as Jon climbed to his feet. He hesitated as the bright lights glinted off the knife.

Another dagger hit the floor of the arena. Batterson grinned at me through bloody teeth and picked it up.

The only way I stood a chance was to keep inside and control his blade arm. I narrowly avoided a sweeping slash to the midsection, forced his arm up, and whipped a shallow cut across Jon's torso. He staggered back in surprise. The spectators bayed.

He didn't stay surprised for long. Jon's blade raked across my bicep in our next pass and sliced it open. Pain forced its way out in salt tears that mingled with my sweat in stinging vision. I blinked to clear my eyes. Batterson played the crowd as if he were back home in a tournament game, sweeping his bloody blade in front of him as the screams rose. His arrogant confidence returned, making him sloppy and easy to read with my empathic senses.

With his next wild thrust, I swept his blade arm to the side, trapped it between my arm and body, and pulled him off balance. I struck him in the throat with a fist still wrapped around the hilt of my dagger. As he choked, I hooked my leg around his knee and rode him down. We hit the floor together, and the knife fell from his hand on impact.

I dropped my blade and punched him until my knuckles dripped blood, my vision dimmed by rage, each blow for Rasida, Gresh, and every other soul who died in the terminal because of the weapons his company created. For each changeling he ripped from their home. When my breath grew too ragged to continue, I grabbed the dagger. The razor's edge kissed the pulse in his neck.

One quick stroke, and it would be over. Shrieks of encouragement in a dozen languages washed over me, urging me to finish the job. Jon stared up at me, a bizarre mixture of hope and defiance in his bloody eyes, his torn and swollen mouth a sneer. He wanted me to kill him.

I dug my knee into his diaphragm instead. He doubled up in a convulsion of pain as I stood and kicked his knife away, arcs of fire and electricity spitting as it collided with the energy barrier. The crowd made a collective noise of dissatisfaction.

BOOM.

On the opposite side of the arena, the metal door shuddered with the force of a large and insistent creature demanding entrance. The grilled viewport darkened as something moved behind it. Silence fell as the sound echoed, and then wild, hoarse cheers erupted in anticipation of the finale, a cacophony from the throats of multiple species. The hair on the back of my neck prickled in the wave of bloodlust breaking against my mind.

Jon lurched upright. "What are you waiting for?" He screamed and paced the circle as far from the door as he could get. "Kill me, you cockless freak!"

"I don't want to kill you."

BOOM. The door buckled.

The crowd leaped to its feet in rising frenzy. Batterson's agitation climbed, the slick, ammonia-laden scent of fear sharp in my nose and ripping my senses. His worst nightmare was about to come to fruition. "Do it!" His eyes bulged. Blood and saliva flew from his lips. It would have been a mercy killing at this point, but the crowd's eager hysteria bombarded my mind. Their anticipation, fear, and excitement muddled my thought processes.

The door slid partway open and stuck fast with a metallic shriek as the warped port tried to recede into its slot. Four enormous hands curled around the edge of the door and ripped it out of its housing. Ouros lurched through the caged tunnel with eyes fixed on Batterson, mouth open to filter the scent of blood and terror through jagged teeth. It glanced at me only once. The mind-nudge it gave me served blunt trauma to my empathic nets, a warning to stay away. Getting between the Shontavian and its prey was an imbecilic move, but Jon's panic in my head told me I would experience every moment of his death with him. I couldn't just let Ouros have him.

Shit. Self-preservation or guilt, it made me do the stupid again.

I stepped between them and faced Ouros down. Every ounce of psychic energy I had—granted, not much—went into a mental push. *I forbid you to do this.* The creature hesitated for less than a second before blasting me with a numbing telepathic flood of desperation. Its gnawing hunger, never satisfied; the drive for violent feeding in the absence of the specific purpose for which it was created—battle. The monotony of gray metal bays and corridors of the ship without end. Boredom. The arena granted its only mechanism of release.

It tried to make me understand. So help me, I almost did.

The second Shontavian unexpectedly barreled through the door. Pandemonium erupted in screams of excitement. A few mercenaries lingered in the doorway. The bastards were going to make sure I didn't make it out of here alive.

Unlike Ouros, its silent counterpart held no restraint. Batterson ran like a trapped rat in the cage until it picked him up. He screamed in its face, daring it to kill him, and pounded it with his fists.

It ripped Jon's arm off with its teeth. Batterson's shrieks rose to a skin crawling pitch and drowned in the cheers of excitement. His agony and gibbering terror blinded me and turned my insides to water. Ouros pushed me into the floor in its haste to join the feast.

Oh god. Oh god. Ouros still held my mind in its telepathic grip. I didn't just experience Jon's terror as he died, but the Shontavians' pleasure at the saltiness of blood, the slide of entrails down my—their—gullets. Every last, bite, chew and swallow.

Thankfully, Batterson didn't live long. His torment ended abruptly and hurtled into darkness with the snap of his cervical spine. Still long enough to reduce me to a vomiting, quivering mess on the metal floor, curled into a fetal position with my hands clutched in horror to the sides of my head. The crowd's roar became far away and soft. Shock took me down a tunnel never entirely black, but splattered in crimson and echoing with the crunch of bone, copper sharp at the back of my throat.

When Ouros loomed over me and blocked out the retina-searing lights, I was too far gone to care. Death would bring an end. I closed my eyes and waited to be torn apart.

Instead, it cradled me like a child in those four massive arms, its hands still wet with Batterson's body fluids. The mob's noisy exhortations went high-pitched with disbelief, echoed in the ringing of my own ears as Ouros carried me back through the ripped door. It crooned to me in the rumble of an earthquake, its mind touched mine with soothing, gentle reassurance. Bits of Jon Batterson were still caught in its teeth.

My brain gave up trying to understand.

SHIVERS RACKED MY body as I opened my eyes on the floor of a cramped metal capsule. Disoriented panic buzzed through me, certain I lay naked and cold on board the Nos ship. A gentle nudge against my mind brought me back to sharp focus, and I raised my head.

Ouros, wearing a four-armed environment suit and the helmet of its battle armor, peered through the narrow hatchway at me. Six empty seats lined the constricted walkway where I lay, beyond the reach of Ouros's long arms. But the Shontavian appeared uninterested in me as a meal. I was still in one piece. What I felt from it now seemed anything but violent. Its mouth sifted the air from the capsule, the jagged spikes of teeth shiny and clean again.

The objections of my battered body forced a groan from my throat as I sat up. The laceration across my bicep had been treated and covered. Still-fuzzy thought processes recognized Simish's hand in this, and in the clean clothes I wore. Red. The color made me recall Batterson's blood, a queasy memory of the taste of copper.

An old life-support pod, rimmed thick with dust, provided this refuge. Overhead racks where environment suits had once been kept lay empty, save for one. It held a suit, too high-tech and clean in this can not to be a recent addition—say, in the last few hours.

Ouros made a motion to its head. On the seats behind me, a stack of items waited. The helmet from a set of composite armor leaned among them. I slid it over my head and left the visor open.

"Master's orders," Ouros growled in Ursetu. The translation sounded a moment later in my ear. "You. Go. Not come back."

What? It took me a minute to understand. "Lord Rhix told you to do this?"

"Life for life." Behind Ouros, the second Shontavian glanced in, as placid as these creatures could ever appear, I suppose. Stomachs full, both of them broadcast happiness. "You go. We see stars."

The viewport at the front of the capsule gave out on a small airlock, not a launch tube. It wouldn't require authorization or sequencing, so this operation would go unnoticed. The Shontavians sealed their own helmets and hooked into tethers before they started to prepare the capsule's external components. I turned to Ouros and attempted to convey my gratitude for its help, though my mind-brush remained tentative after the events in the arena. It blinked at me and nudged back in farewell. The port slammed and sealed shut.

I scrambled unsteadily into the waiting environment suit. I didn't trust this battered, oxidized boat not to be leaky. The other items I stowed quickly in bins under the seats—nutrition and water packets, analgesics. With characteristic efficiency, Simish had thought of everything. The whine and pop of metal in depressurization warned me to put on the helmet and strap in. I dropped into the pilot's seat. Gloved and sealed, a cool wash of oxygen reassured me I wouldn't suffocate and die in vacuum.

Clamps disengaged with a grind and jolt. Space swallowed the viewport; the capsule and I released from the bonds of artificial gravity and propelled gently outwards by the Shontavians' immense strength. Without propulsors firing, the lifeboat spun in slow revolutions. As it turned back on the Market, I glimpsed Ouros and its counterpart, straining at the end of the tethers to see their longed-for stars.

Thirty-Four

COM FREQUENCIES OSCILLATED on the instrument panel. I set one scanner frequency to monitor continuously and tested the others one by one, avoiding Sol Fed, Nos and Ursetu traffic. At each stop, I spoke a single word and my chosen waveband into the mic.

"Inconceivable. 76084.37." A speck of dust in the cosmos, it would be damn near impossible for them to find me without my tracker or implant com.

"Inconceivable. 76084.37." Silence. The call repeated a hundred times before I took a break for food and water. The relentless cycle of transmission and monitoring each silent band for a hint of reply defined my concept of time. The beacon switch that would alert any nearby vessel to my location, I left untripped. The titanic silhouette of the Market ship and its trailing flock made regular appearances around Sedna's dark visage. I didn't want to draw the wrong attention.

Repeat. Wait. Adjust frequency and try again.

Repeat.

By the third day in an environment suit, I reeked. The antique capsule might be airtight and without leaks, but its bodily waste disposal system? Not so much. The confines of the claustrophobic lifeboat started to close in. I clawed the walls of paranoia, afraid to sleep and miss a reply, panicked the transmitter on this archaic piece of shit didn't work; sure the oxygen would run out prior to rescue. My coded distress calls went on until I was hoarse.

The Market ship made one last appearance around the curve of Sedna's cheek, turned back toward deep space and vanished from my sight. The session had ended. All other ships would soon be gone as well.

An upper band of frequencies, only scanned five hundred times, seemed worth another shot.

"Inconceivable. 76084.37."

"Inconceivable. 76084.37." My voice cracked in conjunction with my sanity.

"Incon—"

A blare and hiss of static filled the cabin. "You keep using that word," Ozzie's sibilant voice said. "I do not think it means what you think it means. Well, fuck me sideways. Why didn't you contact the Man in Black? We thought you were dead!"

Relief flooded me, and I laughed in near hysteria before replying. "Only mostly dead. Implant's broken."

"Location."

"Uncertain. I'm orbiting Sedna in a can. I have a distress signal available, but I'm afraid to draw attention here."

"Hang on. Turn your beacon on in twelve hours. We're coming to get you."

TWELVE HOURS CONSTITUTED an eternity. I needed a long session in the cleanser and as much unconsciousness as I could manage. Mental and physical exhaustion made me hallucinate points of light among the starfield moving toward my lifeboat. Half an hour before their ETA, I feared I had imagined the entire conversation with Ozzie and almost didn't turn on the beacon.

A needle-sharp prow approached in the darkness outside the viewport. Only when I stumbled over the airlock threshold into *Thunder Child's* corridor, did I start to believe it was real.

When I saw the welcoming smile on Tella Sharp's face, I snapped. It took both Ozzie and Ziggy to keep me from throttling her, inarticulate threats spilling from my lips in delirium.

"Dalí, stop!" Ozzie shouted in my ear as Tella cowered against the wall of the bay. Tommi finally took me down with a hypospray. I got all the unconscious time I wanted.

I woke up clean and tucked into a bunk in medical. Tommi heard me stirring and approached, the whispery Cthash language gentle in my ears. I shook my head. Her talon made an exaggerated motion to tap my implant. A smooth bump met my fingertip, broken edges gone.

"There you go. I replaced it while you took a nap. Still feeling homicidal, or are you ready to listen?" Tommi's words chided me good-naturedly, but she kept her distance. One eye engaged mine, and the other watched my body for signs of agitation.

A hot flush of embarrassment rose. I took in a slow breath, held it, and blew it out. "I'm sorry."

She relaxed but didn't touch me. "You dug in deep, and it will take some time to come back. I need to debrief you as soon as possible and make a record of all you remember. Stress can make those memories vanish. It might be difficult to think about now, but I can induce a hypnotic recall to keep you calm and safe if you prefer. It's important we document everything you know immediately."

In the end, I chose hypnosis. I wasn't certain I wanted to relive fresh events without a level of detachment. Tommi led me through the questions and the timeline with quiet persistence. I didn't remember crying. The evidence remained when she brought me out, uncomfortable damp in my ears and the stiffness of dried salt on my skin. Afterward, Ozzie, in command with Sumner's absence, came to visit me.

"Welcome back, Dalí." He leaned against the desk, and I raised myself slowly to a sitting position. I'd spooked them with my meltdown in the bay.

"Are Kai and Dru safe?"

"Yeah, they are. You did it, my friend."

Tension embedded for weeks unspooled with a shuddering sigh and left me lightheaded. I impatiently knuckled a fresh batch of relieved tears out of my eyes as Ozzie continued.

"We tracked Kai down not long after he left the ship, and they gave him up without much of a fight. The buyer is well-known in Remoliad circles and anxious it not get out she purchased a sex slave. He wants to see you, but I told him you need some time." Both Ozzie's eyes fixed on mine. "Stay here for twenty-four hours and decompress. Convince me you're not a danger to Dr. Sharp or anyone else, including yourself."

"Yes, sir." I swallowed. "Did I hurt her?"

"No. She's fine. I listened in on some of the recall session and understand why you reacted that way. We need to talk about a few things that happened after you went under. Turn off your implant."

Ozzie settled in more comfortably against the desk when I complied. "First, Dr. Sharp did contact Jon Batterson back in the early days of the mission. Sumner grounded her back on Zereid with the changeling you replaced while Melos tracked you. They're all doing fine, by the way. Ambassador Martinez is a good guy."

"Something happened to change your mind about her. What?"

"An attempt to remove the kidnapping victims from the Embassy and 'escort them home.' Apparently, the extended vacation on Zereid made somebody nervous. They refused to leave, and the Zereid government granted an emergency request for asylum before the goon squad showed up."

"Who?" Ozzie had to have been watching old movies again.

"Friends of Dr. Sharp's husband. Martinez evacuated the citizens and sent them somewhere safe. They didn't find them but found William Farmer and killed him. Then they came for her."

"A cleanup operation."

"Embassy security neutralized them before they could execute her. That was the end of any loyalty she had to Batterson. She confessed she'd told him about your mission. Our arrival at the Market was delayed because of all the excitement, but when we got there, obviously, there'd been trouble. We couldn't wrangle another invitation into this session. Sumner went under as a Nos merc when he learned they were hiring. Might take him a little longer to rendezvous with us. In the meantime, Dr. Sharp gave up some valuable intel about the less public business ventures of Batterson Robotics."

"Batterson's dead. Does she know?"

"Not yet. I'll break the news later."

"So, you trust her?"

Ozzie shrugged. "No. We're only bringing her home. She'll be cut loose when it's safe."

"Safe..." I jerked. "Did Tanaka and Hyatt leave with the toxin?"

"They took off with their purchases the day after the arena. Melos is following them at a discreet distance." He cocked his head. "The camera you set in the cargo bay hasn't yielded much, but audio in the cabin was a stroke of genius. Hyatt talks a lot and loudly when he's scared. We're on an intercept heading now."

"That's a huge head start. The shuttle is well into Sol Fed space by now. Can we still catch them? Is *Thunder Child* really that fast?"

"You have no idea. The boss would marry this ship if he could." After seeing Ouros's maw up close, Ozzie's openmouthed grin no longer frightened me, downright sunny in comparison. He straightened and waved at me. "I'll brief you on the plan after you wake up. Tommi will give you meds if you can't sleep."

Drowsiness struck with such paralyzing quickness, I suspected a posthypnotic suggestion. Dreams proved inescapable this time. The images didn't replay the horrors of the arena or Luna Terminal. I dreamed of Rhix, a white-hot sexual fantasy that ended with me stabbing him through the heart.

Guilt much? In the chill of the darkened med bay, I woke. It was time to move on.

I staggered into the cleanser's vibration field. Bruises complained against the pressure. Afterward, I stood in front of the mirror and examined my battered frame. New scars would soon fade, but the deeper ones in my conscience would take some time. Dark hair lay long against my shoulders and reminded me of the role I played for the last two months. It had to go.

Clippers borrowed from Tommi buzzed the sides close to my head. The top I kept long, but pulled back, and asked my crewmate to cut a hand's width off the end of the ponytail. New look.

New life.

A uniform waited for me. I dressed and we left the medical bay. On the command deck, the Andari stayed busy at holoscreens, and Ziggy pored intently over an astronomical chart of the solar system. All the crew wore the same gray fatigues I did as they went about their duties.

"Dalí." Ra'sho greeted me. "Welcome back. I crosschecked the data you downloaded to us. The anonymous accounts used for the arms transaction traced back to two corporations." A flick of her hand produced a holographic document from the sensor on her glove. "Batterson Robotics and Mars Hydroponics."

No surprises there, but I read the report with grim satisfaction. "Thank you. Is a dump compiled for the authorities?"

"Ka'pth is working on adding the human trafficking evidence now. We'll deliver it on an anonymous channel. It was too far out of range to record when we turned back, but there is enough audio to charge them with the purchase and transport of illegal weapons. The conversation, however, leads me to believe they plan on disrupting the Remoliad membership treaty presentation." Ra'sho skimmed her fingers over the heads-up display and enlarged a voice pattern bite.

"...*Can't be allowed to come to a public vote*," Hyatt's voice said. "*He's too weak to resist the progressives alone.*"

"We won't make the session now. It's a lost cause." That was Tanaka. *"However...if our operation were scheduled on a specific date, I'm certain President Batterson and his chosen few could ensure they won't be in attendance. But there are times he couldn't justify his absence, though members of the Senate would be free to boycott the proceedings. The hearing for ratification of the Remoliad treaty terms, for instance. Highly covered by the media. The chamber would be full of those who support galactic interference, and the President himself."*

Hyatt's laugh chilled me. *"The same idea crossed my mind. It moves our timetable up considerably. I should thank Lord Rhix for getting rid of Jon. With him out of the operation, there's only one Batterson left to eliminate."*

"Are you ready to take on such responsibility?"

"I'll do what I must to keep Sol Fed an independent system."

"I bet you will," I muttered. My lip curled in revulsion. "This is more than we thought."

"What is it?" Ra'sho eyed me.

My mother and everyone else in the chamber during the Remoliad membership treaty hearing would be killed. With President Batterson assassinated, Hyatt, the Head of the Senate, stood next in line to become president.

"They aren't planning a disruption. It's a coup."

Thirty-Five

"GRESH?" KAI'S UNCERTAIN voice came from behind me. To see him standing on the deck with a face-cracking smile hit me harder than expected, and my eyes clouded. He embraced me at length, arms tight around my shoulders, his gratitude spilling over into tears. Both of us staggered as Dru launched herself at me in a stealth attack, and I was sandwiched between them. We clumped together, bound by the horrors we'd shared early in our captivity, but no longer trapped by them.

"What happened after I got out?" Dru wiped her eyes when they allowed me to breathe at last, and I shook my head.

"You don't want to know."

"You look different." Kai tugged on the short queue at the back of my head. "I guess your name's really Dalí, right? It might take me a while to remember."

"Yeah, it is. You doing okay?"

"I am. I don't think I can ever repay you." Dressed in plain coveralls, he seemed more at ease than he ever had in nanosilks at the Market. "The captain said we can't stay up here long, but I just wanted to see you and say—" Kai waved in helpless emotion. His eyes grew shiny again, and his voice rough. "Thanks."

"Me too." Dru's shoulder twitched in a half shrug. "I'm still not sure I want to go back to Mars, but Captain Ozzie says he can take me to Zereid with Akia and the others if that's what I want. I have a choice. Thank you, Gresh—Dalí."

"You're welcome." Too much still bubbled below the surface of my mind to put the mission to rest, but Dru's happiness soothed me, and Kai's joy glowed like bright sunlight against my empathic nets, warm and comfortable. Enviable.

"Attention, crew. Some unanticipated action is coming our way." Ozzie's voice came urgently across my implant. "Dalí, Zig, will you join me in the cockpit? Everybody prepare for a quick sublight transition. Five minutes."

"On my way." I turned back to my friends. "Go strap in. We'll talk later."

"Yeah. We usually hang out in the mess area with Dr. Sharp. She plays a mean game of chess." He gestured behind him. Across the command deck I exchanged a single glance with Tella, her outsider status proclaimed by civilian clothes. Fiddling with her earpiece, she looked away first.

Huh. It was doubtful she had come clean about her role in their kidnappings, but I refused to destroy Kai's mood. He was too happy to be here.

A blank viewport, still covered by metal shielding, hung in front of me when I ducked into the cockpit. Ozzie motioned for me to sit in the copilot's seat. Ziggy followed and slid into position at the weapons console behind their brother. With the five-point harness snugged tight over my chest, I donned the headset the pilot gave me.

"Melos contacted us—a Nos frigate intercepted the Sol Fed ship in the disputed trade corridor. Seems like maybe they know what they're carrying. Even with pirates up their ass, those guys still aren't yelling for help. They definitely don't want the authorities to learn what they're up to."

"They're close to Enceladus. The fleet's got a reading on the frigate by now. What about us? Do we have permission to be in Sol Fed sovereign space?"

"Not exactly. We didn't check in at Neptune Station, and we aren't broadcasting any ID. But the Nos will pick them clean before the fleet arrives. They'd probably like to see a friendly human face about now. Too bad it will be yours." Ozzie's wry mischief danced across my senses. "Up to another rescue mission?"

"Hell, yes. They won't expect me." This would be fun.

The effects of rapid deceleration took my breath away, my weight straining against the harness as the blockade runner transitioned from EM drive. Metal shields across the viewport retracted into *Thunder Child's* hull to reveal Saturn off the port bow, a tawny jewel wrapped in ribbons of silver. Ahead of us, Tanaka and Hyatt's shuttle raced toward the inner Colonies. A blocky frigate loomed in relentless, patient pursuit, a proverbial bigger fish closing in on its prey. The smaller ship's flight path zigzagged in futile evasion. The Nos maneuvered in behind the other craft and fired. A searing beam of cadmium light notched the Sol

Fed vessel's topside thruster and turned it to slag. The ship began to falter as its engines struggled.

Ziggy shifted in the seat. "Weapons online. Do you want to give them a warning?"

Ozzie gripped the yoke in front of him, and *Thunder Child* swept in a curving dive toward the frigate. "No, let's just get to the point."

"I hoped you'd say that." Ziggy turned back to the console. The deep thud of an energy cannon vibrated my internal organs. Dazzling beams sketched argent lines against the void of space. Metal smoldered in brief, angry red wounds on the hull of the hostile craft as it shuddered away from its trajectory and banked sharply, coming around to return fire. Rays of yellow plasma blazed in front of us.

"Now that I have your attention..." Ozzie muttered. He keyed his mic and spoke in Nos. "Conglomerate vessel, I suggest you set a course out of this system immediately before the fleet arrives."

"This is our trade corridor." The furious translation carried its own heat. "We claim rights predating Sol Fed and its arrogance."

"They're coming around again," Ziggy announced.

"Time to show them we're serious." Saturn's rings blurred in my vision as Ozzie put *Thunder Child* into a steep, upward arc. Below us, the Nos ship completed its ponderous turn. *Thunder Child* screamed down and curled into a raptorial position behind the frigate. "Target their weapons system."

"Torpedo away!"

The frigate's ventral cannon fused violently into a lump of tangled metal.

"Outstanding, sibling." Ozzie keyed his mic again. "I repeat, Conglomerate vessel, leave this system, or we will disable your engines. You can deal with the fleet on your own, without a cannon or propulsion systems."

The answering snarl from the Nos was untranslated by my implant, but the pilot laughed. "Yes, my mother *is* a lizard. No need to be obscene."

"Picking up some chatter. Military vessels will arrive in about five minutes, and they aren't happy." Tommi's warning rang over the headset.

"Guess my new friend decided not to risk it." Ozzie waggled his talons at the Nos vessel as it pivoted toward open space and fired its engines.

"We don't want to stick around and wait for them either, until we receive proper clearance," Ziggy suggested.

The crippled shuttle still limped on its arrow-straight course toward the Colonies, and I had a bad feeling Hyatt and Tanaka could still talk their way out of this. "How close can we cut it?"

"Right up to the time they drop out of EM drive." Ozzie's eyes rotated between instrument panels. "What do you have in mind?"

I adjusted the mic of my headset. "Ka'pth, is the evidence file ready to transmit?"

"It is prepared."

"Send it to the approaching vessels. Give them warning the shuttle is carrying explosives, arms, and chemical weapons. They can't have the option to refuse boarding."

The com rustled again. "This is Sol Fed 626. Thank you for your assistance." The voice of the pilot, breathless and relieved, carried a grateful note I didn't need empathic senses to interpret. "Who are you? Are you Remoliad?"

At Ozzie's invitation, I answered the call. "Negative, 626, we are a private vessel. Happy to help, but we prefer not to identify. Tell Senator Hyatt and Mr. Tanaka they're welcome."

Another voice took over the com, Hyatt's smooth, suspicious tones easy to identify. "Who is this?"

"No one of consequence." I couldn't resist. Behind me, Ziggy and Ozzie hissed with laughter.

"I demand you tell me."

Oh, this was too good. Hyatt was feeding me all the straight lines. "I am the Dread Pirate Roberts."

Another voice took over. "Are you finished mocking us, Ambassador Tamareia?"

"I think you mistake me for another, Mr. Tanaka."

"What do you want?"

"Your cooperation. The authorities are on their way. Just be polite and do what they tell you."

Static crackled in protracted silence.

"I've been watching you a long time. Back as far as your university days when you and Andrew Gresham began working toward third-gender rights." Tanaka's voice was quiet, meditative. "I found efficiency in recognizing one's potential enemies early in their careers. You were marked for brilliant futures, you and Gresham—your wife as well. Such a shame, the explosion in the terminal, but it saved us the trouble of dealing with them later. The Remoliad knew all about the danger, but they didn't make an effort to save those people."

The air evaporated in my lungs. "What are you talking about?"

"The terrorist who set them didn't realize the scanners on the enhanced technology still shared a frequency with every other media bot in the terminal. The signals were linked. You and your family held priority facial recognitions that day for the networks. The Remoliad knew the bombs were there."

The familiar, numb feeling began to creep over me and blanketed my better sense in the fallout of rage. Sumner told me he tracked the shipment to Luna Terminal. Next to me, Ozzie shook his head vehemently in negation.

"You are a liar." I managed.

"Oh, they would never admit they missed a known galactic terrorist in plain sight...or they chose to overlook one of their own. Too many of the citizens the Remoliad wants under its thumb perished because of their inaction. Bad form, you must agree. Ah." He paused. "You saved me the trouble of activating a few of the bots. Well, this will be quick."

"No. No!" My voice escalated.

"What's going on?" Ozzie hissed.

High volume and strident, Hyatt's voice demanded, "Tanaka, what are you doing?"

"The survival of the movement is everything, Edward. We'll be martyrs to the cause, you and I."

"Are you insane? Give me that!" The sounds of struggle came over the com. "Help me!" Hyatt shouted. "He's trying to blow up the ship!"

"Oh, no you don't!" Ozzie bellowed. "Tommi, jam all standard frequencies on—"

An explosion enveloped the craft, the white heart of a small sun. Another followed in rapid succession. The wake bludgeoned *Thunder Child* with savage fists and debris before Ozzie throttled up and away with urgent speed. Shields slammed across the viewport as we gained velocity.

"Did the evidence file transmit to the authorities?" In the sober quiet of the cockpit, my words echoed dully in my own ears.

"Yes. Anonymous channel," Tommi confirmed. "The ships are dropping out of EM now."

"Did they see us?" Ziggy asked softly.

"Negative. Chatter is still focused around a Nos frigate."

"All right. Setting a course for Neptune Station to make our presence legal. We'll wait there for Melos and Sumner to catch up." He said nothing for a moment as he tapped in coordinates and then turned to me, as earnest as a Cthash could manage without lips. "Dalí, I know you have questions about what you just heard."

"You think?" Caught between anger, betrayal, and a thick edge of disappointment, my careful sarcasm spat all three.

"The truth isn't what he insinuated, I swear to you. I don't have clearance to share any details. When Sumner gets back, I'll make sure he tells you everything."

OUT OF EMBARRASSMENT for my behavior in the bay as much as my distrust, I avoided Tella after we docked at Neptune Station. We didn't speak until the day she left when I literally ran into her at the top of the narrow stairs leading to crew quarters. I retrieved the bag our collision sent tumbling back below decks, and we stood for a long moment in uncomfortable limbo. Words failed me. I couldn't decide whether to apologize for attacking her, bid her farewell, or tell her not to let the door hit her on her way out.

"Dalí, can we please talk? Just for a few minutes?" she blurted at last.

I jerked my head toward my quarters. Tella perched on the jump seat, hands twisted in her lap, and I sat in the bunk.

"Nothing I can say will change what I did."

"No. It can't."

"When Jon's friends came to kill Bill Farmer and me, I realized just how insignificant I was to him."

"As insignificant as the changelings you put in stasis."

She flinched. "I deserved that. One day, I hope you can forgive me."

She'd gained my trust and used it against me. I'd earned Rhix's and manipulated him to my own ends. The only thing separating my actions from Tella's were our goals. I met her eyes.

"I am sorry for what I did in the bay." I meant it.

"After what happened, I understand." Her lip quivered. "Jon. Did he...was it quick?"

"No. It wasn't."

"Damn you." She swiped at her eyes. Angry tears sparkled on her face. "Can't you feel anything for me at all?"

I couldn't give her the absolution she wanted. Not yet, anyway.

She stood and walked out. "Don't let this work make you heartless, Dalí. Not after everything you've been through."

"Goodbye, Tella." For a long time, I thought about what she said, and her uncanny insight into my psyche.

It was something I worried about, myself.

Thirty-Six

MY INSOMNIA IMPROVED over the next few weeks, but there were still plenty of nights I needed distraction. I instructed Ziggy in *zezjna* fundamentals and showed Melos the Ursetu knife-fighting style Rhix taught me. After a couple of endless, stupid movie marathons with Tommi and Ozzie, I started to learn how to laugh again. Nothing in the galaxy is funnier than a lizard with the giggles.

Some nights I just wanted solitude.

Like every space station, Neptune was a hollow cathedral of transparent alloy and steel. Spates of travelers from outbound vessels and inbound cargo ships paced the corridors in search of diversion. Three places served synthetic alcohol. The two on the arrival decks gleamed bright and spotless, crowded with travelers. The one on the second level held a vaporous, sticky ambiance, a collection of a dozen scarred tables and fewer customers. It boasted a synthetic bartender, too, slinging drinks like a pro. The robot didn't resemble a media bot in the least, but I still didn't like it. The stuff dispensed out of the barrel-shaped chassis was not bad, though. I practiced alcohol-enhanced invisibility, while we waited for Sumner to rendezvous and watched the news feeds.

Furor over the destruction of an intersystem shuttle registered to the Batterson empire was short-lived. Not much remained of the craft, but in the end, enough debris was left to show the explosion came from inside its own hull. The toxin scattered, harmless and inert in an airless void.

The evidence file detailing the company's involvement in the manufacture and sale of illegal weapons—including those used in the Luna Terminal bombing—reached ears other than those of the fleet. Discretion had not been observed in our broadcast. Kiran Singh chose to release his exclusive expose of the human trafficking operation once the other details came to light.

No evidence existed the president had any knowledge of what Jon Batterson, Senator Edward Hyatt, and Edo Tanaka, all presumed to be on board the ill-fated shuttle, conspired to do. But President Batterson's position was severely compromised. Politicians scrambled away from the NPM, leaving him a small man facing the consequences alone.

Third-gender rights still had a long way to go. No doubt Akia Parker and Singh would use the new goodwill of a sympathetic public and introduce movements to repeal the restrictive laws against us.

It was such a media circus, it almost eclipsed the coverage of the Remoliad treaty hearing. The diplomatic team, headed by Marina Urquhart, triumphantly presented the terms for ratification. It filled me with a strange, bittersweet feeling. In a different lifetime, it would have been me standing at the podium. Where my father sat in the audience and watched her with pride, Gresh and Sida might have watched me. The brief sadness didn't diminish my admiration for her in the least— this formidable, history-making Ambassador was my mother.

The terms were overwhelmingly approved for referendum. Citizens registered consent or dissent within forty-eight hours of the hearing.

It passed with a majority of sixty-five percent. After the results came through, I contacted Mom from one of the public subspace booths on Neptune Station.

"Dalí!"

"Congratulations, Ambassador Urquhart. How does it feel to be an official member of the alliance?"

"Exhausting. I told you, I'm too old for this shit. Where are you?"

"Edge of the system. I'm heading back out in a few days."

"You're in the Fed? Why didn't you call sooner?"

"Busy with work."

"Uh-huh." Her eyes studied me in shrewd Mom calculation. "Kiran Singh asked me if I knew where you were. He's got a wild idea you were involved in the rescue of those human-trafficking victims from the Shontavian Market." Her voice was too light, too innocent.

"Kiran has delusions."

"I take it you won't be visiting on this trip?"

"Not this time. I suspect you might be appointed to the Remoliad in some permanent capacity, though."

"Rumor has it. If it happens, Paul is going to retire and join me there."

"No way." My eyes widened. Dad, retired?

"I do get to choose my own staff. I'll find something for him to do. Maybe cook."

"Dad's cooking is worse than Gresh's was."

"I heard that." My father's voice rang from offscreen, and he leaned in. "It's good to see your face, Dalí."

"Yours, too." Glances passed between them, easy to read, so I offered the information. "I'm doing all right. Don't worry. I'll be in touch as often as I can."

"There's still a place for you in the Diplomatic Corps. Like I said, I get to choose my own staff." A wistful curve to Mom's lips caused me a pang of momentary regret.

"Not yet. There are still things I need to do." The sweep of the one-minute limit on my transmission dwindled. "I love you both."

The call timed out before she or Dad said anything more. My own face reflected in the blank, dark screen. I did have other plans. Sticky, booze-filled ones, for now.

I SPENT ENOUGH time in the gloomy bar in the small hours of night people started to think I was "working." I got propositioned more than once. That kind of contact was the last thing I wanted at the moment.

Yeah. Inconceivable.

Another shadow blotted out the glare from the holo screen on my battered tabletop. I sighed and didn't even look up.

"I'm not interested."

"So I take it flirting is out of the question?"

Surprised, I glanced up. Rion Sumner grinned at me.

"I'm not drunk enough yet." I motioned for him to take the seat across and signaled the robotic bartender. "I believe I'm supposed to buy the first round."

"Ozzie said I could find you here." He took in the bar with a glance. "Interesting place."

"It isn't fancy, but it's...a dive."

"I've been in much worse." The robot wheezed up to the table and pissed out a weak stream of whiskey into a flimsy recyclable cup. "Classy." Sumner raised his drink as the 'bot creaked away. "Here's to making it back in one piece."

I could toast to that. We sat in silence for a few minutes.

"How did you get out of the Market so quickly?" I finally asked.

"Short-term contract. I signed on for one session and bummed a ride out with some Ferians. Got a nice bonus, though. I didn't expect it."

I laughed briefly.

"I couldn't decide whether to kick your ass or throw a party when I heard you weren't dead. What happened to not drawing attention to yourself?"

I gestured helplessly. "None of it was planned. I made it up as I went along, just like on the *Bedia*."

"Your 'making it up' is better than a lot of operatives' best-laid plans. You have a gift for this kind of work. Not everybody rescues kidnap victims and prevents a coup their first time out." He knocked back another slug of whiskey. "Did the information you got out of the Market give up what you were looking for?"

"No." Each time Rhix had called out to me, the data stream faltered. Blank gaps like surgical strikes punctuated the dates I estimated the sale of the media bots might have taken place. "Not a goddamn thing."

"I'm sorry." Whiskey swirled in a vortex inside his transparent cup. "Ozzie told me what Tanaka said."

"I wondered when we would get to it."

"I told you I was undercover on the *Bedia*. I didn't tell you why." Sumner finally met my eyes. "Sol Fed's acceptance into the Remoliad has mixed support. The majority of galactic citizens are happy to welcome another member of the club. There are a few less enthusiastic. I have to admit, I'm one of them. The government's xenophobia and resistance to galactic protocol make it a questionable ally at best, but its needs are clear.

"Growing up off world, the way you and I did, we had an opportunity to see how things can be. If we'd grown up here, we wouldn't be the same." He eyed me through narrowed lids. "Not everybody had the same chance."

"Who are we talking about?"

"My mother was only one of three female officers on board the Europan vessel captured by the Nos. Another became pregnant during their captivity as well. The Europans hated me enough in utero to make my mother flee the system, but her shipmate stayed on Europa and raised her child there. She and my mother kept in contact. Mom tried to get her to join us, but she was a loyal Europan. Her daughter left as soon as she could and looked us up. I gathered her mother never let her forget she was the product of rape."

Sumner's jaw set. "She was the most angry, most vulnerable person I've ever met. I didn't work for the Penumbra yet. I was serving in a mercenary unit. She signed on with me and made officer herself. I left when I was recruited, and we lost touch. She's now one of the leaders of an anti-Remoliad group. They foster any hint of dissatisfaction in Alliance members and create chaos whenever they can. She's found someone who accepts her, and offers an outlet for her rage."

He signaled the bartender again, and the 'bot creaked over to squeeze out another measure of booze. "She traveled on the same passenger starship as the crate of explosive media bots purchased from the Market, a week before the Luna Terminal bombing. The group never claims responsibility for their acts, but they leave a calling card, if you know what to look for."

"Any idea where she is?"

"She's traveled on Andari-registered passenger liners every six months to Rosetta Station. It's why I was on the *Bedia*. I hoped to find her, but for now, she's disappeared. Since Sol Fed got so twitchy and installed DNA scanners everywhere, she had a little trouble getting through customs even though she's still a citizen. I resemble my mother, but she has some of the Nos paleness about her. Yellow hair, eyes like ice." He met my gaze, tossing back the whiskey in one gulp. "More like the bastard that fathered both of us."

"She's..." Stunned, I couldn't form the words.

"Her name is Skadi. Miriam Skadi. She only uses her surname now." He cleared his throat. "The transaction you wanted might not be there, but there might be others we can use to trace the group she works for. Ka'pth and Ra'sho are analyzing the data. What you gave us was practically a directory to every underground account in the galaxy conducting business with the Market in the last fifteen hundred cycles. We just need time to sort it out. We'll have plenty of work cut out for us if you haven't changed your mind. I have to offer you a chance to walk away. You went through a hell of a lot. None of us will hold it against you. You can stay here, or go back to Zereid. We'll get you where you want to go, if that's your decision."

Zereid's peace tempted me as much as it ever had. My career in Sol Fed might be over, but work remained for third-gender rights; efforts Gresh and Sida would have wanted me to continue.

I hoped they'd forgive me for being selfish.

I'd learned who I was, and who I wasn't, on this mission. Part of me got off on the danger and wanted another taste. But *zezjna* remained at my core. The path of the peacekeeper—a road I wouldn't know I could follow unless I tried.

"I think I need a few more missions before I make a choice."

"Most of our jobs aren't as exciting." The slow grin lit up his face. "Some of them are downright boring."

"Might not be a bad thing." I leaned forward. "Will you answer a question, Rion?"

"What do you want to know?"

"What if we find Skadi, and she is the one who bombed the terminal?"

A flush started to work its way up his neck. A shadow crossed his ocean-colored eyes, the dark sapphire of fathomless waters. Damned null. I still couldn't read him at all. "I will help you take her down. I promised you, and it is my duty as a Penumbra agent. If she isn't—"

"Then we'll find out what she knows. There's always room for negotiation."

Glossary

Terms

Third-gender: An intersex human being, usually with a dominant set of male or female reproductive organs.

Changeling Third-gender: A genetic mutation within the third-gender population, these individuals possess neither male nor female gonads and are incapable of reproduction. Their anatomy has specialized hormonal glands, which allow them to assume the secondary sexual characteristics of a male or female, at will. They possess a vaginal-like organ without a cervix or uterus, and spongy, nerve-filled tissue in the mons, or pubic area, which can become internally or externally engorged. When externally erect the mons can serve the sexual function of male genitalia.

The New Puritan Movement (NPM): A human purity movement that stresses survival of the genetically pristine human race by isolation and parthenogenesis (reproduction without fertilization, which allows unwanted genetic traits to be edited out.) Quasi-religious and fanatic in that NPM wants to legislate mandatory genetic editing and reproduction for the citizens of Sol Fed. NPM views third-gender citizens, especially the increasing number of sterile changeling citizens, as a threat to humanity's survival and discourages galactic contact with humanoid races for fear of contaminating the gene pool.

The Penumbra: A covert agency attached to the Remoliad, responsible for gathering intelligence and investigating violations of galactic law.

The Remoliad Alliance: A local galactic coalition similar to the United Nations, which facilitates trade, diplomacy, and aid to the member planets. It also enforces galactic laws.

Shontavian Market: A black market on board a starship that remains in constant motion through the galaxy to avoid authorities.

Dealing in illegal weapons for sale and trade, the Market derived its name from the sale of genetically engineered creatures called Shontavians, bred solely for fighting wars.

Sol Federation "Sol Fed": The United Colonies within the solar system that originated from Earth's survivors: Luna, Mars, and Jupiter's moon, Europa. Each colony has its own militia and governor. The citizens of the solar system elect Senators and a President to determine federal law. Also referred to simply as the Colonies.

Zezjna: A philosophy of peace through empathy developed by the Zereid, a highly empathic/telepathic species. The term is also used to encompass a non-lethal defensive martial arts style that relies on empathic senses as well as physical skills.

Enemies and Allies

All the races depicted here are bipedal unless otherwise noted and are both humanoid and oxygen breathing.

Andari: A diminutive, ichthyoid race. They live in groups led by a female alpha. Members of the Remoliad.

Cthash: A reptilian species from an arid planet system. The Cthash are born in trios. Each set of siblings is comprised of a male, a female, and an ix. The ix gender is required for mating purposes and produces an enzyme that allows the hard-shelled eggs of the female to become temporarily porous for fertilization. Members of the Remoliad.

Ferians: A feline-like race, bipedal and covered in short fur. They walk on two or four limbs. Remoliad members.

Nos Conglomerate: A starfaring race that has plundered less developed civilizations for thousands of years. Opportunistic pirates and mercenaries. Genetically, they are closely related to the human race and are nearly identical in physiology. They are not allied and take advantage of any other system not affiliated with the Remoliad.

Ursetu: Another race similar to humanity in appearance and genetic traits, the Ursetu possess a strictly divided social hierarchy: the ruling caste, the intellectual caste, the warrior caste, and the working caste. Their planet created and sold genetically engineered creatures for servitude and battle for thousands of years. They are not allied with the Remoliad.

Zereid: A highly empathic/telepathic race. The species is bipedal and covered in short blue fur. They are skilled in diplomacy due to their ability to sense emotion. Pacifist in nature, they have developed a non-lethal martial arts form for personal defense, and all serve time in their military, which defends when necessary, but primarily offers compassionate aid to other planets. Members of the Remoliad.

Characters

Aja: A third-gender changeling kidnapped and sent to the Shontavian Market for sale as a sex slave.

Akia Parker: A third-gender changeling. A human rights solicitor kidnapped by a human trafficking ring.

Captain An'ksh: Captain of the Andari passenger vessel Bedia

Constable Caniberi: Law enforcement chief on board Rosetta Space Station

Dalí Tamareia: Former ambassador to the Remoliad. A third-gender changeling.

Dru: A third-gender changeling kidnapped and offered to the Shontavian Market for sale as a sex slave. One of three changelings whom Dalí goes undercover to rescue.

Edo Tanaka: The head of the New Puritan Movement, one of the president's most influential advisors behind the scenes.

Edward Hyatt: Senator from Mars, an isolationist who opposes Remoliad membership.

Gor: Dalí's Zereid crechemate (blood brother). A large bipedal humanoid from Zereid, Sol Fed's first allied galactic neighbor.

Gresh—Andrew Gresham: Dalí's late husband, whose nickname Dalí takes as an alias during the mission. A human rights solicitor.

Jon Batterson: The head of Batterson Robotics and a high-ranking member of the New Puritan Movement on Europa. Son of the president of Sol Fed.

Kai: A third-gender changeling kidnapped and offered to the Shontavian Market for sale as a sex slave. One of three changelings whom Dalí goes undercover to rescue.

Ambassador Marina Urquhart: Dalí's mother. Former ambassador to Zereid, now head of the Remoliad membership negotiation team from which Dalí was removed after the Luna Terminal bombing. Ambassador Urquhart is a female-dominant third-gender human.

Ambassador Michael Martinez: Current ambassador to Zereid.

Captain Paul Tamareia: Dalí's father. Commanding officer of Rosetta Space Station in Jupiter's orbit.

Lord Rhix: An Ursetu mercenary, head of the Shontavian Market

Rion Sumner: Commander of a covert operations team who recruits Dalí to the Penumbra.

Sida—Rasida Gresham Tamareia: Dalí's late wife, pregnant with a child who possessed genetic material from both Dalí and Gresh when she was killed. A genetic research scientist.

Simish: A small humanoid, genetically engineered for servitude on board the Shontavian Market ship

Dr. Tella Sharp: Surgeon and medical officer on board Rosetta Space Station who treats Dalí's injuries after a near-fatal fight.

William Farmer: An executive at Batterson Robotics. A passenger on board the Bedia.

Dr. Yesenia Atassi: Geneticist whose flawed research was glorified by the New Puritan Movement in its campaign for mandatory genetic editing of the species.

The Crew of the Thunder Child

Ossixiani clan Sustrix – "Ozzie": a Cthash pilot, second in command. Male reptilian. One of three siblings.

Tommizax clan Sustrix – "Tommi": a Cthash medic and communications officer. Female reptilian. One of three siblings.

Zigoxanian clan Sustrix – "Ziggy": a Cthash weapons officer and engineer. Ziggy is "ix" — a Cthash third gender. One of three siblings.

Ka'pth and Ra'sho: a mated pair of Andari. Intelligence officers.

Melos: a Nos engineer and navigations officer.

About the Author

E.M. Hamill is a nurse by day, sci-fi and fantasy novelist by night. She lives in eastern Kansas with her family, where they fend off flying monkey attacks and prep for the zombie apocalypse. She also writes young adult material under the name Elisabeth Hamill. Her first novel, *Song Magick*, has won multiple awards for young adult and fantasy fiction.

Facebook: https://www.facebook.com/EMHamill

Twitter: https://twitter.com/songmagick

Website and blog: http://www.elisabethhamill.com

Also by

All That Entails (Beneath the Layers anthology)

Also Available from NineStar Press

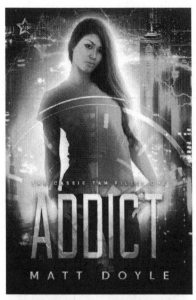

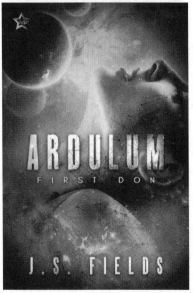

www.ninestarpress.com

Made in the USA
Lexington, KY
12 August 2017